DATE DUE

MAY 1 7 1996		
NOV 2 5 1996		
DEC 1 2 1996		
FEB 2 5 1998		
NO 0 8 0?		

D0812333

HEARTFELT PRAISE FOR
SARA FLANIGAN'S *ALICE*

St. Martin's Paperbacks Titles by Sara Flanigan

ALICE
SUDIE

ALICE

SARA FLANIGAN

SMP

ST. MARTIN'S PAPERBACKS

ALICE

Copyright © 1988 by Sara Flanigan Carter.

All rights reserved. No part of this book may be used or reproduced in any manner whatsoever without written permission except in the case of brief quotations embodied in critical articles or reviews. For information address St. Martin's Press, 175 Fifth Avenue, New York, N.Y. 10010.

Library of Congress Catalog Card Number: 87-36703

ISBN: 0-312-92784-3

Printed in the United States of America

St. Martin's Press hardcover edition published 1988
St. Martin's Paperbacks edition/March 1989

10 9 8 7 6 5

*In loving memory of my sister
Lavon Flanigan*

Thank you God

and also

A special thank you to my dear friends Floy Moore, June and Sam Wininger, Joyce Cofield, and Joyce Jacoby, who kindly shared their homes with me as I wrote this book.

ALICE

Chapter 1

Sometimes I git so happy I have to run through the woods hollering. It's the trees and the mountains and the flowers most times, on account of they's the happy stuff, if you know what I mean. Then sometimes it's the deer or the squirrels or the birds. It might even be the rain when it comes soft and sweet and splashing into a zillion swirling circles into Cherrylog Creek. And one time, when I was real sad on account of Sammy was sick, it was God, 'cause he made me a sunset that lit up the fluffy clouds over the mountain behind our cabin like sideways streams of red and orange embers, glowing, glowing, and changing shapes, and singing in my mind like whispers from Him.

My cousin Morgan, who's mean as a shot bear, says I'm teched in the head, but I ain't. He's the one, if you ask me. Like that time when he followed me all the way to Ormond Guthrie's place and seen me go into that shed room where they keep Alice. He threatened me with telling if I didn't let him see my bosoms, but I told Morgan that he wadn't never seeing me and if he tried I'd blow his guts to Kingdom Come with Daddy's shotgun. He laughed like crazy and chased me down the mountain, but he didn't catch me.

Anyhow, today is the day of all days. Today is the day of rejoicing and singing and squealing out. Today is the

1

day of running through the woods. Of calling to the creatures. Of telling the trees and the violets and the ferns. Today is the day me and my big brother Sammy has been planning on for way over a year. Today is the day we gonna git Alice out of that shed!

My name is Louellen Perkins and the reason I'm gonna tell you this story is on account of Love. Some folks may not think love is much of nothing, but I do. I think love is God and you sure can't say God is much of nothing. Leastways you can't say it if you know Him. I know Him. Oh, I ain't never *seen* Him. Or I ain't never heard his big voice come out of the clouds, but I know Him.

It's a feeling. Well, no, maybe not a feeling, maybe it's a thing in my heart, or gut, or head. Maybe it's my spirit that gits a glance or a hearing of His spirit. Whatever it is, it's way beyond what I can tell about.

The first time I knowed I knowed Him I was eleven. I was setting on a old log down by Cherrylog Creek watching minnows scooting like tiny silver flashes around a pine branch that had fell into the water. Dozens of them. Scoot and circle and gather up, then separate to scoot and circle some more. A brown water snake was snoozing on a limb not far from my head, and Under, our hound dog that Daddy named Under cause he's always under something, was laying there sniffing at a turtle that didn't pay him no mind.

Then I heard the soft crunching of a animal walking close, stepping slow on the dead leaves and pine straw. Under raised one ear and I glanced across the creek to see a doe ambling toward us.

I didn't blink a eye and whispered to Under to stay down. Deer can sense a movement in a flash. She stopped to drink a dozen or so feet from us and I could of cried with

2

the joy of it. I guess I love deer more than any other animal nearly.

The doe didn't glance our way and when she was done drinking I crossed my fingers that she wouldn't go off right then. And she didn't. She twisted her neck back and forth. Then she moved from behind a clump of cattails and I could see her sides was all swole. She was so heavy and awkward I was scared she'd drop her baby as she walked. She moved only a few steps and my heart raced as I watched her body tighten. She twisted her neck back and forth some more and then she sunk onto the mossy bank.

I set froze to that stump as she laid there heaving with the movements of birthing. Under showed no interest atall and didn't even notice the turtle slide into the water. In a minute he was snoozing away.

Tears run down my face and dropped down on my dress and I didn't move a twitch. I never been so still in all my life. It seemed like hours passed or years or lifetimes and ever muscle in me hurt. My stomach knotted up ever time the doe's did. Then I seen the head come out. Wet and slick and limp. I waited. I strained inside as though I could help her. The longer I watched the agony of the doe, the more I panicked. How long does it take? Oh, how long?

Finally the doe laid its head down. Its eyes closed. I thought it was dead. I raced across the creek, slipping on the slick rocks. The doe's head jerked up and for a second or two she looked like she was gonna try to stand. But then her body convulsed nearly like Alice's does when she has them fits and in a minute there it was. I thought my heart would explode just seeing it. A gooey, slippery glob that was all skinny legs. The cutest, sweetest little thing I'd ever seen. I had to drop to my knees, I got so weak.

That's when it happened. I looked right into the eyes of the doe and my life ain't never been the same since.

How can I tell you what it was like? How can you tell about the end of lightning? How can you tell about the stopping of rivers, or the turning off of the night? What's to say? Right in them big liquid, sad and wise, dark eyes was the story of Life. And the story of God, and the story of Love.

I seen a picture of Jesus once. He had blue eyes and I remember thinking it just wadn't right. The eyes was blank and pale and they didn't know nothing. And right then, right there in them quiet woods with the gentle sounds of nature all around me, I knowed if I could paint the eyes of Jesus they would be just like that doe's.

And the quiet and the calm overcome me, like pouring sweet, warm peace into the top of my head and it flowing slow, oh so slow, into my face and neck and shoulders and all the way down, till the peace left me limp as the baby deer.

I didn't touch the doe. All I done was squat there on my knees and stare in them eyes. I had to touch my face to see if I was still there. Then I whispered to the doe and the baby. To the trees and the bushes and to the creatures. I whispered, "Thank You."

I told Mama about it as best I could. She hugged me close and called Daddy and I tried to tell him and he got right misty-eyed and patted my head. And when Mama had diphtheria later on, and all of a sudden took a turn for the worse, she held my hand and said it. Right as she laid there, while Daddy was racing over the mountain to git Doc Murphy, she said it. I knowed she was dying and she did, too. She held hard on to my hand and she said, "Remember the doe, Louellen. Always remember the doe. Don't never forget about love. Don't never."

And I never did.

Chapter 2

*T*he first time I ever heard of Alice it was winter. I had rode Poke, our old mare, down across Yager Valley where me and Sammy had set a lot of rabbit boxes. Snow had covered the ground for days. That day a new storm had started, at first soft and timid, and the flakes fell on my face and hands like little kisses, as I coaxed Poke up the mountain. The three rabbits from the boxes was calm and still now in the croker sack tied to the old saddle.

I hated it. I hated killing rabbits to eat, but since Mama died, Daddy was in such bad shape that me and Sammy had to help git meat. In the summer me and Aunt Bessie, Morgan's mama, canned vegetables.

Daddy and Uncle Will, Morgan's daddy, run a sawmill down close to Bolton. Ever since I can remember we had enough to live on. Enough food and warm clothes. Daddy had been a good provider. Now Uncle Will brings flour and meal, and when he kills his hogs he brings pork shoulder and ribs and sausage.

When Poke finally got me to the top of the mountain I seen smoke coming from over the trees. I knowed it was from the Guthries' chimney. The Guthries had moved up there two years before but I hadn't never met them. They didn't go nowhere like church or town meetings. Daddy

5

said he heard they had a pile of little younguns. Uncle Will said neither Mr. Guthrie or Mrs. Guthrie could read or write, and don't send their younguns to school.

As I got close to the cabin I could hear the children. One screaming and another crying. I thought about trying to be neighborly and meeting them, but then I got this funny feeling in my stomach. A scary feeling. I brought Poke to a stop behind some pines and set quiet a while. The snow-flakes was bigger now, floating like whispers.

The crying finally stopped but the screaming got worse. Goose bumps come up on my arms. I never heard nothing like it. A dying animal was what it sounded like. A terrified dying animal.

Then a woman come out of the front door. She was carrying a dishpan full of something. She toted it around to a shed that was hooked onto a half fell-in barn. I watched her set the dishpan down in the snow and lift a heavy log that run all the way across the door.

Then she hollered real loud, "GIT BACK! GIT BACK IN THERE AND SET DOWN OR I'LL TAKE YORE BREAKFAST RIGHT BACK IN THE HOUSE, YA HEAR!"

She was feeding a animal. But what kind? A animal that screamed like a person. I crouched down into Poke's neck as she dropped the log back into the latch with a crash. Then the animal cried Ma-ma, a sound that broke my heart in two. Ma-ma, Ma-ma, over and over and over.

They was a *girl* in that shed! Oh, Dear God in Heaven, a *girl*! My mind raced with all kinds of thoughts. What is she doing in that shed? Is she being punished for something? Could that be it? Maybe her mama would let her out in a little while. She must be freezing out there in this weather.

Then I seen a little trickle of smoke coming out of a pipe on the roof of the little room. I breathed a sigh of relief. At least she had heat. But her mama fed her with a pan! A shiver run over me and I hugged Poke's neck. I could feel the sack of rabbits moving against my leg. I nudged Poke's ribs with my knees. I better git out of here, I thought, before I git caught snooping. Anyhow, that girl ain't none of my business.

"Ma-ma, ma-ma, uhhh, Ma-ma."

Chills run right down my spine at the sound. The awful sound. I knowed I couldn't go. I knowed I had to see that girl for myself. I dropped to the ground and led Poke, slow and quiet, back into the trees and then around in a half circle to behind the barn. When I peeped around, the woman was gone back in the house.

I stayed still a while, trying to think what to do. They was two little windows in the shed. One faced the house and the other one faced the woods. Nobody could see me if I snuck to the back window. I looked in ever direction to make sure nobody was around, then I run to the back of the shed.

It was a little room, maybe eight foot by nine or ten foot, and the tin roof probably wadn't, say, seven foot at the highest part. My heart was pounding hard as I pressed my nose against the glass. I couldn't see a thing. Something was covering the window on the inside. I felt right sick. What could I do? Did I dare try to whisper something to the girl? I tried. I whispered, "Hey! Can you hear me?" I put my ear against the pane. I couldn't hear nothing. I tried again and again, but she didn't answer me.

When I got home I run in and told Sammy. He was reading his history lesson, but put his book right down when I got to the part about the girl. Me and him puzzled over it and he asked me questions time and again but we couldn't figure it out. We finally decided I had to be right about the girl being punished for something, so Sammy went back to his studying and I got out my spelling book.

Trouble was, I couldn't think about spelling. I was think-

7

ing of the girl all alone in that awful shed. Then I got to thinking about me and Sammy being alone so much since Mama died. I got real sad and started sniffling.

Sammy put his book down and asked me what was the matter. Sammy is nice. Ever since Mama died he has been real nice to me and watched after me and all. I was eleven when Mama died and Sammy was fifteen. Now he was seventeen and I was thirteen.

He patted my hand and asked me if I wouldn't like to play checkers, but I told him no. He knowed I was crying over Mama. Finally he went out back to clean the rabbits and I went to the kitchen and started a fire in the stove to cook supper.

The next day we was snowed in. I was glad. We don't git snowed in much. North Georgia don't git as much snow as some places. Daddy took one look out the back door and hollered at us to stay in bed. Sammy jumped up and run to the kitchen and I could hear him and Daddy talking about the weather. I got up to use the slop jar, and it was so cold to my butt I squealed out.

"What is it, Ellie?" Daddy called.

"The slop jar is ice cold!" I yelled.

Him and Sammy laughed and I set there shivering. When I was done I dived back under the quilts. As I was dozing I heard Sammy tell Daddy about the girl in the shed. Then Daddy called me.

"Whatcha want?" I asked.

"Come in here."

I wrapped a quilt around me and run to the kitchen. Daddy and Sammy was standing next to the stove, holding their hands over it.

"I don't want you a-going back up to that house, ya hear?" Daddy said, as I snuggled up to him. He put his arm around me and pulled me up tight.

8

"It was awful," I said, "the girl sounded so pitiful, Daddy."

"It ain't none of our business. They trashy people. Will says he heard old man Guthrie would just as soon shoot you as look at you. Now, you stay away from there. I mean it, girl!"

I looked at Sammy and he nodded.

"I'll stay away," I said.

Aside from worrying about the girl, that day was the best day me and Daddy and Sammy had had in a long time. I'm gonna tell you about it, but first I want to tell you about our cabin.

It's made out of logs and chinked with white clay. Daddy built two of the rooms before him and Mama was married. Later he added two more rooms. A front room with a big rock fireplace, and a kitchen with four windows. Mama liked windows. He put in plank walls and ceilings in all the rooms but the kitchen. Me and Sammy sleeps in the two original rooms. Sammy's room has got the old potbellied stove. Mine ain't got no heat, but it's the biggest and that's why I chose it. Daddy sleeps in the front room.

Mama sewed everthing by hand. Purty quilts of all colors. Fluffy curtains on ever window and, except for the bedroom set that was Mama's before they married (and mine now), Daddy made all the furniture, even the rocking chairs.

Daddy was good at all sorts of stuff till Mama died. Then he seemed to give up. He took to drinking corn liquor. At first it wasn't so bad, but it got worse. He got to where he drunk it ever day. It changed him a lot. He went from nice to mean when he was drinking.

Me and Sammy got to where we stayed out of his way, but at times Sammy has got rough with Daddy. Even though Sammy is skinnier than Daddy, he's taller. And he's strong. Maybe not as strong as Daddy, but when Daddy is drunk he gits floppy, if you know what I mean. So twice when he got to hollering and raving on, Sammy wrapped his arms around him, pinning his arms to his sides, and held him till he shut up.

I pray ever day that one of these days my daddy will quit drinking that moonshine.

Anyhow, that snow day was so good it brought my spirits up high and flying. The world outside them windows was pure as the sky. Clean and white and fluffed up like fat pillows. The snow mounded against the big oaks, snuggled around their giant trunks, and laid like cotton on their bare limbs and branches. The tall green pines, heavy to sagging under their white covers, was cracking and swaying in the icy breezes, the only sounds in our forest. It was magic.

I cooked a big breakfast while Daddy built a fire in the fireplace. Plump sausage patties sizzled and the smell of good strong coffee filled up the cabin. While we eat, Sammy and Daddy talked. Good talk, without no wishy-washy words. Things to be done, fences to mend, stuff like that.

I listened. It felt good listening. Good for the first time in years, it seemed like. Warm and cozy and tickling my heart. I knowed Mama was smiling.

We decided not to go outside. We wouldn't mess up the world with footprints. No snowmen. No snowball battles for me and Sammy. It was a whole new feeling. Grown-up.

We played checkers and popped corn. Daddy helped me with my spelling. I sewed up a tore place in my dress while Sammy and Daddy fixed the slats in a chair.

And I prayed silent prayers that they wouldn't be no footprints in the snow all day and all night. No footprints to the barn where Daddy hid his liquor.

And they wadn't.

The big snow magic lasted only one day. On the second morning I looked out the window to see deep footprints leading to the barn. Daddy was in a fog all day, sleeping off and on and then going back to the barn, so me and Sammy went on out and built a snowman. He was big and round and I got Daddy's straw hat and put it on his head. Then we pounded it with snowballs, patted hard as rocks, till it got chunked out with icy gouges and holes and ridges. Then it fell and I cried.

We went back to school six days after the big snow. We don't git much of a education in these mountains. We still got a three-room schoolhouse down in the valley, but it's hard to keep good teachers. Also, younguns are out a lot on account of helping on the farms, and sickness keeps them out, too. Like measles or mumps or whooping cough that goes through all the family. Some die. I was in the sixth grade and Sammy the eighth. Don't hardly nobody graduate. When Mama was alive, her and Daddy said no matter what it took, me and Sammy would graduate, and if God was willing, Sammy would go to a college down in Atlanta. We don't talk about things like that nowadays.

Chapter 3

For the rest of the winter I thought about the girl in the shed. I didn't go there. I kept my word to Daddy. But then one day in early spring I went. I didn't go on purpose. I went 'cause Leety, our cow, had got out and I followed her tracks in the fresh thawing ground up the mountain. They led right past the Guthries'.

When I come in sight of the house, I stopped to listen. I didn't hear a sound. They wadn't no smoke coming out of the chimney or out of the pipe on the shed roof. It was Saturday, and lots of the mountain families go into town on Saturdays. Maybe they had gone, too, I thought, and that means the girl is all right. If she's gone to town then she's fine.

Leety's tracks crossed the front yard, so I decided to follow them right into the yard. If the Guthries was at home, and if they come out, I could just explain about our cow.

The whole yard, front, sides, and back, was littered with trash. Rags, broke plows, rusty tools, and buckets. A old wagon with two wheels missing leaned against a tar paper chicken house down past the barn.

I walked slow across the yard, straining my ears for any sound. Except for chicken clucking here and there, it was dead silence. I stared at the shed and was tempted to walk back to it, but I didn't.

The tracks led me back into the woods. When I'd gone a few yards I heard the cry. Ma-ma, Ma-ma, over and over. I stopped still, my heart racing. Somehow I couldn't seem to believe it. I couldn't believe she was in that shed again and she was alone. Everbody else was gone.

Then the voice inside my mind, or heart said, Go to her.

Oh, no! Oh, I can't. I don't want to.

I argued back and forth to myself a few seconds. Then I did it.

I run to the shed.

I knocked on the door. They was no answer, only the awful cries. I pounded louder. Still no answer. I stared at the log that bolted the door.

I wanted to run, I wanted to run home to Sammy, but I didn't. I lifted the log out of the latch. It was heavy. I let it fall to the ground and jumped back as it fell. I waited.

The cries stopped.

"Hey!" I called. "Hey in there!"

She didn't answer.

I pushed at the door very easy. I think I hoped it wouldn't open. It opened. Slow and sure. Then I seen her. She was laying curled up like a baby on a old cot, and if I live to be a hunderd I won't never forget the sight and I won't never forget the smell. Both made me sick. One was as bad as the other.

The shed was filthy. Nothing but filth. The terrible mess of quilts she laid on was bunched up and so dirty I couldn't see the colors. Beside one window was a potbellied stove, and all around it was a fencelike thing, made out of logs and wrapped in animal hides shrunk and black from the heat. They was a big homemade box, and on it set a dishpan with

13

mush dried to its side. Beside it was a washpan and a jar of water.

When the light hit her she jumped and raised her head. A mess of long black tangled hair covered her face. She wore ragged, faded men's overalls and a man's shirt.

I stared at her. I was struck dumb. Her hands moved toward her face, skinny with ragged nails that was crusted with the mush.

I backed to the door in horror. Then I seen her eyes. She pushed the hair away from her face, and the eyes struck me like a blow. Big, dark, sad liquid eyes. I thought I'd faint.

Mama's words pounded my mind. Remember the doe. Don't never forget about love.

The eyes didn't show no fear. No surprise. They stared at my face, gentle and quiet and sad. They broke my heart.

"Hey," I said, real quiet, "ah, my name's Ellie."

She didn't say nothing.

"I live down the mountain a ways. I'm Ellie. What's your name?"

The eyes didn't leave my face.

"How come—well, how come you out here? How come you in this shed?"

She moved her mouth but no words came. She wet her lips with her tongue.

"Whooooo?" she whispered, in a voice craggy like laryngitis, "whooooo?"

I stared at her. The odor of pee was so strong I felt sick.

"Whooooo youuuu?"

"Oh—oh, I'm Ellie." Then the thought hit me that she must not could hear so good, so I yelled, "I'm Ellie!"

"Ethie?"

"NO. ELLIE!" I screamed.

Her eyes changed. She had heard me!

"Ellie?"

14

"YEAH, THAT'S IT. ELLIE! WHAT'S YOUR NAME?" I hollered and moved closer.

"Al–ice. I Al–ice." She pulled herself up to a sitting position. "Where Ma–ma?" she whispered.

"I—I DON'T KNOW. MAYBE SHE WENT TO TOWN. I'M SURE SHE'LL BE BACK SOON."

"Huh?"

I said it again. Louder.

She leaned toward the hide-covered fence and grabbed it with both hands. She pulled herself to her feet. I backed toward the door again, afraid. I don't know why.

She was taller than me and older, maybe by two years. She looked fifteen or sixteen. That matted hair fell almost to her waist. Her dirty bare feet seemed too small for her height. I noticed her toenails were long and jagged.

"Wa–t. Wa–ter." She pointed to a empty jar. "I ditta water."

I watched like somebody dazed as she got the jar and moved past me. She walked slow, stumbling, almost like she had forgot how to walk. I followed her to the wellhouse. In the sunlight her skin was white as a sheet. She looked sick, real sick. I was going to offer to draw a bucket of water, but a thought hit me.

Oh, my God! That's it. She's sick. She's got some bad disease, and that's why she's in the shed. She's quarantined!

I wanted to run again, but I couldn't. I stood several feet from her and watched her hold the windlass as the bucket dropped into the well, then I had to ask.

"ALICE? ARE YOU SICK? WHAT'S THE MATTER?"

She didn't answer.

I moved four steps closer and yelled again. Still no answer.

As she poured water into the jar, she looked at me.

"Huh?" she asked.

I screamed the question again as she watched my mouth.

"Nooooo."

"YOU'RE *NOT* SICK?"

"Noooo."

"THEN WHY ARE YOU IN THERE?" I pointed to the shed.

"Hit wher I at. I haf fit."

"WHAT?"

"I haf fit."

"FIT? FITS?"

"Mmmmmm."

I backed away so fast I backed into a tree. Fits? Oh my Lord! Has she got rabies?

I leaned against the tree and watched her walk slow back toward the shed.

"I GOTTA GO, ALICE!" I screamed. "ALICE?"

She didn't turn around. She disappeared into the little dark room. I stood froze with fear and questions. I said a prayer and asked God what was wrong with her. Did she have rabies? What should I do?

I didn't listen for a answer. I didn't want one. I run, forgetting the cow, forgetting the tracks. I run all the way home. Later that day Leety come home.

That night I asked Daddy what happened to somebody who had rabies. He said they went mad and died, in a matter of days or weeks, he wadn't sure.

Alice couldn't have rabies. She'd been locked up for months, maybe longer. What did she have? What awful disease was it? I never felt so upset in my life. I wanted to tell Sammy, but I didn't. I couldn't tell him, 'cause I'd promised Daddy I wouldn't go back.

The whole thing drove me crazy nearly. I went up there the next Saturday, but the Guthries was home. Three kids was in the yard, the oldest probably six or seven. I went the Saturday after that and they was gone.

I waited in the woods close to a hour, I bet, just to make sure. The only sounds I heard come from the shed, moaning and screaming and shaking the door. They was no calls to Mama. The sounds scared me bad. Those animal sounds again. Wild.

I stood listening a while longer before I decided I wouldn't open the door. I did go up to it, though. I stood close and heard her screams and heard her say words. The screaming would stop for a minute, then she'd say stuff like, "Ooooh, how do? See, ooooh, see. How do?" Then she would scream, "Aaaaghhh."

I couldn't stand it. It was the most awful thing I ever heard. I asked God why.

Oh God, why? What's wrong with Alice, God? She's so pitiful. So sad. Why? Why? Help her. Please help her!

When I got home, Uncle Will and Morgan was there. They was setting on the front porch talking with Sammy and Daddy.

"Where you been?" Daddy asked as I rode up on Poke.

"Nowheres. Just down to Cherrylog."

"You see Under?" Sammy asked.

"Nah, I ain't. Hey, Uncle Will. Hey, Morgan."

They both said hey, then went back to talking. I put Poke in the barn, gathered up some eggs, and went on in the kitchen.

Sammy come in.

"Under's been gone all day," he said, gitting a dipper of water.

"I ain't seen him."

"Ellie?"

"Huh?"

17

"I went to Cherrylog. You wadn't there. How come you told Daddy you was?"

My heart sunk. I can't stand to be caught in a lie.

"'Cause I was," I stammered.

"I was there all morning. You wadn't. Ellie, you been up the mountain? You been to the Guthries?"

I stared out the window and didn't answer.

"That's where you been, ain't it? You been there, you better tell me."

I took the eggs out of the basket, slow, and put them in the cupboard.

"Ellie? You better tell me!"

"I can't," I whispered.

"Then you been there."

I turned and looked at Sammy.

"I had to. Oh, Sammy, she's so pitiful! You ain't never seen nothing like it. Something awful is wrong. Please don't tell Daddy. Please," I begged.

Sammy patted my shoulder. "It's too dangerous," he said. "The man is mean."

"They go off. The whole family goes off 'cept her. I think they go in town on Saturdays. They was gone today."

He took my arm. "Come on," he said, and pulled me out the back door.

"You gotta tell me about it, Ellie. Tell me about that girl."

We went to the barn and I was gonna tell, but Morgan come around the house looking for us, so I couldn't.

Morgan's such a fat pest. Aggravates the daylights out of you. He's a year older than me. He looks like Aunt Bessie, round as a butterball. Mama used to say he acted too big for his britches and one of these days somebody was gonna take him down a peg or two.

Oh, he acts all right in front of grown folks, but just git

18

by yourself with him and he'd drive you crazy. Always poking at me or pinching me, and he always called Sammy names, like Purty Boy or Sissy.

Sammy *is* purty. Well, no, not purty. He's nice looking. He looks like Mama in a way. Red hair bright as copper, and them gray eyes. Clear as Cherrylog Creek. The girls at school giggle and titter and act plumb silly over him. Makes me sick.

He likes Bertha Langford. Him and her is sweethearts, sort of. Least she claims him. Hangs around him blinking and sniggering and flirting. She's a real snot, if you ask me, but I can't say nothing. If he likes her, it's his troubles. I told him he ought to claim Lillian Mosley 'cause she's sweet and smart, but he said she's too fat. Hurt my feelings 'cause I ain't no string bean myself.

Aunt Bessie says I'm going through a stage. She says some girls plump up at my age.

Anyhow, that night Daddy got purty drunk and passed out, and me and Sammy set on the front porch steps and talked. I told him everything.

He said he didn't think Alice could have rabies neither, but she sure must be bad off.

"Ain't nothing you can do," he said, "you ought not of gone in that shed. Whatever she's got you could of caught it. Did you touch her?"

"No."

"Daddy's right. You stay away from there. Some diseases you can catch even by being in the same room. Why you think they got her out there? A quarantine means stay away, Ellie. Now promise you won't go back. You promise?"

"Yeah."

We set quiet a while, then I thought of something.

"Sammy?"

"Huh?"

"Maybe she ain't got a sickness. Maybe she's crazy."

"Could be."

"Maybe she won't die."

"Might not."

"Is there any medicine for crazy?"

"I don't know. But I tell you one thing, crazy is dangerous, too. Never can tell what crazy people will do."

Right then Under come trotting up and me and Sammy jumped off the steps to pet him.

I tried my best to forgit about Alice but I couldn't. I thought about her all the time. Them eyes stayed in my mind. Even when I was studying my lessons. If I had been stuck in the house I think I'd of got the jitters bad, but the weather was so nice I stayed outside a lot. The biting cold was gone and the days was warming.

Spring was poppin out all over them mountains, turning the hardwood trees into all shades of tender greens. The violets busted through the dead leaves and pine straw on the forest floor, and tiny curls of fern peeped out of the creek banks, and my heart sailed along with the wonders as it always does. Sammy says I git plumb wild come spring.

One Sunday after church me and Sammy rode Poke down to Cherrylog to wade in the cold water and lay on the mossy bank and dream our dreams. We been dreaming our dreams on that bank since we was kids. Just a-laying there, sometimes with our eyes closed, and sometimes squinting up through the tree branches at the fluffy clouds drifting and changing into faces and animals and things. Springtime is the best time for dreams. Ain't no doubt about it 'cause everthing is new, and if you lay real still the creatures come out with their babies and the birds tweet and sing and court, and birds is Sammy's favorite. Like mine's deer.

I don't never fall asleep while we're dreaming, but sometimes Sammy does and that Sunday he did. Under was sleeping too, so I was the only one paying attention. And I heard it. The sounds of a animal walking. My heart started beating faster, hoping it was a deer, but I dared not raise up to look. Finally I couldn't stand it no longer so I set up to look, but I didn't see nothing. Then I seen Alice. I nearly fell over. She was down the creek close to where me and Sammy keep one of our rabbit boxes. She was walking slow as a snail, touching everything she saw. Leaves, branches, tree trunks, rocks. That matted black hair hung down past her waist and her face and arms was pale as snow. The overalls hung on her slim body and I was shocked out of my senses to see she didn't have on no shirt. The bib of the overalls didn't cover her top up. I could see the sides of her bosoms plain as day. I sucked in my breath and said, "Oh my gosh!" Sammy set up quick.

"Whatsa matter?" Then he looked and his mouth fell open and his eyes bugged out and he whispered, "Is—is that *her?*"

I shook my head.

"She's—she's—Ellie, she's the purtiest thing I ever seen. My Lord! Why is she so white?"

"'Cause of the sickness," I whispered.

Then a man run up to her and grabbed her arm and jerked her so hard she almost fell. It had to be her daddy.

Sammy jumped to his feet but I grabbed him around the legs. "No! No, don't, Sammy. He'll hurt you."

Sammy stood with his fists clenched up as we watched them disappear into the woods. He set back down and stared into the water.

"She *is* sick," he said finally, his voice low. "She must be real sick. I wonder what she's got. Ellie, she looks fifteen or sixteen. Uncle Will said the oldest one of them younguns was six or seven. I reckon they don't tell folks about her."

I nodded.

"She must be dying. It's hard to think of somebody that young dying, ain't it? 'Specially somebody that purty."

"But she *might* not die," I said, trying to make him feel better 'cause I can't stand it when he's sad. "She might git well."

"How could her daddy be so mean to somebody sick as her?"

I stared at the place where Alice and her daddy had been. "He must drink liquor," I said.

Chapter 4

*E*ver spring we have a all-day doings at the school. It was planned for that next Saturday and Aunt Bessie had made me a new dress and camisole and bloomers. The dress was a purty pale blue with white polka dots and white rickrack on the collar and sleeves.

Aunt Bessie makes my clothes. She likes to sew girl stuff 'cause she ain't got a girl. Only Morgan. I wondered why they didn't have but one kid. I asked Mama once and she said Aunt Bessie had some kind of woman problem.

Anyhow, I just loved my new dress. I'd made up my mind that I'd quit worrying and thinking about Alice and I'd go to the meeting and have me a good time.

I got up real early Saturday morning to git ready. Everbody brings food, but Aunt Bessie said she'd bring ours so I had a long time to git myself fixed up. We ain't never had a bathing tub, just a washbowl. When Mama was alive she'd heat up water and bring in the washtub from the wellhouse and bathe us in it. The night before I'd told Sammy I was gonna bring the tub into the kitchen and for him to stay out.

I'm purty big, so setting in a washtub ain't easy. All I could do was set my bottom in it and hang my legs over the side, or either squat down. The truth is, you don't git no cleaner than if you was using a rag and the washbowl, but somehow you feel like you do, 'cause you set down in the soapy water. Aunt Bessie makes the soap and it smells like lilacs nearly. She says she's gonna show me how to make it one of these days.

When I was done bathing they was more water on the floor than in the tub. I swept it out the back door.

Then I put on my new clothes. The new bloomers and petticoat and camisole was white. The dress fit perfect. I stood in front of my dresser a hour, I bet, fixing my hair. Mine ain't as red as Sammy's, sorta brown red. I had rolled it up on rags and when I combed it out it stuck out in a kinky mess. I looked like I had been scared senseless by a booger or something. If I hadn't of looked so funny I would of cried. Sammy got up and took one look and busted out laughing, so I throwed the comb at him.

"Leave it like it is," he said, "it'll scare everbody away from the table and I'll git all the chicken."

"What if it scares Bertha away? Then yore heart would break and fall into the chocolate cake."

"At least Bertha don't have a head that looks like lightning struck it." He laughed and leaned on the dresser.

I stuck my tongue out at him.

"No, she don't. She has a head that looks like it ought to set on a moose! And she's so stuck up somebody ought to hang her from a flagpole."

"You're just jealous 'cause boys look at her and don't look at you."

"They do too look at me."

"Ha! *Who* looks at you?"

"Lots of 'em."

"Who? Tell me just one."

"Git out of here and leave me alone!"

"Who looks at you? Elephant ears?"

"Git out," I said, "or I'll call Daddy."

"Won't do no good. He ain't come to yet. You and elephant ears would make a good pair. Yore hair sticks out and his ears sticking out. Folks could see you coming a mile off. Maybe you could fly away together."

I kicked his leg.

"Huh!" I said. "You think Bertha has got such a good figger. Lisa Mae told me she's got a bale of cotton wadded up on her chest. She said if they took her to the gin her daddy'd be a rich man."

Sammy flopped on my bed and put his hands behind his head. I could look in the mirror and see his face. He got this silly wicked look and said, "*I* happen to know they ain't cotton."

"You lying!"

"I ain't lying."

"How you know?" I was shocked.

"*That's* the big secret."

"Sammy Perkins, did you touch her bosoms?"

"I ain't telling."

"Well!" I snorted, "I always knowed she was a harlot."

He laughed. "You don't even know what a harlot is."

"I most surely do!"

"What is one?"

"Bertha's one."

"See. You don't know."

"One is a girl that—well—"

"That what?"

"That *does* it!"

"Does what?"

"*It*, stupid. Now will you git out of here?"

"What's *it*?"

I was gitting embarrassed. Sammy likes to git me embarrassed. Makes me furious, so I thought, well then, I'll show *you!* I stuck out my tongue and wiggled it.

"Does *that*, smart britches!"

I thought Sammy would fall off the bed laughing.

I whirled around. "What you laughing at?"

He got off the bed and pointed at me. I grabbed a pillow and pounded his head. He still laughed.

"If tongue-kissing ain't a harlot, then what is?" I yelled.

Sammy run in the kitchen and I run after him with the pillow. He took it away from me and took holt of my shoulders and pushed me into a chair. Then he set on me and patted my head like he pats Under.

"I think you better have a talk with Aunt Bessie, sis," he said, still grinning like a fool.

When Aunt Bessie and them got there I was ready. I'd finally twirled my hair round the comb into lots of curls and tied them with a ribbon. Sammy said I looked like a old-fashioned old maid. Aunt Bessie said I looked sweet, which didn't make me any happier than what Sammy said, but it was too late to do anything else.

I never seen so many folks at the school at one time. Tables was set up under the trees, made out of sawhorses and planks, and covered with stiff starched tablecloths that was white as the little wood building. Right away me and Sammy spotted Bertha. She had on a dress red as Georgia clay and she was prissing around, giggling and carrying on. It didn't take her two minutes to lay her eyes on Sammy and come sashaying over.

"If she ain't a harlot I ain't never seen one," I hissed at Sammy, poking his ribs.

"Mighty purty harlot," he whispered and winked.

"Hey, Bertha," Aunt Bessie said, then everybody but me said hey.

"Y'all gonna stay for all the games?" Bertha asked.

"I reckon," Sammy said.

"Bess won't leave till the food runs out," Uncle Will said.

"How's Russ?" (Russ is Bertha's daddy who has got rheumatism.)

"Oh, he's fine," Bertha said, pointing across the school yard. "He's right over yonder. I baked yo' favorite cake, Sammy." (All the unmarried girls over fifteen brings special lunches that the boys bid on and whoever gits the bid gits to eat lunch with the girl. Everbody there knowed her mama baked that cake but nobody said nothing.) Sammy grinned. I pinched him on the arm.

When the bidding started for the girls' lunches, Sammy was right up front. I knowed he'd brought thirty cents he'd saved up. I hoped to goodness he didn't waste it all on that harlot's lunch.

When they helt up Bertha's basket Sammy said, "I bid ten cents." (Everybody starts at ten cents.)

Lamar Williams said he'd give fifteen and Donna Hood got mad as a hornet 'cause she likes Lamar. Van Cofield said twenty and Sammy said twenty-five. Then that cute Christopher Hays said thirty, and his sister Holly laughed out loud 'cause she knows Bertha is a snot.

Then out of the clear blue steps up David Bettler and said half a dollar! I thought Sammy was gonna cry, and for a minute I felt right sorry for him, though I was glad. Sammy ended up with Lisa Mae McClung for twenty-five cents, who is my friend and is cuter than Bertha any day in the week and don't stick out a mile in front.

Me or Sammy neither one won none of the games. Mark Hudson won the sack race. I forget who won the rock throw, but Jennifer Williams won for telling the funniest story.

Me and Lisa Mae stayed together a lot of the time. She was heartbroke 'cause of David bidding on Bertha's lunch. I told her she ought to think of it like I do. Think of that Bertha is just one of them kind that boys lust after like in the Bible.

27

"Whatcha mean, lust after?" she asked. "Is that 'pose to make me feel better 'cause he lusts after her?"

"'Course it is. Lusting is a bad sin."

"What you reckon it means?" She set down on the grass under a big elm. I set down beside her.

"Ah, *you* know."

"Well, I don't neither."

"Well," I said, "it means that the boy—he gits this yearning to kiss a girl with his mouth open and all. And sometimes if he gits to lusting real bad—then sometimes he'll even try to touch her bosoms."

Lisa gasped. "Louellen Perkins, you're just making that up!"

"I ain't neither. They's a lots of lusting in the Old Testament, Preacher McKay said so. Ain't you ever listened to him preach about lusting?"

"Yeah, but I didn't know it meant *that*."

"Well, it does," I said. I was feeling real good telling Lisa something she didn't know. I like to tell her stuff 'cause she gits so carried away with things. Aunt Bessie says Lisa is so dramatic she ought to grow up to be a actress or something.

When me and Sammy got home Daddy was setting at the kitchen table drinking his liquor. I guess he didn't expect us that soon 'cause usually he drinks it in the barn.

"You eat anything?" I asked him. He didn't bother to move the jug off the table. He didn't answer me, neither.

"I brought home some chicken and beans and biscuits Aunt Bessie give me. You want some?"

He still didn't answer. He stared down at the table with his head in his hands. I got a plate out of the cupboard and set it on the table and put some of the food in it. He didn't look up.

Sammy had gone to the toilet. When he come in and seen

28

the jug he picked it up and set it on the cupboard. Daddy still didn't say nothing.

"Cat got ya tongue?" I asked, trying to be cheery, and set down across from him. Sammy set down beside me.

"How was the meetin'?" Daddy mumbled.

"Oh, it was fun," I said. "But I lost the egg toss. Elephant ears splattered me. Aunt Bessie and Uncle Will said they believed they was as big a turnout as we ever had. Uncle Will pitched six horseshoe ringers against Nell Green's daddy. Sammy eat lunch with Lisa Mae. He bid on Bertha but lost to David, who give half a dollar. Can you believe any fool giving half a dollar to eat with that har— that stupid girl? I just couldn't . . ."

"You have a good time, Sam?" Daddy asked.

"Yep," Sammy said.

"And you won't *believe* how many cakes they was. I counted fourteen. 'Leven of 'em chocolate. Doc Murphy was in seventh heaven and Lorraine Hood brought a platter of caramel fudge with peecans. Mmmm, was it good. I nearly got sick."

"You want to go lay down, Pa?" Sammy asked.

"Guess I will, son."

"You want me to help ya?"

Daddy pushed away from the table and stood. He wadn't drunk yet. He went on into the front room and laid down.

"You want some tea or anything?" I asked Sammy.

"Think I'll go to bed, too."

"But it's just barely dark. Don't you wanna play some checkers?"

"Nope." His shoulders sort of sagged as he headed to his room. I started clearing the table.

29

Chapter 5

Sunday after church Aunt Bessie and Uncle Will and Morgan come. Aunt Bessie brought jars of green beans which we cooked with 'taters. She made a big pone of cornbread.

After Uncle Will said the blessing, Morgan said, looking me straight in the eye, "I heard the Guthries' place is hainted. Calvin Martin said one night when he was coon huntin' he could hear a haint's echo halfway down to Cherrylog. You heard any haints, Ellie?"

Sammy looked at me and scrunched his eyes up in warning.

"Haints?" I said. "I ain't never heard no haints."

"I seen you up thataway. Thought maybe you heard 'em."

Daddy stopped chewing.

"I thought I told you to stay away from the Guthries," he said.

"I was just looking for Leety, Daddy."

Morgan reached across me for the butter as he talked.

"Calvin said he heard old man Guthrie is teched. Said he's crazy as a loon and mean as a rattler and has got the skins of two men he kilt hanging in his barn. He said the barn is hainted and the ghosts scream all night and one time when

30

he was riding up the mountain he seen a big white ghost floating right in amongst the trees like a . . ."

"Quit making up tales, Morgan," Aunt Bessie said.

"I ain't!" Morgan said, opening up them squinty eyes. "It's the truth, Mama, Calvin told me."

"Calvin Martin ain't told the truth since he was borned. Ain't no such thing as ghosts and you know it. Hand me the pepper."

I giggled, looking at Aunt Bessie. Her big bosoms hung over her plate as she reached for the pepper. Aunt Bessie is mighty fat. One time me and Sammy bet on how much one of her bosoms would weigh. I bet they'd weigh five pounds each and Sammy said heck no, said he bet they weighed twelve or fifteen. Then one time when me and him went into Bolton with Daddy, we went in the store and scooped up three big scoops of crowders that we thought was as much as one bosom and put them in the scale. Sammy said three scoops wadn't enough so we scooped four. I jumped up and down and clapped 'cause four scoops was a little over six pounds, so I come closest to winning.

"Any of them Guthrie younguns in school yet?" Aunt Bessie asked.

"Nah," Morgan said.

"You ever seen any of them, Jack?"

Daddy shook his head.

"I ain't never seen none of them," he said. "Saw Guthrie once at the mill. Spoke to him, but he acted like he didn't see me."

"Trashy bunch," Aunt Bessie said. "Where you reckon they come from?"

Uncle Will crumbled a big slice of pone into his buttermilk.

"Doc Murphy said they come up here from south Georgia, down around Waycross."

We talked on and on, catching up on the gossip and news.

Then the menfolks went out to set on the porch and me and Aunt Bessie washed the dishes.

After Mama died Aunt Bessie took to coming a lot and showing me about cooking and how to can stuff from the garden. She showed me about sewing. Aunt Bessie is real good with a needle, like Mama, and she makes the purtiest doilies that she puts on all the furniture. Lacy and ruffledy, and she's even got a whole crocheted bedspread. The purtiest thing you ever seen. And she showed me how to dry wildflowers by using sand and sometimes by just hanging them upside down from the barn rafters. I got bouquets setting all over the house in baskets and jars. Aunt Bessie wanted to teach me to crochet, but I don't want to learn. It takes too long to crochet things. Hours and hours of setting still, and I don't like setting still all that long.

I don't know what I'd do without Aunt Bessie to talk to. That night I had two big things I wanted to ask her. The first was about Alice's fits and the second was about harlots and boys lusting and all. While we was doing the dishes I asked about Alice. I said, "Aunt Bessie, you ever seen anybody have a fit?"

She laughed.

"Lordy yes," she said. "Morgan pitches a fit ever time he wants to do something and I don't let him do it."

"Not that kind of fit. I mean a real fit, you know, them kind where they can't help it."

"Sorta like a crazy fit?" she asked.

"Well, I don't know." I handed her a plate. "Ain't they no other kind?"

"Well, they's epileptic fits. Spells. Is that what you mean?"

"What's them?"

"I never seen nobody have one but I heard of them. Homer Summers' uncle had them till he died."

"Did the fits kill him?"

"Yeah, you could say that. When he was having one, he fell off the porch and broke his neck. How come you wanna know?"

"Was Homer Summers' uncle real pale and white?"

"I don't know. I never seen him. Now what's this all about?"

I told her all about Alice. The whole story about me sneaking up there and everthing. Aunt Bessie was shocked.

"You mean she's locked in that shed? She lives in that shed?"

"Yessum," I said. "She lives in it. It's the awfulest place you ever seen. And the stink is so bad you can't hardly git your breath. She's real sick. She may even be crazy, and she don't hear good atall. You reckon she's dying?"

Aunt Bessie shook her head.

"Ain't no telling. Will says that daddy of her'n is such a strange one. I doubt anybody'll ever know. He won't let nobody near the place."

"Is epilepsy catching?" I asked.

"No, it ain't," Aunt Bessie said. "If they got her quarantined, she's got to have something else. Something bad. Can't think of what would cause any kinds of convulsions 'less maybe high fevers, or maybe some kinda brain disease. I just don't know. It's plumb pitiful, Ellie, but ain't nothing nobody can do. Surely they has had her to a doctor. We could send food up if old man Guthrie would let us, but you know he won't, and whatever the pore chile has, I don't want you and Sammy gitting close to her. All I know to do is pray. That's all I know to do."

We finished up the dishes and then we went out to look at the garden and the flowers. I showed her where I had put two rose cuttings she had give me. It was a warm sunny day and two butterflies was flitting around a yellow rosebush that Mama had set next to the chimney. I opened my mouth I bet five times to ask her about lusting but couldn't ask. Finally I blurted out, "Aunt Bessie, does all boys lust?"

She was knocking a black bug off the leaves of the bush. She squinted her eyes at me.

"Lordy mercy! How come you asking that? You got some boy after you?"

I know my face was red as a beet.

"N-no, no I ain't, but, well, ah, ain't I old enough to know all that stuff?"

She looked at me a long time. A sad look come on her face. She took holt of my hand and led me to the back steps and we set down. She stared at the ground a while, then sighed and said, "I been dreading you growing up, Ellie. You been my little girl. Time flies, don't it? I sure hate the way it flies." She looked in my face. "I reckon you old enough to be told, but I sure hate it. What was it you asked me?"

"If, well, I asked if all boys lusted."

"Yep. All boys lust. All men lust and a lot of women lust." She smiled a little.

"*Women* lust?"

"Uh huh."

"Gosh! Uh—do *you* lust?"

She squinted her eyes at me again. "You know what lust means?"

I told her what I thought it meant. She told me what it really meant. I was shocked.

"Women's lusting is different," she said. "The difference is that women's is mixed up with loving most of the time. You see—well—you sure you want to hear all this, honey?"

I looked down at the steps and nodded.

"Go git us a glass of tea," she said. "Then we'll set here and talk."

That night I prayed a long time. I prayed about growing up and falling in love with somebody. I prayed about

34

Sammy and Bertha. I prayed about what Aunt Bessie had said about Daddy being so lonesome without Mama. All them prayers about man and woman stuff made me nervous so I prayed about Alice. I asked God to please not let Alice die. To please talk to Mr. Guthrie so's he wouldn't be so mean. To please do a miracle with Alice and do a miracle to git all the liquor off this mountain and to please let me not think about Alice so much. Not think about them eyes.

Chapter 6

School let out for the summer on Friday and Aunt Bessie come over Saturday. She drove that prissy little buggy Uncle Will bought for her the year they got married. She said why didn't me and her go down to Bolton and she'd git some cloth to make me a summer skirt. Sammy sort of hinted around, but she didn't ask him to go, so he went fishing. Daddy wadn't home. We didn't know where he was. He left before sunup.

I love riding in that buggy. It ain't got them leather seats on account of Uncle Will bought it secondhand and they was wore out, so he took them off. But you ought to see it. Last year Aunt Bessie made new cushions out of flowerdy cloth. She put ruffles on them. Then she had Uncle Will make a top for the buggy out of canvas and she made a cover for the canvas that hooks on and it matches the cushions and has got a crocheted scalloped edge, I reckon about a foot wide. She painted the buggy herself. Blue, nearly like cornflowers, and she painted the spokes white. That buggy is the talk of these mountains.

When they done all that, Aunt Bessie even had a bonnet to match the buggy cushions, but their goat eat it. Daddy laughs evertime he sees the buggy. Uncle Will said they couldn't just call it Bessie's Buggy, so him and Daddy got to thinking of the right name for it. We laughed at all the silly names they come up with, like Bessie's Bosom Bouncer. (Uncle Will thought of that.) Daddy thought of Bustie Bessie's Blue Belly Laugh. Aunt Bessie laughed the hardest at that one. Then she fussed at both of them and said she thought it ought to have a real romantic name, but she couldn't think of one. Then she said that, okay then, by cracky, *she* was calling it the Calico Carriage, and that was that.

But that wadn't that. Uncle Will calls it B.B. (Bosom Bouncer). Daddy calls it Allembees (for all them B's).

Anyhow, back to Aunt Bessie. When we got to Bolton, we went in Blackburn's General Store, but they was out of the cloth Aunt Bessie wanted, so we was standing there talking to Mrs. Blackburn when who should come in but that Bertha Langford.

"Hey, Mrs. Perkins," Bertha called. "Hey, Ellie, how y'all doing? Did Sammy come down with you?"

"Naw, he went fishing," I said, hoping she'd go on. She didn't.

"Did Sammy tell you we tied in the story contest?" she asked.

"He didn't mention it," I said, and it made me mad that Sammy hadn't told me. That's the way he is lately. He don't tell nothing. Me and him use to write stories all the time. Daddy said they was good. I wondered why he'd kept this a secret.

"Well, ain't that nice," Aunt Bessie said. "Did y'all win first place?"

"Uh huh."

"I'm right proud of you. Sammy didn't tell us nothing about it. He always was a purty good storyteller. Ellie, too. How's your mama?"

"She doing fine."

"That's good. You give her my regards, ya hear?"

"Our teacher is gonna send both our stories to the University of Georgia contest. Whoever wins first place gits to go to Athens and wins two dollars."

"Two dollars!" Aunt Bessie said. "Lord mercy! Ain't that wonderful! Did you read Sammy's story, Ellie?"

"No, I didn't," I said, gitting sicker of Bertha ever minute.

"His was about Indians," Bertha said.

Aunt Bessie grinned. "Yeah, he always has liked Indians. What was yores about?"

"I wrote about a family who was real rich and the daddy got killed and they lost all their money and the girl had to go to work and the boy stole a horse and wagon and got put in jail."

Aunt Bessie made a face.

"Sounds like a mighty sad story," she said.

"Oh, it don't end sad. The girl marries a rich boy and saves them."

"Well, that's nice. You must of . . ." Aunt Bessie stopped in midsentence and stared toward the door with her mouth open. I looked. It was the Guthries and all the younguns, 'cept Alice. They walked in and went on to the hardware. Me and Aunt Bessie kept staring as Bertha kept talking. I never seen such filthy younguns. Mr. Guthrie stayed in the hardware and Mrs. Guthrie went to the grocery and picked up a few things, then got some Bruton snuff and walked back to hardware. The kids stayed with their daddy.

They didn't stay long, and when they left, Aunt Bessie said, "Them two ought to be horsewhipped, leaving that sick girl by herself."

Bertha looked at the family and wrinkled her nose.

"Phew!" she said. "Who *are* they? What girl they leaving?"

I give Bessie a pinch and shook my head. I was scared she'd forget and tell Bertha about Alice. So she changed the subject to what purty hair Bertha had.

After we left the store we walked to the post office and talked with Miss Grace a while. Then we went down to the livery stable so's Aunt Bessie could pick up some leather Uncle Will had ordered. While we was there we seen the Guthries ride by in their old wagon headed toward Elijay.

I says to Aunt Bessie, "How come you reckon they going thataway? Surely they don't go to two towns to buy goods."

Aunt Bessie got a funny look and passed off my question with a shrug, which of course means I'm too young to know, which of course made me want to know all the more. So while Aunt Bessie talked to Mose and Elton, I set down on a old saddle and thought about it. It didn't take long. Daddy goes down that road lots. Ever week. Why? Now the Guthries was going. What's down thataway that they can't buy in Bolton? It had to be liquor. My heart sunk thinking about it.

Nobody was home when me and Aunt Bessie got back, so she come on in and helped me start supper. We put on a pot of butter beans. Then she sent me out to pick blackberries for a cobbler. I hate to pick blackberries. You git stickers all over you and have to watch out for bees and snakes. The blackberry patch is down the bank on the side of the road. The only good part is you got a good view of the valley, a sight that is as purty as a picture.

Yager Valley is the second biggest valley in these mountains. It's like a long green bowl. Its dirt grows just about anything you want to put in it. I looked down on the patchwork valley, divided up by the farmers in squares and rectangles—of blue-green cabbages, tall swaying corn, fat cotton stalks, gardens and grassy meadows.

Cherrylog Creek comes off the mountain and runs through the west side of the valley, spilling and gurgling over rocks for miles. River oaks, willows, and maples cling to its banks along with cattails, ferns, and a bunch of other bushy plants nobody's told me the name of. And at that time of the year (which was late June), the fields was surrounded by wildflowers. Tucked in and amongst the trees and undergrowth was sky-blue phlox, pink sweet peas, orange daylilies, and bunches of wild daisies and black-eyed Susans and then the brightest of all, the chigger weed, a flashing orange. It was enough to put lumps in your throat. Sammy has found more arrowheads in the valley than everywhere else put together. In fact, Yager Valley is Sammy's favorite place on earth, he says. He's found chunks of Indian pottery and one time even found some beads made out of copper and silver.

Morgan rode up while I was picking and asked his usual stupid question.

"Whatcha doing?"

There I was, bending into that briar patch with berry-stained hands and a bucket, and he asks whatcha doing.

"I'm shucking corn," I snapped.

"You don't have to be such a turd," he said, and rode off to the house.

When my bucket was half full and I was straightening up to take another look at the valley, I seen a speck of a person walking slow through one of the cabbage fields. I squinted my eyes against the sun, but all I could see was the speck moving. I had this strange urge to run down the mountain to the speck, but I didn't. I went on back to the house.

As it turned out, the strange urge wadn't so strange. The speck was Alice. Sammy found her in the fields down close to the gristmill. He was fishing down at the shoals right at the mill and looked out across the valley and seen her.

Here's how he told it to me.

"I couldn't believe my eyes, Ellie. I happen to glance over toward the cabbage field, and there she was, eating a whole cabbage, setting down between the rows with them filthy overalls and shirt, and that hair hanging ever which way, chomping on them huge cabbage leaves. I throwed down my pole and started to run to see, but decided I might scare her off. So I walked real slow with a big smile froze on my face. She never did hear me coming or look my way. I stopped about ten foot from her so's I wouldn't catch what she's got. Finally, she looked up.

"She didn't even flinch or jump or nothing, just kept on eating as fast as she could eat and staring at me without blinking with them big cow eyes."

"Deer eyes," I said.

"Huh?"

"She's got deer eyes, not cow eyes."

He looked impatient and went on.

"Okay, deer eyes. So I stood there smiling and saying, hey, over and over. Then I remembered she's hard of hearing so I yelled.

"'HEY! I'M SAMMY. I'M ELLIE'S BROTHER. YOU REMEMBER ELLIE?' Then she said, 'Ellie?'

"'UH HUH. SHE COME TO SEE YOU ONE TIME. REMEMBER?'

"I didn't think she remembered, so I said, 'PRETTY GOOD CABBAGE, HUH?'

"She tore off two big leaves and helt them out toward me. I was so surprised I started to walk up and take 'em. Then she patted the ground beside her like she wanted me to set. I didn't do that, but I did walk closer. I wadn't, oh, four feet from her, I bet and oh, Ellie, she stunk bad."

"I know," I said.

"Anyhow, I made up my mind I wouldn't act like I noticed the stink. I pulled my own cabbage and took a bite and she smiled. Did you see that girl smile when you was up there?"

"No," I said, "I don't think so. What's the matter with her smile? Her teeth rotten?"

He shook his head.

"I never seen a purtier smile. Sweet, you know, sweet. Kinda sweet like a baby's. Ah, you know. And that white skin, 'cept for the dirt, that skin was white as cotton nearly. And . . . well, all I can say is that's the purtiest girl I ever seen in my whole life. I mean it. My whole life. And them cow eyes."

"Deer eyes."

Sammy grinned.

"Deer eyes. Ellie, her eyes was wet looking. I mean she looked like she had tears that never come out."

"I know."

"And her hands, purty little hands, so dirty, and her fingernails. Ugh! I squatted there, not talking to her. All I could do was stare. Then you know what she said?"

"What'd she say?"

"She said, 'Ellie purree.'"

"She *did*?"

"She sure did, and I said, 'ELLIE *IS* PURTY. DO YOU LIKE ELLIE?' Then she said, 'She tum? She tuma see me?'"

"'YEAH. SHE COME TO SEE YOU.' And she said, 'She tumaback?'

"'YEAH. WELL, I DON'T—WELL, YEAH!'

"Then she tore off another cabbage leaf and got up and started walking. I jumped up and walked behind her and yelled, 'WHERE YOU GOING, ALICE?'

"She didn't answer, just kept walking. She got to the creek and waded in and laid on a big rock. Then she put her face in the water and drunk awhile. That hair hung in and flowed all around in a circle.

"Then she stood up and started walking. 'WHERE YOU GOING?' I yelled again, and she said, 'Where I liva.'

"So I asked her if she was going home and she said, 'I go home.'

"I'll tell you, Ellie, I panicked. It was crazy. I didn't want her to go back to that shed. I wanted to bring her here. Take her to Aunt Bessie. Anything. Then she said, 'You tum fixa limb?'

"And I said, 'DO WHAT?'

"'Fixa limb.'

"I couldn't figure what she was saying. 'FIX WHAT LIMB? WHERE?' And she said, 'You tum?'

"'WELL—AH, YEAH—I'LL COME.'

"She walked so slow it took over a hour to git to the Guthries'. She didn't talk. I said a few things about the weather and about fishing, but she acted like she didn't hear. When she got to the shed, she went right in. She pointed to the log that latches the door and said, 'You fixa limb?'

"I couldn't believe it. She wanted me to lock her back in! I saw that rat hole and I felt like busting them Guthries in the face, both of them.

"'You fixa limb?' she said again.

"'YEAH, YEAH. I'LL FIX IT,' I said.

43

"Then she asked, 'Ellie tum?'

"'I'LL TELL HER.'

"My stomach knotted up when I laid that log in that latch. I swore to myself I'd do something, but what? What in God's name can I do, anybody do? She's gonna die in that rotten stinking hole and we can't do a thing about it."

That evening Daddy come in sober. While we eat supper I wanted to talk about Alice. I wanted to tell Daddy but I didn't. I decided to talk about the story Sammy sent to the contest. I asked Sammy how come he hadn't told me and Daddy about it.

"What contest?" Daddy asked.

"It's a statewide contest," Sammy said, "put on by the University of Georgia. The one that wins gits to visit there."

Daddy smiled a big smile.

"Now ain't that something! I always said one of y'all would end up writing stories. Why ain't you let me read it?"

Sammy shrugged.

"Go git it. I want to see it."

"I ain't got a copy, Pa."

"Well, tell us about it," I said, passing Daddy the beans.

"Yeah," Daddy said. "What's it about, son?"

"Ah—it ain't much. I mean, I didn't think it was all that good."

"Other folks must think so."

"It's about Indians," I said. "Bertha told me. Tell us about it, Sammy."

"Well," he said, "it's just a story of a Cherokee boy. I named him Long Runner. He lived with his family in Yager Valley, though I couldn't find out what it was called then. I called it Yager, and he made a necklace out of copper and silver for his mama, and she lost it. It's sort of a funny story about how he thought his friend had stole it, so his friend was determined to find it to prove he didn't steal it. It ain't very exciting."

"All stories ain't exciting," Daddy said. "The main thing is the writing, the way you tell 'em. You must of done a fine job."

We set up a long time talking. I made a pot of coffee and we went out on the porch. It was a good night.

Chapter 7

*T*he next Saturday me and Sammy rode Poke over the mountain to see Doc Murphy. We had to talk to somebody who knowed something about sickness. When we got to the little white house, Doc was hoeing his garden. He put his hoe down and took off his straw hat and told me and Sammy to come set on the porch 'cause he needed to git cool.

We set on the porch swing and Doc set in the pine rocker and Mrs. Murphy brought us all some ice tea and chocolate cake.

"Now what's your problem, Sam?" Doc asked, pinching off a big bite of cake. I had started the swing swinging but Sammy stopped it.

"Oh, it ain't me, Doc, or Ellie. What we was wondering is, well, it's about that Guthrie family. You ever seen any of them, sir?"

"Can't say as I ever seen any of them but the ole man. Seen him once. Somebody sick up there?"

"He's got a real sick girl."

"What's wrong with her?"

"We don't know. They keep her locked in a shed outside the barn. She must be quarantine. She's real pale."

46

"Locked in a shed! What you mean? Does she go to school?"

"No, sir. Ellie seen her in the shed. She told Ellie she had fits, some kind of fits."

Doc took a big swaller of tea to wash down a big bite of cake. A dab of dark chocolate clung to his nose. Doc's a little man with not hardly no hair and he's got a big nose.

Doc shook his head.

"Damn shame," he said. "Hard dealing with ignorance. Some of these mountaineers let their kin die because of ignorance."

"Reckon you could go see about her, Doc?" Sammy asked.

"I'll ride up there tomorrow, son. Doubt they'll let me in. Seen a case about a month ago over close to the mill. Youngun died of the measles. That youngun could of lived. Plain carelessness. How old is the girl?"

"Maybe sixteen," Sammy said.

"Y'all want some more cake? Trudy baked two. She always bakes two at a time. Best cakes in the county."

I said I'd like some more and Sammy did, too. Doc called Mrs. Murphy.

Doc Murphy rode up to the Guthries' the next day, but he was right. He didn't get in. He told us all about it. He told us Mr. Guthrie answered his knock toting his shotgun and when Doc said he'd heard they had sickness, Mr. Guthrie lifted the gun and said we ain't got no sickness.

Doc backed up a little so's he could see the shed.

"Whatcha got in that shed?" he asked. Then Mr. Guthrie leveled the shotgun at Doc's big nose.

"Settin hens," Mr. Guthrie said. "Now I say you git offen my land."

"I ain't had much luck with my hens this spring, Guthrie. How yours layin?"

"You gonna git or am I gonna hafta blow that hawk beak offen yore face?"

"My wife says my henhouse is too cold. I ain't much of a handyman. I see you got that shed heated. Smart thinking."

"I said git!"

"What kind of heater you got?"

Doc said Mr. Guthrie took steps forward till the gun wadn't two inches from his face.

"All right—all right, Guthrie," Doc said. "I'll git. Put the gun down. Nice day, ain't it? Thought I'd go down to Cherrylog and catch me some trout. If you ever need me, holler."

When Doc rode back by our house to tell us what had happened, he said, "Sam, you know what Saturday the Guthries go into town? They go ever week?"

"Don't know," Sammy said.

"Here's what I want you to do, son. Ride Poke up there every Saturday morning early. If they leave, come tell me. We'd have plenty of time. We'll go up and I'll look at the girl. It's the only way."

"Yessir, I'll do it."

He helt out his hand and Doc shook it.

"Thank ya, sir," Sammy said.

The Guthries went into town the next Saturday, so Sammy rode Poke to git Doc Murphy as fast as Poke would go, which ain't very fast. By the time Doc and Sammy got back up the mountain, Alice had left the shed.

Sammy showed Doc how he figgered Alice got out. He had noticed it when he locked her in. She had rigged up a lever kind of thing out of a long thin piece of iron that

48

Sammy figgered come off the old wagon. She would push it through the wide crack in the door till it was under the heavy log latch. Then she stood up a old plank under the iron to get leverage. Then she pushed down on the iron to raise the log.

Doc Murphy said he didn't see how anybody that had to live in filth like that was alive, let alone had enough sense to figger how to git out.

They decided to look for Alice. Sammy rode toward Yager Valley. Doc found her at Cherrylog Creek. He talked to her as best he could. He said she didn't act like she was afraid of him atall. She let him check her throat, ears, eyes, heart. She told him she had fits but she couldn't describe them. According to Doc, she said, "Ooooo, dey tum on. I feel whooooom. Dey tum on."

"DO YOU WANT TO GO BACK TO THE SHED, ALICE?" Doc screamed.

"Mmm, you fixa limb?"

Doc Murphy told us he thought Alice probably had epilepsy. He told us what the seizures was like, and he told us they wadn't nothing could be done.

"The girl is not crazy," he said, "and she's not dying. She seems to be in fairly good health. Decent food and a little sunshine would make a difference. And the youngun needs a bath." He shook his head. "Damned shame. Seems like a smart girl."

"Why they got her in that shed, then, if she ain't got a catching disease?" I asked.

"Like I said, ignorance. Ignorance is worse than sickness, Ellie. Sad case. Seen a lot of sad cases in these mountains."

"Can't the law do nothing?" Sammy asked. "Can't the law—ah—take her away or something?"

Doc patted Sammy's shoulder.

49

"Afraid not, son. Nobody can tell a man how to treat his younguns."

"Can't nobody do nothing? Can't *we*?"

"If they was anything to be done, I'd do it," Doc said. "And I think you two better forget it. Guthrie is not to be fooled with."

Doc changed the subject to Daddy. We told him the drinking was worse. He said he was sure sorry to hear it. He said if we needed him, come on down. He got on his horse to leave.

"Y'all are mighty young to be facing all this," he said. "Sometimes life gives us problems too big to handle. I don't know the answers. Don't know who does."

I looked down at my feet.

"I reckon God does," I said.

"Sometimes I wonder," Doc said, then rode on.

Me and Sammy couldn't talk about it. We both moped around. Sunday after church, I got Mama's Bible and got on Poke and went to Cherrylog. I don't read the Bible. It's too hard to understand all them funny words, but sometimes I like to hold it. Makes me feel closer to Mama.

Under followed me down and laid on his usual spot and went to sleep. I set on the moss and leaned up against the log. I set a long time listening to the trickle of water and watching the minnows play. A cardinal had built its nest in a patch of thick shrub across the creek. She had laid her eggs and the babies had long since flew away. Now she was back. I figured she was ready to do it all over again.

I thought about it. How sad it was. She had her babies and now they was gone. Did she ever see them? If she ever seen them, would she know they was hers? How come God give her babies only to let them go away? Under had made babies with Aunt Bessie's dog one time. He didn't even know it. How come in the animal and bird world the daddies make babies and don't take care of them? Do creatures know about love? Is it only the mama creatures that love?

I thought about people. About Mama and Aunt Bessie, doing all the taking care of while the daddies tended man business. But daddies love. I knowed Daddy loved us. Uncle Will loves Morgan (though I don't see how). Do daddies love different? How come God made a man like Mr. Guthrie who don't love atall? Does *Mrs*. Guthrie love? If she loves Alice, how come she lets her stay in that shed?

I watched Under start scratching. He was laying close to a ant hill. A long row of ants was circling a little pine and toting food to the hill.

I heard a swooshing in the ferns on the other side of the creek. In a minute two chipmunks come onto the bank and darted around, playing and chasing each other. They moved like squirrels, quick and jerky. Stop, start, look around, sniff, chase. They was so cute.

Does Alice love animals? Has she ever had a pet? Does her family talk to her? Has she ever had a friend? The thought made me bust into tears. The awful thought that she ain't never had nobody that loved her.

Oh God, why? Why don't she have nobody? Mama said you love us all the same. Don't you love Alice? *Don't* you? Was Mama wrong? The preacher says you know what we need before we even ask. Is that true? Don't you know Alice needs somebody, God? Don't you even *care*? What good are you anyhow if you don't help us?

Then I got so mad at God I jumped up and stomped my feet. Scared Under half to death. His eyes popped open and he shrunk up and started whining.

Then I really pitched a fit. I told Under to hush up his silly whining. Then I picked up rocks and throwed them in the water, then at the trees. I tried to throw one at God but it hit a limb and clonked to the ground. I picked it back up and was gonna try again, but a thought hit me and I looked up through the trees to the puffy white clouds and hollered as loud as I could holler.

"Do you drink liquor?"

Chapter 8

I heard Daddy bust through the kitchen door, cussing and stumbling and as drunk as I ever seen him. I was at the stove stirring gravy. I thought my heart would jump out of me, he scared me so bad. I backed against the wall, still holding the stirring spoon. It dripped on the floor.

Daddy didn't even see me. He fell onto the table, knocking over two chairs. Under, who was sleeping under the table, yipped and whined and run to the door. Daddy pushed hisself up and tried to focus his eyes on Under. He cussed some more, then picked up one of the chairs and throwed it at the dog. I screamed and run to Under. The chair leg had hit him in the face and cut his nose. He was whining loud.

Daddy then tried to focus his eyes on me. His head swayed from side to side. I tried to drag Under out the door.

Sammy wadn't due home till dark. He'd gone down to work at the sawmill. I couldn't think of what to do. I knowed Daddy couldn't chase us. He couldn't even walk. I pulled Under off the porch and half toted, half drug him to the barn and laid him down. Then I hid in the loft and laid on my stomach in the hay and stared at the kitchen door.

In a minute Daddy busted through it, falling all over the

porch, carrying his shotgun, hollering for Under. I went down the ladder steps in a flash and grabbed Under and dragged him out the barn into the pasture. He was yipping and whining all the way. Then I crawled into a chicken coop and drug him with me. He kept whining.

"Shush! Oh, Under, shush!" I whispered. I heard Daddy hollering, cussing. He stumbled into the pasture.

Me and Under both was laying in piles of chicken doo-doo. Tears run down my face as I watched Daddy weave around. He fell and managed to git up. I don't know how long I laid there watching my daddy, stumbling and falling. I prayed, please let him pass out. Oh, please, please let him pass out. Don't let him hurt us. Don't let him hurt hisself. I prayed over and over and over with my eyes squeezed shut. When I opened them, there my daddy laid, still as a plank. He'd passed out.

I went in and got him a pillow and quilt. When Sammy come home, he drug him into the house and put him to bed. Then Sammy got Daddy's shotgun and his rifle and wrapped them in canvas and hid them under the house.

"He's gitting worse," Sammy said. "Ain't no telling. He could of shot you. He could shoot anybody. You. Me. Under. What we gonna do? Hiding his guns don't solve nothing. Uncle Will says he ought to be beat, but who's gonna beat him? I don't want to beat him." Sammy put his face in his hands.

We couldn't think of nothing to do about Daddy, so me and Sammy made a pact. I told him that since Doc Murphy couldn't do nothing about Alice and since it looked like God wouldn't do nothing, I reckoned we'd have to do something. He said he'd already thought of it. He said what we was gonna do was one or the other of us would spend the day with Alice on the days the Guthries went into town. But that wadn't all. He said that we would go up there at

54

night and sneak her out of that shed and into the woods or down to Cherrylog. He always has lots of ideas. That's the way he is, thinks up ideas real fast. Uncle Will says he's like Daddy used to be.

"You got to show her how to bathe, Ellie," he said, "and we're gonna cut some sweetgum and make some toothbrushes and show her how to clean her teeth. And somehow or another we gonna wash them clothes she's got on. And I was thinking, maybe we could even teach her to read a little. Maybe how to write her name. And I tell you one thing, Ellie, I'm gonna try to git on speaking terms with Mr. Guthrie—if it kills me. I'm gonna find out what's going on!"

All his plans set my heart a-pounding. The only plan that upset me was the one about gitting on speaking terms with Mr. Guthrie. I'd just as soon kiss a bear.

That night we went up the mountain. It was close to ten o'clock. They wadn't no lamps burning nowhere. Everthing was dark. A sliver of a moon hung amongst the zillion stars. We was scared to death. We tiptoed to the shed door and both of us lifted the log so as to be as quiet as we could. If Alice screamed out we'd have to run. That was all we could do.

Sammy pushed the heavy door open real slow. It was too dark to see inside. Alice didn't hear a thing. I moved to where she was sleeping on them quilts and bent down. I could just make out where her head was. I patted her shoulder. She moved. Then she lifted her head. We couldn't say nothin 'cause we'd have to scream it. She set up. My eyes was gittin use to the dark and I could see her face. She didn't say a word and all we done was smile at her. It was purty scary and strange, standing there in that stinking shed, not being able to talk. I patted her again. She was not scared; her face was calm and them eyes looked us over as though we come there ever day, big and shining and star-

55

ing, from me to Sammy. No question was in them eyes and no fear. Just staring at us straight as a arrow without a blink.

Then she smiled.

Sammy was right. She has the purtiest smile I ever seen, as sweet and bright as a baby's. I patted her hand. Then Sammy patted her shoulder. She looked at my hand patting her. Then she looked at Sammy's. Her smile went away and her eyes scrunched up like she was in pain—looking at our hands patting her. Looking and looking. Then we both moved our hands 'cause she looked so funny. She still stared at our hands.

Then she reached over ever so slow and helt out her hand, dirty with them ragged fingernails. She helt it next to mine. She wanted me to pat her again! Me and Sammy looked at each other and I started patting and Sammy started patting till her smile come back and lit up her face. Then with jerky movements that was a little timid, she started patting us.

If anybody would of seen us three in that stinking filthy shed in the dark of the night just a-patting, I reckon they would of laughed till their stomach hurt.

The next Saturday she let us lead her through the woods toward Cherrylog. The crickets and birds filled up the day with their songs but I knowed Alice didn't hear. We both helt her hands and Sammy toted the rags and soap and stuff and it's hard to tell you what I was feeling. It was like a secret big adventure. Dangerous and scary and fun. My stomach was full of butterflies and when we got far enough away from the house, I busted into giggles.

When we got to the creek, Sammy dumped the stuff and said he'd go on down a ways till I give Alice a bath. All of a sudden I panicked. How in the world was I gonna git her to bathe? I got mad at Sammy's fancy ideas. Whoever heard of taking a stranger to a creek and telling her to bathe? It was the awfulest idea I ever heard of. What if I hurt her feelings so bad she run home? What if she was so shocked she hit me or something? I could of just choked Sammy. She smelled so bad I knowed we'd have to bathe her sometime, if we was gonna start seeing her and teaching her and all, like Sammy planned, but *how*?

Then a thought hit me. I would act like *I* wanted to take a bath. I'd git in the water and soap up, then I'd ask her casual like if while we was down here she wanted to bathe, too. I got the soap and a rag and waded in till the water come to the bottom of my dress. I put soap on the rag and washed my face. Alice stood on the bank watching.

"WATER SURE IS NICE AND COLD," I screamed. She didn't hear me. I waded back toward her and screamed again.

"Mmmm," she said.

"MY AUNT BESSIE MADE THIS SOAP. YOU WANNA SMELL IT?"

She stared at me with her face blank. I climbed the bank and helt the soap under her nose.

"SMELLS SWEET, HUH?"

She nodded and smiled.

"I THINK I'LL TAKE ME A BATH. I LOVE BATHING IN THE CREEK."

I waded back out and soaped my arms. Then I waded over to the bank again.

"YOU WANNA WADE A WHILE?" I helt out my hand to her and she took it. I helped her down the bank into the water. Then I told her to roll up the legs of her overalls. She didn't understand, so I did it.

"Oooooo hit told!" she said.

"YOU'LL GIT USE TO IT. IT FEELS GOOD WHEN YOU GIT USE TO IT. WANNA SOAP YOUR FACE?" I handed her the soap and rag. She ran it over her face and arms. I stood there feeling like a silly stupid fool. This wadn't gonna work. She needed a all-over bath. She needed that hair washed. I wished Sammy was there to see how stupid his idea was.

We stood like two idiots looking at each other. I was frantic, trying to think of a answer. How *could* I ever git her to take a real bath? I remembered when I was little and Mama would bring me down and let me splash in the water naked. It was such fun. How can I git her to git naked? Is she too timid to git naked? The smell of her so close was gitting to me. I waded to the deeper part, pulling my dress up. She followed me and got the overall legs wet.

"DON'T GET YOUR OVERALLS WET, ALICE!"

"Huh?"

I pointed to the breeches legs, feeling more silly by the minute. The thought come that the only way I'd ever git her to take a real bath is take one myself. Show her. Right then I *really* got mad at Sammy for all *his* ideas that *I* have to work out. Well, it might as well be now or never, I thought. We're here and I got the soap and rags, and her overalls are wet anyhow. I waded away from her and played like I stumbled. I fell into the creek with a big splash. I squealed and carried on and turned to look at Alice. She had copied what I done. She was setting in the water! I got up and went to the bank and she did, too.

"WE MIGHT AS WELL SOAP UP NOW THAT WE'RE WET ANYHOW," I said.

I took off my dress and stood there in my camisole and bloomers.

"TAKE YORE CLOTHES OFF IF YOU WANT TO. IT'S ALL RIGHT."

She unhooked the big overalls and pulled them down. Her daddy's shirt hung nearly to her knees. It took her a long time to unbutton it. I was standing there shivering. When she took it off she was stark naked. She didn't have

58

on no camisole or bloomers. All of a sudden I felt awful for what I'd tricked her into. I could of just kicked myself. She was standing there stiff and straight and didn't look atall timid or embarrassed, but I still felt awful. All of a sudden I decided to git naked, too. After all, we was both girls, and after all, it was the least I could do. So I did.

I showed her how to soap up and rinse off. I washed my hair so's I could wash hers. I scrubbed her head till my fingers hurt. When we got done we had to put our sopping wet clothes back on, but I couldn't help that.

Sammy came back, giving me his whistle signal. I whistled it was okay. I was so mad at him I could of busted. He said why didn't we go set in the clearing in the hot sun so's our clothes would dry some. He tried to say a few things to Alice. It was pitiful how hard it was to git her to understand. Finally, we took her back to the shed, and my heart sunk as we dropped the log back into the latch.

On the way home I told Sammy off good and proper.

Chapter 9

Monday noon Sammy rode up to the Guthries. The day had started off cloudy and hot. Thunderstorms threatened. He tied Poke to a pine and went up them front porch steps. He said he was mighty scared. He knocked on the door and hollered out.

"Anybody home?"

He had to holler three times before the door opened. There stood Mrs. Guthrie with three younguns hanging on her. Sammy said she was just a regular woman. Sorta fat. Hair twisted up in a knot. She had on a old brown housedress that hung on her. She had a dip of snuff under her bottom lip.

"Yeah?" she said from behind the screen.

"Howdy, ma'am. I'm Sammy Perkins. We live down the mountain a ways. Heard y'all raise chickens. Pa sent me to buy some eggs from you."

"We don't sell eggs. Sell chickens."

Two of the kids pushed the screen open and come out to stare at Sammy.

"Oh, well, ah, I guess Pa heard wrong."

"Yeah." She spit a brown glob off the porch.

Sammy shuffled around a minute.

"Nice warm day, ain't it. Might rain," he said.

She didn't answer.

"Pa said anytime y'all need anything we . . ."

"We don't need nothing."

"Uh—well—ah, it's nice meeting you. You must be Mrs. Guthrie. Mr. Guthrie at home?"

"He ain't here."

Sammy backed to the steps.

"Well, y'all come to see us anytime," he said. "Nice meeting you."

"Yeah," she said and closed the door.

By the time Sammy got home, dark clouds was hanging heavy over the mountains. He was disappointed and mad when he come in.

"I don't see how anybody can git to them!" he said.

"That's what Doc Murphy said. He told us not to risk it."

"I never seen the like."

He set at the kitchen table and I poured him some coffee. Thunder rolled nearby. The clouds was getting darker.

"Them folks ain't even natural! What time did Daddy leave?" he asked.

"A while ago. He didn't take his liquor as I could see."

"He's due for a sober-up. Must be purty sick by now."

"Yeah."

"I was thinking, Ellie, that woman might be right nice. I mean, I think they all scared of the old man."

"How could she be nice? For gosh sake, Sammy, she feeds her girl out of a dishpan. She don't see she gits a bath. You call *that* nice?"

"Yeah, but trashy people is like that. Aunt Bessie said so. They can learn better."

"Who's gonna teach them?"

He shrugged and give me a smile.

"Any biscuits left?"

I got the biscuits out of the warmer and give him the

butter and soggum, then put a plate in front of him. We heard the first raindrops on the tin roof.

"You going to help at the sawmill today?" I asked.

"Nah. We caught up. Mr. Hudson is bringing in a load late afternoon if it clears up. Reckon I'll fix them planks in the barn."

"We going to see Alice tonight?"

"Depends on the weather."

We didn't git to go that night on account of Daddy. Sammy was right. He was due for a sober-up. He come home and wadn't drinking. I made us a nice supper. Fried 'taters, cornbread, crowder peas, and sliced 'maters. Daddy eat purty good. After supper he milked Leety. He looked rough. Eyes and face red.

"You got a headache, Daddy?" I asked when we was setting on the porch.

"Had one. Supper helped. Good supper, girl."

"Tomorrow I'm gonna make a strawberry pie. Picked nearly a quart down close to the branch. We nearly out of sugar though. You going into town tomorrow?"

"Might—it's according."

"Better git some coffee, too. And Daddy, you reckon you could git a comb?"

"We got a comb."

"Yeah—well—I know, but I sure would like to have one of my own."

Sammy looked at me and grinned. He knowed I wanted to give it to Alice.

"Can't see as we need two combs. Money don't grow on trees."

"How much they cost, Ellie?" Sammy asked.

"I don't know."

"Uncle Will paid me for two days, nearly a dollar. I'll git a comb."

"No sense wasting money, son," Daddy said. "Our comb ain't broke."

"Girls need stuff like that," Sammy said.

"Don't need it if they got it—ought to spend money on things you need."

Sammy was setting on the steps with me. He got up and took a step or two in the yard.

"How much a quart of liquor cost, Pa?" he asked.

Daddy was rocking in the rocker. He stopped. He was quiet a while. I got nervous. Me and Sammy don't never git snappy with Daddy.

"You planning on buying some?" His voice was like a warning.

"If it don't cost too much," Sammy said. "Thought maybe I'll try to grow up to be like my daddy." His voice cracked.

"You talking mighty smart, boy! You buy liquor and you'll git a knot jerked in yore tail. You ain't old enough to talk to me like that. You don't know what you talking about. Drinking liquor is man's business. You ain't lived long enough to know nothing about living, about what a man goes through."

Sammy climbed the steps past me. I looked up at his face. His square jaw looked like a vice clamped. He stopped on the top step and looked at Daddy.

"Looks to me like," he said, "drinking liquor keeps a man too drunk to go through life atall. How can you go through life when you don't even know you're alive?"

"Hush up! Ya hear me, boy? You hush up or I'll be obliged to hush you."

I could see Sammy shaking. I moved up two steps and pinched his leg, hoping he'd keep his mouth shut.

"Me and Ellie is tired of not having a daddy, Pa." He looked Daddy straight in the eye. "We tired of you gitting

63

drunk. We scared you gonna hurt yourself—or somebody. Daddy, you got to quit. You got to!"

I couldn't believe Sammy was talking like that. He knows when Daddy's just got off a drunk he's ill as a hornet. He knows to leave him alone. Daddy's eyes got narrow and he helt on to the chair arms.

"Cut it out, son!"

"I hid your guns."

"I noticed."

"You tried to kill Under. Pa, you was gonna shoot Under. Can't you see how dangerous you getting?"

"What ya mean, I tried to shoot Under?"

"Uncle Will says you're blacking out. Says you don't know—don't remember. Pa, you could of killed Ellie!"

"You lying! I never pointed no gun at that girl, or Under!"

Sammy looked at me.

"Am I lying, Ellie?"

I could feel my palms sweating. The night air was still heavy with dampness. A rolling fog covered the valley below us.

"Am I, Ellie?" Sammy asked again.

"He ain't lying, Daddy."

Daddy got out of the chair so fast he set it rocking. He bounded down the steps past me. He went through the yard and across the road to where the blackberry patch is. Then he stood staring at the foggy valley.

"You shouldn't of done that," I whispered.

"I got to do it sometime. Waiting may be too late."

"He can't *help* it. You know that. He can't help drinking. It ain't his fault."

"It ain't mine neither, and it ain't yore'n. We suffering more than him. You need a daddy. I do too. Ellie, something's got to stop him."

"I pray all the time," I said. "Mama would cry if she'd of heard you talk to Daddy like that."

"She'd cry harder if he'd of shot you."

"Oh, just hush!"

"I can't hush. Somebody has to talk to him."

"Mama'd turn over in her grave!"

Sammy turned around and took holt of my arm. "Come on," he said.

He pulled me up and made me walk, half run, around to the backyard.

"Where we going? Turn loose of me!"

He didn't turn loose. He pulled me through the garden, down past the cornfield and to the spot next to the branch where Mama is buried. I looked at the huge rounded creek stone that Daddy carved my mama's name on.

MARY ELLEN PERKINS
1901–1937

The grave site was purty. We kept it that way. Petunias was Mama's favorite. We planted them ever spring, all around her grave. Lavender and white and pink. The grave was covered over with creek sand. We never did let one weed stay on it. I looked at the marker. She had been dead two years. It seemed like forever.

The sweet smell of the flowers hit me and I started crying. Sammy put his arm around my shoulder.

"She wouldn't want Daddy to shoot us, Ellie," he said.

I nodded. "I'm sorry," I said, and buried my face against Sammy's chest.

Chapter 10

It rained off and on for four days. The third day Sammy said we ought to go see Alice anyhow. He said we could take her a coat and we'd take her to the rock overhang over at Lookout where we could stay dry. Lookout ain't far from Alice's house. All it is is a bunch of rocks, but you can stand there and see a long ways over the mountains. We had a school picnic there once.

The night was black dark on account of the rain, and even with the lantern it took us a long time to git to Lookout. By the time we got there we was all purty wet and shivering. I was sorry we had come.

"We ought to have waited," I said to Sammy as we ducked under the big rock. "I'm freezing and Alice is, too."

It was dry under the rock 'cause it hangs out over a washed-out place like a cave. Piles of dead leaves had blowed up against the back wall, so Sammy told us to set on them.

"We'll cover up with the leaves," he said, pushing them with his foot and lifting bunches to put in one spot.

"I wish I had some dry wood," he said. "I could make us a fire."

"Leaves don't burn long," I said, shaking.

"Yeah, that's right."

I huddled on one side of Alice and Sammy on the other. We scooped leaves over our legs and piled them against our chests. All that was hanging out was our shoulders and heads.

"THE LEAVES WILL GIT US WARM," Sammy yelled to Alice. "ARE YOU OKAY? ARE YOU REAL COLD?"

"I cold mmmm," she said.

I put my arm around her and snuggled closer. In a little bit I could feel the chill leaving. Sammy piled more leaves under her neck.

"YOU EVER BEEN HERE BEFORE?" he asked.

"Nooo, I not." She shivered against me.

Sammy had set the lantern away from the leaves. Its flickering light made spooky moving shadows on the dirt and rock walls on both sides. The rain fell slow and steady, its big drops making plipping noises on the trees and bushes. The peaceful sound helped me forget the moving shadows.

"THIS PLACE IS CALLED LOOKOUT," Sammy said. "ON A CLEAR DAY YOU CAN SEE TWO STATES."

"Wha? Wha dat?"

"STATES? WELL, A STATE IS A PLACE. A REAL BIG PLACE WITH LOTS OF TOWNS AND CITIES AND LOTS OF LAND."

Alice didn't say nothing. She ducked her chin into the leaves.

"WE LIVE IN A STATE CALLED GEORGIA. STATES HAVE DIFFERENT NAMES. FROM HERE YOU CAN SEE INTO NORTH CAROLINA AND TENNESSEE. WE'LL COME BACK SOMETIME AND SHOW YOU. WOULD YOU LIKE TO COME BACK?"

"Mmmm."

"ARE YOU GETTING WARMER?"

"Mmmm." Her eyes followed the moving shadows.

"YOU SCARED? YOU SCARED OF THE SHAD-OWS?"

She shook her head no. "Dey jumpa. Dey jumpa hurry, huh?"

"YOU LIKE TO SEE THEM JUMP?"

"Dey jumpa makea swoom ona hit." She pulled her arm from under the leaves and made a swoop.

"OH, LOOK!" I said. "LOOK AT THE SHADOW OF YOUR ARM ON THE ROCK."

She moved her arm back and forth, looking at the shadow.

"I CAN MAKE ANIMAL SHADOWS, ALICE," I said, and lifted my arms. I put my hands together with my thumbs separated and my little fingers separated from the others to make a dog face. My shadow didn't show up clear.

"Let me try it," Sammy said. He was in a better spot. His dog shadow was perfect. He moved his little finger to make the mouth move.

"Ooooooh!" Alice said. "Hit look lika dog, hit do. *I* do hit?"

Sammy took her hands and fixed the fingers. Then he moved them to get the best shadow.

"THERE!" he said. "YOU DID IT. NOW MOVE YOUR LITTLE FINGERS UP AND DOWN."

She did and the dog's mouth moved. She giggled.

"I do hit! I do hit!" she said.

Sammy showed her how to make a horse face and a rabbit and he showed her how to do funny birds pecking each other. She squealed out and giggled and her eyes never left Sammy's face. For a while all of us forgot about being wet.

After the game I noticed Sammy staring at Alice's face. We had buried down into the leaves again. I glanced at Sammy and he was staring like in a dream nearly, watching the shadows move across that white face. His eyes didn't blink and his mouth was open a little. Alice was staring with half-closed eyes at the lantern, her thick dark lashes almost touching her cheeks. When he seen I was watching him, he turned his head.

We didn't stay long on account of I was afraid Alice would git sick. When we got back to the shed, I felt around for something for Alice to sleep in. I couldn't find nothing. Sammy was waiting outside. I motioned for Alice to take off her wet clothes and she did. Then she got in the bed and I tucked them stinking quilts close around her, and hung her overalls and shirt over the rail next to the stove.

Chapter 11

*M*e and Aunt Bessie spent the next week canning vegetables. I went down to her house and helped her, then she come up and helped me. One day we made twenty-seven quarts of vegetable soup out of tomatoes, corn, okra, beans, and peas. We was so proud of them I couldn't wait to show Daddy. We canned blackberries and squash another day, and the last day we made scuppernong jelly.

You should of seen our big cupboard. It was slap full and we wadn't done. We'd keep at it till fall. Then when apples was ready, we'd cut up two or three bushels and lay them out to dry.

Aunt Bessie says I take after Mama about canning, and I reckon she's right. Ever summer Mama filled up the cupboard and she'd just beam. She said they ain't nothing like seeing all them colorful jars of good food laid up to feed yore family come winter.

Morgan come with Aunt Bessie the day we made the jelly. He hung around making a pest of hisself, gitting in the way and licking the spoons and asking stupid questions.

"Why ya use so much sugar?" he asked once. "Ain't that too much sugar?"

"I use it 'cause yore mama told me to," I said.

"What if it's too sweet?"

"Has they ever been too sweet before?"

"Well—no, but sugar costs a lot of money."

"Would you quit standing right in front of the stove! Why don't you go bring in a load of wood?"

"It's hot enough in here as it is," he said, fanning his face with his hands.

"Well, why don't you go draw up some fresh water?"

He glanced at the bucket setting on the washstand.

"The bucket's full. What ya want more for?"

Aunt Bessie come in from the porch with a dishpan full of scuppernongs.

"This is the last of 'em," she said, and set the pan on the table. Morgan reached over to grab one. Aunt Bessie slapped his hand.

"I wish you'd of gone with yore daddy this morning," she said. "A kitchen ain't no place for a boy. Why don't you git Sammy's pole and go down to Cherrylog. Maybe we could have fish for supper."

Morgan flopped down in a chair with his legs stretched out into the middle of the kitchen.

"I'm tired of fishing."

"Why don't you git a bucket and pick us some blackberries?"

"I'm tired of pickin."

"Tired? You ain't picked nothing all week. Move ya legs! If we waited on you to help, everbody'd starve. Now git on outa here."

"Ain't nothin ta do," he said. "Can I take the buggy?"

Aunt Bessie looked at him, disgusted. "If I've told ya one time I've told ya a hunderd, you can't use my buggy! Now move yore legs."

"Grant Campbell's daddy lets him use his."

"*I* said move!"

"His daddy let him take it all the way to Bolton. I don't

71

never git to do nothin. How come I can't take yore silly buggy?"

Aunt Bessie slapped a dishrag against the table.

"Oh, so my buggy's silly, huh? You think it's silly? And just when did my Mr. High and Mighty decide my buggy was silly?"

Morgan scratched his fat stomach.

"Ain't just me. Everbody thinks it's silly."

"*Everbody?* Who's everbody?"

"Ellie thinks it, don't ya, Ellie?"

I was by now so mad at the stupid idiot I could of poured hot jelly on him.

"Me!" I squealed. "You better shut yore mouth. I love that buggy and you know it!"

"Ha!" he said, staring me straight in the eye. "You and Sammy makes fun of it alla time."

I was stupefied. I whirled around with my wood stirring stick dripping with jelly and I slapped it across his cheek.

"Liar!" I screamed.

He jumped up so fast the chair fell on Under, who yelped and run. He lifted his arm to hit me. Aunt Bessie hollered and jumped for his arm across the table. She missed and fell into the pan of scuppernongs, knocking them all over everwhere. Morgan swung at me and I dodged and the fool hit the pot of bubbling jelly and knocked it off the stove. It's a wonder we all wadn't scalded. I never in my life been so mad. Aunt Bessie shrieked and Morgan took off out the door with her trying to chase him. I run right behind them swinging my stick. Morgan run out to the road. Aunt Bessie's so fat she couldn't chase him but I could. I'm a dadgummed fast runner, so I hauled off after him and caught him before he run two hunderd feet, I bet. I grabbed holt of his overall straps, then I started pounding his head with the stirring stick. In a minute Aunt Bessie was there.

"March!" she ordered, pointing back to the house.

He marched.

When we got there she said, "Into that kitchen!"

He went in. We followed him. Aunt Bessie pulled out two chairs and set them against the wall. "Set down, Ellie," she said, and I did.

"Now, clean it up, Mr. High and Mighty!"

"But, Ma," Morgan whined.

"Now!"

Aunt Bessie got two glasses and poured me and her some tea. Then she set down beside me and we gossiped and giggled while Morgan spent way over a hour mopping up that sticky jelly and picking up the scuppernongs.

"It's just a pleasure, ain't it, Ellie, honey," Aunt Bessie said, "watching that sweet boy clean up yore kitchen. I don't think I've had so much fun since Will slipped in the hog pen and fell into the slop. Men folks has a tendency to git a little spoiled, don't ya think? We wait on 'em hand and foot all their life. I wish you coulda seen Will with slop dripping off his face. I musta laughed a month!"

I just love Aunt Bessie.

Chapter 12

*T*he next Saturday we spent with Alice was real hot.
We had decided this was the day to give Alice the
whole cleanup. Wash her clothes, bathe her, cut her nails,
wash her hair, and show her how to clean her teeth. I had
brought everthing. Rags, soap, soda, scissors, and a dress to
put on her while her clothes dried.

Sammy left us at the creek and went looking for arrowheads. He hadn't been gone five minutes before Alice
simply walked to the creek bank, stripped, then waded into
the water. For a minute I thought about letting her bathe by
herself, but then she looked at me like she was disappointed.

"Whaa?" she said. "You tum?"

I got naked and waded in.

We splashed around a little, then I scrubbed her overalls
and shirt and showed her how to help. We both wrung
them out and took them to a clearing and laid them on
some bushes. Then I showed her the sweetgum toothbrushes. I dipped one into soda and rubbed my teeth. Then
I handed her one. She made a big face over the soda taste
but she did it.

Then we bathed.

She soaped herself three times. Then we washed her hair.
Alice was having a good time. She giggled and splashed and

laughed. I wondered if she's ever played before in her whole life.

We dried off and I put the dress on her. Then I got myself dressed and combed her hair. Never in my life have I ever seen as many tangles. I must of worked on that hair a hour. Then I cut her fingernails and toenails.

When it was all done I looked at her. She stood there in my school dress, a blue and green sorta flowerdy pattern. She stood straight and clean with that white skin and that long black hair shining around her face and I had to suck in my breath. I couldn't wait to see Sammy's face when he seen her.

I heard his whistle. I pulled Alice behind a big tree. When Sammy walked up, I pulled her out. His face was something to see, I can tell you that. But more than his face, was her face seeing his face.

At first he stopped dead, still staring like he couldn't believe his eyes. He didn't ever glance my way.

Her face seeing his face was scared looking at first—like she didn't understand why he was looking at her thataway. Then the most amazing thing happened. Here was a girl who didn't even know she was one, who hadn't never had no friends, nobody who cared, nobody to look at her. Here was a girl who all of a sudden was one. I know that when this boy at school whose name is Randolph passes me, I git this knowing—whatever it is, this tickly feeling in my stomach when he looks at me. And when I looked at Alice's face, I knowed she had the feeling. Scary and tingly and makes you want to giggle and cover up. That's just what she did. She giggled and jumped back behind the tree.

Sammy said, "I can't believe it."

"Ain't she purty, though?"

He walked to the tree she was hiding behind.

"ALICE?"

"Mmmm?"

"COME OUT."

"Noooo."

"COME ON OUT."

"Nooooo."

"YOU LOOK PR . . . YOU LOOK BEAUTIFUL. COME OUT."

I went to the tree.

"IT'S OKAY," I said. "LET HIM SEE YOU."

"Noooo."

"BUT YOU LOOK SO BEAUTIFUL."

I suspected she'd never heard the word *beautiful*. I wondered if she had ever even looked in a mirror. I bet she hadn't. I bet she didn't even know what she looked like. I took her hand and patted it. Then I pulled her out.

She covered her face with her hands. Me or Sammy neither knowed what to do then, so we stood there. She kept her face covered.

Finally Sammy said maybe he ought to go on and leave us alone. I didn't know nothing else to do so I said all right. I said we would stay long enough for her clothes to dry, then I'd take her to the shed and come on home.

Alice uncovered her face when Sammy got out of sight. We waded down the creek a ways, then walked to the clearing where her clothes was drying. They was still real wet, so we picked some wild daisies. I didn't know what to do next 'cause she was so quiet and had quit smiling. Seemed like she wadn't with me, if you know what I mean. Seemed like her mind was somewhere else.

We laid down on the creek bank at mine and Sammy's favorite spot. She dozed off for a few minutes, but I wadn't sleepy. I laid there and tried to imagine all the stuff that Alice didn't know. It was a lot. I had asked her once what she was thinking, and then I found out she didn't know that word. How could she be fifteen or sixteen and not know that word? I thought of word after word I knowed she wouldn't know. I laid there watching a squirrel sail through the trees like it had wings, scooting up the treetop limbs and then jumping to another tree, then another. It looked like fun.

Then all of a sudden Alice started jerking and making the awfulest noise you ever heard in your life. "Aaghhhhh," on and on. Her whole body was jerking so bad that for a second I was so shocked I couldn't move.

"ALICE!" I screamed. Then I grabbed her shoulders. I knowed that, oh, my God, she's having one of them fits! I went into a panic. I didn't know what to do. I screamed her name over and over. She was jerking so hard if she'd of been on a bed she'd of jerked off of it. Her eyes was half rolled back. Slobber was coming out of her open mouth. The noise in her throat sounded like rocks rolling down a hill. It was the horriblest thing I ever seen.

Doc Murphy had tried to tell us what they was like. He didn't tell us *this*! He didn't tell us what to *do*! Oh, God. Oh, dear god, I screamed out loud. What do I *do*? Oh, God, how long will it last? She ain't breathing! She can't breathe. She's gonna die!

I screamed, "Sammy! Sammy!" but I knowed he wadn't nowhere around. What was that awful sound in her throat? She's choking to death! She's dying! Oh, God! God! Oh, dear Jesus. Please, please don't let her die. I didn't mean it. I'm sorry I got mad at you, God. I won't never throw a rock at you again. I won't never. Oh, please don't let her die. I lifted both my hands toward Heaven. I bowed my head and closed my eyes.

Please, God. Please.

When finally it ended, I was as limp as her. She had caught her breath with a deep gasp and it was over except for the rock sounds in her throat. She laid there with the slobber still coming out and the rocks rolling. She was not conscious. I laid beside her and put my arm around her and helt her. Then the tears come. I tried to stop them, but I couldn't. They run down my face onto her shoulder. I cried and cried. She was still unconscious. I set up beside her and took her limp hand and patted it. I looked at that purty white face that was finally relaxed. I wiped the slobber off her mouth with my fingers and wiped it on the dress. My heart had finally slowed down. The noise in her throat finally ended. It must of took close to a hour.

When she come to she was like a dazed person. I screamed at her not to move, to stay there. I'd go get her clothes. Her eyes was blank and she didn't try to move. I raced through the woods to the clearing. The shirt was dry but the overalls was still damp. I took them anyhow.

I thought I'd never git the dress off of her. When I did, I saw the back of it was soaked with pee. I used the dry part to wipe her bottom, then I put her clothes on her. I let her rest a while longer but I knowed we had to git back before the Guthries got home. I half pulled, half toted her back to that shed. I laid her on them stinking quilts. Then I patted her hand. She was too dazed to notice. Then I locked her in.

Chapter 13

*T*he next day I told Sammy all about the fit. We was both real sad and moping around all day. We tried to talk about good things so as to git cheered up, but it didn't work. Late that afternoon Uncle Will rode up and brought us some news that cheered us up good. He brought a letter from the University of Georgia.

"Who you know at the University of Georgia, Sam?" he asked, and handed Sammy the letter.

I jumped up and squealed. "Oh, you must of won the contest!"

Sammy ripped open the envelope and read the letter out loud. He didn't win, but they said his writing showed real promise. He was disappointed, but me and Uncle Will bragged on him so much he got to grinning. Uncle Will told him that he bet one of these days he would write books and be famous. He said good writers made a lot of money.

Uncle Will couldn't stay, but after he left I kept talking about Sammy being a big writer. Then I teased him about how he'd probably marry that snotty Bertha and have a bunch of younguns and live in a fancy house and never speak to us again.

"Would you marry her? Huh? Would you?" I asked.

He smiled. "If she'd have me, I would."

I could of just puked. I changed the subject quick.

When Daddy got home from the sawmill, Sammy showed him the letter. Daddy was real happy about it. He shook Sammy's hand and patted his back.

"You need to practice your writing, son. Maybe we could find out from Flossie Moore"—(she's Sammy's teacher)—"if they's some place we could send off and git you some kind of book on writing. Maybe she knows about some kinds of study you could get in the mails."

Sammy looked at me, then at Daddy.

"Flossie ought to know about stuff like that," Daddy said. "Why don't you ask her about it when school starts back?"

"I'll do that, Pa," Sammy's voice was flat.

"It'd be somethin to have a author in the family, wouldn't it, Ellie?"

"Sure would," I said.

"What we having for supper?"

"I was fixin to go and pick some okra and squash. That be all right?"

Daddy got up out of his chair.

"Sounds good. I'll go help ya."

Sammy decided he wouldn't wait for school to start back to talk to Miss Flossie about gitting some books on writing. He said since we knowed neither one of us would ever git much education, and since he didn't want to be a pore farmer all his life, or work at the sawmill, he better learn something quick. He went to her house the next morning.

Miss Flossie is real sweet. She talked to him a long time. She said she would git some books and in the meantime for him to concentrate on his English grammar and to read a lot and practice writing ever chance he got.

When Sammy got home, we went to Cherrylog. He took his fishing pole. I wanted to lay around at our favorite spot, but he wanted to go down a ways to fish, so I went with him. Before Cherrylog runs into Yager Valley, it is joined up by another stream. They both spill off the mountain in two waterfalls into a basin that's filled with big rocks. It's a purty big pond and has a lot of fish, 'specially trout. I jumped from rock to rock till I was in the middle of the pond. Then I set down. Sammy fished from the bank. The pond is surrounded by rhododendron and laurel as big as small trees. Ferns cover the ground under them. It's a mighty peaceful place. The sounds of the falls splashing onto the rocks gits you sleepy if you lay listening long enough. I looked up into the trees and thought of Sammy gitting to be a famous writer and how I'd tell everbody he was my brother and how their eyes would pop out and they would be amazed.

I don't never go there by myself 'cause Mohawk, who's a big black mama bear, lives close by. Sammy named her Mohawk; for what reason I don't know. She'd been there three years as best we knowed. Last year she had the cutest cub you ever laid eyes on, but we didn't never git to pet it 'cause you just plain don't mess with bear cubs or the mama'll tear you to shreds. Sammy said he hadn't seen Mohawk since last spring.

Next to one waterfall, up on a rock ridge, is a family of gray and white raccoons. Talk about cute, now they is cute. They stand on their hind legs and hold their food in their paws and eat just like humans. They even clean off their face. And fat! They is plumb fat. Round like big fur balls, and has got the sweetest faces. I wished I had brought biscuits to give them. They know we'll feed them. I was waiting for them to show up.

Sammy won't let me talk while he's fishing. I laid there

and watched some butterflies flitting around what was left of a phlox blossom. Sammy got my attention by hissing and pointed to a water moccasin laying on another rock. I nodded so he'd know I'd watch out for it. When I was seven, one bit me. I almost died and would have if Daddy hadn't of cut the place quick and sucked out most of the poison and then put some salt pork on it. He taught me and Sammy how to do it.

I laid thinking of how Daddy use to be, and smiled to myself. I remembered the time we seen two rattlesnakes and a coachwhip in one day and he killed the rattlers with a hoe and left the coachwhip alone 'cause they won't poison you. And I thought about Alice, and how purty she looked in my dress, and how maybe one of these days we could take her home with us so Daddy could meet her.

While I was thinking about Alice, Sammy must of been thinking about her, too, 'cause all of a sudden he told me to come on 'cause we was going to talk to Doc Murphy.

Doc told us that it sounded like Alice had had a grand mal seizure. The worst kind. We talked about Alice's hearing problem and he said it was possible she could be fitted with a hearing aid and he'd check on where to git one, but the Guthries would have to approve. It all sounded so hopeless me and Sammy was sadder than ever.

That night I went up to see Alice by myself. Sammy was busy reading his book. Daddy had went to bed a little after nine. He was sober. When I snuck to the shed I could hear Alice talking to herself and it tickled me good. She was playing like me and Sammy was there. I couldn't hear ever word, but one time she said:

"Goo Ellie?"

"Gooo Sam-my?"

Then she answered for one of us.

"Uh huh, Alice. Gooo."

"Hooow do? Hooow hit do? Hit do da splinch?"

"Nooo, hit not splinch."

I put my ear close to the door crack. Splinch? What's splinch? I giggled. I wanted to listen to more, but she stopped talking.

When I went in the dark shed (there never had been no lamp out there), she started whispering! I couldn't believe it. How did she understand whispering?

"Weee bath?"

I shook my head no and took her hand. I didn't take her to Cherrylog. I took her down to where Poke was and we set on the pine straw.

"THAT'S POKE," I yelled. "HIS NAME IS POKE."

"Mmmm Pote."

She's such a calm girl, I thought. She don't never act upset. She set cross-legged in them overalls with her hands laying in her lap. She set there a long time without hardly moving.

"YOU LIKE THE DARK, ALICE?"

"Wha?"

"THE NIGHT. YOU LIKE NIGHT?"

She nodded yes.

"LOOK AT THE MOON. IT'S ALMOST FULL. PURTY, AIN'T IT?"

"Mmmm."

"HAVE YOU EVER PLAYED—AH—HAVE YOU EVER PLAYED A GAME?"

"Huh?"

"GAME—PLAYED A GAME? HIDE AND SEEK. RING AROUND THE ROSES . . . HAVE YOU?"

I could tell she didn't know what I was talking about.

"HOW LONG YOU BEEN LIVING IN THE SHED?"

"I liva dare."

"HOW LONG?"

"Alla time."

We was quiet a while. Then I decided to try to teach her to play something.

"WOULD YOU LIKE TO DO SOMETHING? I'LL SHOW YOU HOW TO DO IT."

"Wha doooo?"

"STAND UP." I pulled her to her feet.

"NOW YOU GO HIDE . . ."

"Huh?"

I decided not to try that one. I thought a minute. What could we play? How could I teach her? I couldn't think of nothing two people could play in the dark. I wanted to do *something* with her. Something fun. The next Saturday I'm with her, I thought, I'll teach her to play hopscotch. She needed exercise. She sets and lays so long she can't even walk good. I wondered if she had ever hopped, had ever skipped. Then I thought of it!"

"WE'RE GONNA DANCE, ALICE."

"Danck?"

I took her hands. Then I walked us round and round slow. She did that fine. I moved a little bit faster and she did that fine, too. Then I started skipping. She watched my feet. Then I scream-sung:

"FLIES IN THE BUTTERMILK,
SHOO, SHOO, SHOO,
FLIES IN THE BUTTERMILK,
SHOO, SHOO, SHOO,
FLIES IN THE BUTTERMILK,
SHOO, SHOO, SHOO,
SKIP TA MA LOU, MY DARLING."

She smiled big. Then she tried skipping, and in a minute, she was doing it! We skipped round and round.

"LOST MY GAL, NOW WHAT'LL I DO?
LOST MY GAL, NOW WHAT'LL I DO?
LOST MY GAL, NOW WHAT'LL I DO?
SKIP TA MA LOU, MY DARLING."

I knowed she liked it. She was giggling and smiling and
her eyes was big as saucers. I thought of the time at Lookout when Sammy showed her how to make animal shadows. She had been so happy. It was so easy to git her
happy. We skipped till I finished singing the song, then quit
'cause I was afraid she'd faint or have a fit or something.
Then I set on the straw again. She didn't set. She kept skipping. I'd of give anything if Sammy could of seen her. She
skipped around me, then she skipped around Poke two
times. I sung the song again and when I was done, she
flopped beside me giggling. I patted her shoulder.

"YOU DANCE GOOD!"

She kept giggling, covering her mouth with both dirty
hands.

"HOW YOU FEEL?"

She didn't answer.

"ONE OF THESE DAYS MAYBE YOU CAN GO TO
A BARN DANCE. THEY'RE FUN!"

She didn't say nothing. Finally she quit giggling. She set
there smiling at me. Then she said, "I waaana bath."

"WE CAN'T GO TONIGHT. I CAN'T STAY LONG. I
HAVE TO GIT BACK. SAMMY WILL WORRY."

"Sam-my? Where Sam-my?"

"HE'LL COME NEXT TIME."

"Youu bringa chope nes time?"

"BRING WHAT?"

"Chope."

"SOAP?"

"Mmmm."

"I'LL BRING THE SOAP," I said, and give her a hug.

Chapter 14

*B*ertha Langford and Lisa Mae McClung drove by our house in Lisa Mae's mama's buggy early on a Tuesday morning, heading up the mountain. They stopped and Bertha sung out.

"Oh . . . Sammy."

Me and Sammy was on the back porch giving Under a bath in the washtub.

"Who's *that,* you reckon?" he asked.

"Sounds like Bertha to me," I said.

His eyes lit up and he flew, with soap all over his arms, to the front yard. I followed right behind him. Under took off to the woods.

"Hey, Bertha. Hey, Lisa," he said.

They both said hey.

I said hey, and give Lisa Mae a questioning look to mean what you doing with *her?*

"Where y'all headed?" he asked, rubbing the soap on his overalls.

"Oh, we just riding," Bertha said. "Such a purty day. Thought we'd take a lunch up to the Lookout. Y'all wanna go?"

"We too busy," I said quick.

"We got a whole fried chicken," she said. "Mrs. McClung made us some tea cakes. She put peecans on 'em!"

Sammy leaned on the buggy and stared up at the girls. "Well . . ." he said.

"But, Sammy," I poked him, "we gotta wash Under." Bertha laughed.

"You won't wash him today. I seen him hightailing it to the woods."

"Sammy's 'pose to be at the sawmill to help unload," I said.

"Load won't be in till one or two." He give me a dirty look. "It's coming from Dahlonega."

"Aw, y'all come on," Lisa Mae said. "We could come back in time."

Sammy stood a while looking at the buggy. All the ladies was fixing up their buggies since Aunt Bessie fixed hers. Fact is, Doc Murphy said that on Founder's Day (the day the town celebrates the founding of Bolton, which is October the fifteenth), they was gonna have a buggy judging. He said he thought all the menfolk ought to donate fifty cents and maybe give a five- or ten-dollar prize. Aunt Bessie already had big plans to make hers fancier.

Mrs. McClung's buggy was a sight, painted sunshine yellow with the spokes green. Mr. McClung had built a top that beat all you ever seen, up on fancy posts, with lattice around it, hanging down, oh, say, a foot, painted yellow and green, too. Lisa Mae and her mama made cushions out of yellow cloth with green rickrack. I tell you, it was as purty as Aunt Bessie's to me, and I knowed Aunt Bessie was jealous.

"Mighty fancy," Sammy said, grinning.

"I just love it." Bertha smiled at Sammy. "I wish Mama had a buggy for the contest."

"Mama's gonna win," Lisa Mae said, "so ain't no need."

87

"It'd be hard to beat." Sammy shook his head.

We talked about the buggies and the Founder's Day stuff a while. They kept after us (I knowed Bertha didn't want me, just Sammy) to go up to the Lookout and, of course, Sammy said we would.

I rode up front with the girls and Sammy set behind the seat where they's space for a trunk. Up the road a ways Under come out of the woods and trailed along behind. When we passed the Guthries', we all stared at the place, me and Sammy for a different reason than them.

"Lord have mercy!" Bertha said, slowing the horse. "Would you look at that shack? Is *that* where them Guthries live?"

"I think so," I said.

"I can't believe *nobody* would live there," Lisa Mae said. "I never seen such a mess. Have you ever seen them, Sammy?"

"Yeah. I seen Mr. and Mrs. Guthrie."

"Me and Ellie seen 'em all, didn't we, Ellie?" Bertha said. "They was down in Bolton. All of 'em is filthy, even the mama. Daddy said they come from South Georgia. He said they both too old to be having babies. Said Mrs. Guthrie was a widow woman when he married her. Mama says she bets she's forty-eight or -nine."

I whirled around and looked at Sammy. *That* would explain Alice. Maybe Mrs. Guthrie had Alice by her first husband. Maybe that was why they was such a gap in the ages.

"Mrs. Guthrie have any chillun when she married Mr. Guthrie?" Sammy asked Bertha.

"Reckon not. Daddy said they only been married eight or nine years."

"Who told yore daddy all that?" I asked.

"Mr. Guthrie. Daddy hauls some of his chickens to Atlanta when he goes. Mr. Guthrie brings 'em down. He brought some down last September the nineteenth. I remember because it was Mama and Daddy's anniversary. Daddy was taking Mama to Atlanta to let her buy something. Daddy says Mr. Guthrie don't talk much. Said it was hard to git him to talk. Daddy was just trying to make a conversation. You know, telling him it was his anniversary. Asked him how many years he'd been married."

My mind was a-whirling. I knowed Sammy's was, too. I bet *that's* why Alice is locked in that shed! I thought, I bet he can't stand her 'cause she ain't his and on top of that, her having them fits and all!

Sammy nudged my back. I turned and he nodded. I knowed he was thinking about the same thing. All of a sudden I was glad we had come. Now maybe we had some answers about Alice.

When we was past their house a ways we heard the scream. It was faint and spooky.

Bertha stopped the horse.

"What was *that*?" Her hand flew to her mouth. "Lordy mercy, it sounds like somebody dying!"

"I didn't hear nothing," I said. "Did you, Sammy?"

"Nope. I didn't hear it."

"*I* heard it," Lisa Mae said. "It sounded like a woman. Reckon Mrs. Guthrie is in trouble or something? Reckon we ought to go back?"

"We better *not* go back," I said. "Uncle Will said Mr. Guthrie is so mean he'd as soon shoot you as look at you."

Bertha flipped the reins. "My gosh! You reckon he's beating her?"

"Can't never tell." I turned and looked at Sammy. I wanted to run to Alice and I knowed he did, too. I hated the helpless feeling. He patted my shoulder.

"We can't let it mess up our picnic, now can we, y'all?" Bertha asked and looked at Sammy.

"It won't mess it up," Sammy mumbled.

We hadn't planned to go to Alice's that night, but we did. We had to go check on her on account of the scream. I told Sammy she screamed like that lots and it didn't mean she was hurt or nothing, but he said we better make sure.

It was after ten when we got there. They was no lights in the house. Outside the shed we stood a minute and listened. Alice was humming. Nothing like humming a song, just making different humming noises. Low and high and medium.

"I wonder if she ever even *heard* a song," Sammy whispered.

"How could she? She can't hear. Ain't it pitiful? I sung 'Skip Ta Ma Lou' to her but she ain't even heard songs like 'Jesus Loves Me' or Christmas songs."

"Let's sing to her," Sammy said, serious.

"Huh?"

"Let's take her to Cherrylog and sing to her. Whatcha say?"

"Well—okay," I said. "I reckon we could."

Alice was glad to see us. She jumped up and headed for the door.

When we got to the creek we waded a while in the icy water. None of us talked much. Sammy picked up some rocks and throwed them. I helt Alice's hand as we waded. Then we all laid back on the bank.

"Taka bath?" Alice set up and looked at me.

"Not tonight," I said, wishing we had brought the rags and soap. She stunk worse.

"We should of brought the stuff," I said to Sammy.

"I know."

"When we gonna sing? You wanna sing 'Jesus Loves Me' to her?"

"Well, yeah."

"You wanna sing it now?"

He set up and scooted closer to Alice. I set up too.

"You start," he said.

I started. We scream-sung.

"JESUS LOVES ME
THIS I KNOW
FOR THE BIBLE
TELLS ME SO"

Alice's eyes got big and she leaned her ear close to Sammy's mouth.

"LIT-TLE ONES TO HIM BELONG
THEY ARE WEAK
BUT HE IS STRONG
YESSS, JESUS LOVES ME
YESSS, JESUS LOVES ME
YESSS, JESUS LOVES ME
THE BIBLE TELLS ME SO"

Alice smiled.

"Dooo—dooohit," she said.

"She wants us to sing some more," he said. "What'll we sing?"

"'Old Rugged Cross,' all right?"

Sammy started and we sung it all the way through. Alice kept her ear close to Sammy's mouth. She wanted us to do another one and we started 'Santa Claus Is Coming to Town.' She put her hand over Sammy's mouth.

"Dooo—'Chesus Love'—do it."

We sung 'Jesus Loves Me' all over again. When we was done, me and Sammy clapped.

"I dooohit?"

"YOU WANT TO SING?" Sammy yelled.

"Mmmmm." She leaned back to Sammy's mouth. I could tell by his face the smell was gitting to him. He give me this sort of a helpless look.

"WE'LL SING ONE LINE." I leaned toward her. "THEN YOU SING IT, ALL RIGHT?"

"Mmmm."

We sung the first three lines. Then she said—talking, not singing:

> "Cheesus lovvv me
> Dis I knowww
> For tha Bible"

She talked the whole song, then asked, "Whaaa Chessus?"

I looked at Sammy. He shrugged.

"JESUS," I said, "WELL, JESUS IS GOD'S SON. GOD'S BOY."

"Wha—whooo God?"

Sammy looked at me.

"Good luck," he said.

"GOD IS YOUR—OUR FATHER UP IN HEAVEN. HE IS OUR DADDY WHO LIVES IN THE SKY." I pointed upward.

"Mmy daaaddy liva dare," she pointed up the mountain.

"HE'S YOUR EARTHLY—WELL, HE'S YOUR DADDY UP THERE, BUT GOD IS THE DADDY OF EVERBODY. HE MADE THE WHOLE WORLD. GOD LOVES YOU JUST LIKE JESUS DOES."

"He doo wha?"

"HE LOVES YOU."

"Whaa dat?"

I looked at Sammy. He looked helpless again. He shook his head.

"Your turn," I whispered.

He looked in Alice's face a few seconds.

"YOU ASKING WHAT LOVE IS?"

"Mmmm."

He set up straighter. He put one knee up and leaned his elbow on it and put his chin in his hand, still looking in Alice's face.

"What'll I tell her?" he asked me out of the side of his mouth.

"It's a heck of a question, ain't it?"

"What would *you* tell her?" he said.

We set thinking. How in the world can you tell somebody what love is?

"You could tell her it's a, well, a good feeling, maybe, huh?"

"Then I'd have to tell her what feeling is, prob'ly what good is." He scrunched his eyebrows thinking. Alice stared at Sammy's mouth, waiting for a answer.

"LOVE IS," he said, "LOVE IS WHEN YOU LIKE, AH, REALLY CARE, YEAH, REALLY CARE ABOUT . . ."

She stared at him blank. He put his hand across his forehead. I couldn't see his eyes.

"LOVE IS," I said, and she switched her eyes to my mouth, "IT'S THE WAY YOU FEEL ABOUT, SAY, ABOUT YORE MAMA OR ABOUT . . ."

"What if she don't love her mama?" Sammy uncovered his eyes. He set staring at Alice a long time, then he sighed a big sigh, put his arms around her and pulled her head against his shoulder. I was shocked. He rocked her back and forth, rubbing that tangled hair. He didn't seem to notice the smell of her. Then he sung in her ear.

"JESUS LOVES YOU
THIS I KNOW
FOR THE BIBLE TELLS ME SO"

I didn't sing with him. I just set there looking at my
brother with tears sneaking out of my eyes.

Chapter 15

*T*he next two times we seen Alice she had fits. One real bad, like before, and one not as bad.

The first one sent Sammy into a pure frenzy nearly, it scared him so bad. I reckon menfolk can't stand sickness like us women.

We was at Cherrylog. Me and Alice had bathed and I'd brought her the dress to put on. While I helped her into it I thought about the first time I'd put it on her and about the fit she had. Well, she done it again. When Sammy got back he had stared at her and hadn't hardly took his eyes off her, but we didn't brag on her looking purty on account of she got so timid the last time we did.

Sammy was showing her a doodlebug hole when it happened.

"LOOK ALICE," he said, and pointed to a tiny circle of fine sand beside a stump.

"THAT'S A DOODLEBUG HOLE."

She squatted down to look. Sammy picked up a short twig and handed it to her.

"PUT THE TWIG IN THE HOLE."

He showed her how and then how to stir it.

"IF YOU STIR THE HOLE AND SAY 'DOODLEBUG, DOODLEBUG, YOUR HOUSE IS

ON FIRE,' THE BUG WILL COME OUT. NOW STIR IT. GO ON. STIR IT."

Alice stirred the twig into the hole.

"NOW SAY IT WITH ME. DOODLEBUG, DOODLEBUG."

"Dooodlebug, oooodlebug."

"YOUR HOUSE IS ON FIRE."

Alice froze. She dropped the stick, then went backward as stiff as a board and hit the ground with a thud.

Sammy's mouth fell open.

"My God! Oh, my God!"

I had squatted down to watch Alice stir the doodlebug. I dived toward her."

"Ohhh, no! Ohhh, no!" I cried.

"What'll we do? Ellie, what do we *do*? Should I lift her? Should I hold her head? What did Doc say to do? I forgot!"

Alice was jerking all over and the awful noises made Sammy shrink back.

"Let her lay flat," I yelled. "Don't try to lift her."

"What's that noise?" He bent over her. "Is she choking? Is she choking to death? Is she swallowing her tongue?"

"No—no, she's . . ."

"Give me that twig!"

I handed him the twig. He made a face like he was in pain, then put it in her open mouth. He helt her tongue down.

All I could do was watch. He knelt over her, holding that stick, his hands shaking.

It lasted as long as the first one. It seemed like hours but it was only two or three minutes maybe. When it was over, she caught her breath and laid limp. I wiped the slobber off her chin. The sounds in her throat kept up a long time.

Sammy finally fell away from her and set there with his arms wrapped around his knees, staring.

"It's so terrible," he whispered.

I nodded.

"I don't see how she lives through it."

"Me neither."

"Her mama ought to be whipped. Alice ought not to have to go through these all by herself. It's a wonder she don't fall and bust her head or something."

"When Doc looked at her that time he said he seen bruises, and a cut on her ear. She's got a bruise on her shoulder today. I seen it when we bathed."

We set there staring into the trees a while, then I went and got the washrag and washed her face.

"Why don't you go see if her clothes is dry?" I said.

"They can't be dry yet."

"She—well, when she has these fits, she pees on herself. I want to wash her."

He winced. "Oh, yeah. Well, okay. I'll go see about her clothes."

It didn't take her quite as long to git conscious as the last time. Her clothes wadn't dry, so we set a while longer. We couldn't think of nothing to say. I helt her hand. Later I got her dressed and we got her back to the shed.

While we was riding Poke home, me and Sammy talked about the fits and about her hearing.

"If she could hear better it'd be easier on her. She might could go to school. I wish Doc would find out about them hearing aid things."

"What for? You know Mr. Guthrie won't talk to him about it."

Sammy was quiet a minute, then he said, "Maybe they's a way. Maybe we could threaten Guthrie."

"Sammy!"

"Ain't no other way as I can see."

Sammy set Poke to galloping, so I helt on to him tighter.

"But how'll you threaten him?"

"I'll ask Doc."

"You know Doc said a man can treat his younguns anyway he wants to. You heard him say it. Ain't no law that says he has to be good to her."

"I ain't talking about law stuff."

"What kind of stuff you talking about, then?"

"Meanness. Plain meanness. I reckon it's all Guthrie would understand."

Doc said for Sammy to forgit about threatening Mr. Guthrie. He said if they was one thing he'd learned in his fifty-two years it was two wrongs don't make a right.

"Well, I'm gonna talk to the sheriff then," Sammy said. We was in Doc's front yard.

"I've already done that, son," Doc said. "He can't tell Guthrie what room to put that girl in. That shack they live in ain't got but three rooms and a lean-to. Ain't big enough for all of them anyway. You're gonna have to forget about changing Guthrie."

Sammy kicked a tree. "Looks like we could do *something*," he said. Doc put his hand on Sammy's shoulder.

"She could go to school if she had one of them hearing aids, couldn't she?" Sammy asked.

Doc shook his head. "I kind of doubt it. We know the Guthries don't seem to cater to schooling. Can't read themselves."

"Them hearing aids have to be made special?"

"Different people have different problems." Doc squatted down and picked up a twig and drew circles on the dirt. "It's kind of like glasses. Some folks don't need nothing but magnifying glasses. Same thing with hearing aids. If her problem is like that, then we could git an aid."

"How much they cost?"

"A lot of money. Could run up to twenty—thirty dollars."

Sammy's face fell. "We ain't never seen twenty dollars in our whole life."

"I'm sorry," Doc said.

"Me, too," Sammy mumbled.

While we was riding home Sammy talked about how to earn enough money for a aid. We both knowed it was wishful talk. The money Sammy earns at the sawmill has to help make up for what Daddy don't earn, and we still don't have enough.

"Maybe we could sell something," Sammy said. "Maybe I could build something. You know, Mr. and Mrs. Crews, they take a load of stuff down to the Dahlonega highway ever spring and fall and sell to the tourist folks."

"A load of what?" I asked.

"All kinds of stuff. Canned stuff. Quilts and quilt tops. I don't know what things is worth, but I could find out. And Mrs. Crews, she makes baskets. Cotton baskets and them others that hang over your arm."

"If we sold our canned vegetables what would *we* eat?"

"Can't sell them. Have to think of something else."

"I could make quilt tops if we had cloth scraps. Aunt Bessie uses all of hers."

"We have to sell something we can make without it costing us. I know! I could learn to do baskets. You could, too, and I could make bent willow chairs like Daddy use to make. Uncle Will could show me."

"How about if I sold dried flowers?" I asked, getting excited.

"Good idea," Sammy said. "I tell you what, Ellie, if we make up our mind, I think we can git up twenty dollars or even thirty. Whatcha say?"

"Let's make up our mind," I said.

"Mine's made up. Is yours?"

"Yeah."

"Let's go talk to Aunt Bessie."

Before we could tell Aunt Bessie, she started talking about working on her buggy. She had decided since Jeannette Mc-Clung was bound and determined to beat her, she better come up with some brand-new ideas.

"I'm gonna redo the whole thing," she said when me and Sammy got off Poke.

"But it's purty now," I said.

"It ain't good enough to win. I seen Jeannette's, and though I don't approve of her taste, I have to admit it will git attention. And she just started. What y'all think about me painting the Calico Carriage wine-colored? Now think of it a minute. I'll paint all the wood wine. The spokes, too. Then I'm going to copy me some kind of flower design, say to match the new cloth I'm gonna buy for the cushion and top, and paint the design on the back of the seat. Think that'll be purty?"

"I didn't know you could paint flowers," Sammy said.

"How hard could it be?"

"Flowers might be harder than you think," I said.

"Don't matter. I'm gonna beat Jeannette McClung come hell or high water."

She showed us the tassels she was making out of wine-colored cording. She told us all her plans, then told us to come on in and she'd give us a piece of apple pie. While we was eating, we told her all about our plan to make money for a hearing aid for Alice.

"Why, that's the sweetest idea I ever heard of," she said. "What can I do to help? I'll give you all my scraps, Ellie. I got enough quilts anyhow."

"We wanna learn to make baskets." Sammy was real excited.

"Shoot," she said, "I betcha Arlene Crews'll be glad to show ya. Next time I see her, I'll ask her."

"You reckon anybody would buy willow chairs?"

"Can't never tell. Them Atlanta folks will buy anything."

We stayed till nearly dark talking and planning. Before we left, Aunt Bessie give me a quart of apples for a pie. Then we rode home.

Chapter 16

*D*addy didn't come home that night. Me and Sammy was worried sick. They wadn't no sense in us looking for him 'cause we didn't know where to look.

The next morning Sammy headed for the sawmill in a pouring rain. Daddy wadn't there, and didn't show up all day. When Sammy got home around six, he still wadn't home. It had stopped raining. Sammy said all they was to do was wait. I fixed supper while Sammy tended the chores. After supper Sammy read while I cut quilt squares out of the scraps Aunt Bessie give me.

We was gitting ready for bed when we heard him ride up. He busted into the kitchen door raving. Sammy took one look at him and grabbed my arm and pulled me out the front door.

"We ain't facing him no more, Ellie," he hollered as we run to the barn. "We'll go back in after he's passed out."

I was scared he'd come looking for us but he didn't. We set in the hayloft and talked. Sammy said he'd had a long talk with Uncle Will and Uncle Will mentioned us coming and living with him and Aunt Bessie, but Sammy said no. He said we was going to have to stay and do what we could to help Daddy. He figgered that's what Mama would want.

"Do you ever pray about Daddy, Sammy?" I asked.

"'Course," Sammy mumbled the word. He's always been real timid about talking about God stuff.

"Do you think God really hears our praying?"

"I don't know. Sure don't seem like it."

"Aunt Bessie said we can't never give up. She said if we keep a-praying, then Daddy's bound to quit."

"Sure hope God does something before Daddy hurts hisself or us."

After a while I said, "Sammy?"

"Huh?"

"Do you—have you ever had a time when—well, when you felt close to God?"

"Whatcha mean?"

"Well, I don't know, sorta like you *know* he's there. I mean, really know it."

"I don't reckon."

"Don't you ever feel it, say in the woods or down at Cherrylog or when you're fishing and it's quiet and all you hear is the creatures—you know—times like that?"

Before he could answer we heard a distant crash. Both of us jumped up, climbed down the ladder, and run to the house. Sammy stopped me and pulled me to the window of the front room, and we looked in, expecting the worst.

I never seen nothing like it in my whole life. Daddy must have took a running start and dived at the bed, 'cause he'd knocked the whole thing down. There he was on the mattress, which was on the floor, with both his legs sticking between the wood rails of the foot of the bedstead, which had fell on him. He was frantically trying to hold up the head of the bed, which was *fixing* to fall on him, and he was yelling cuss words so loud we could hear them in the yard. His liquor jug was setting on the table next to the bed and he was trying to reach for it at the same time. I helt my breath watching. He helt up the head of the bed with one hand and waved his other hand close to the jug. He couldn't touch it, so he tried to pull hisself over, and when he did, the bedstead fell on his head and he knocked the jug off the table and the liquor spilt all over the bed. You never seen such action. It looked like him and the bed was in a wrestling match. I was rooting for the bed, hoping it'd win quick so all the liquor would pour out before Daddy could reach it. And it did.

Then Daddy got so all fired mad he took his fist and busted it into the heavy wood. Boy, was that a mistake. And boy, did that make him madder. So he flung the bedstead off of him and grabbed the jug, and when he seen it was empty, hit the post with the jug. Hunks of jug flew everwhere.

The bed won. He was too drunk to git untangled from the foot rails, so he laid back disgusted and still cussing. Then in one minute, it seemed like, he passed out.

Me and Sammy went in and cleaned up the mess. We got his legs untangled and got the bed put back together and him put back in it. I went on to bed but couldn't sleep. I heard Sammy pacing in the kitchen.

Chapter 17

Summertime in the Georgia mountains is a time when everthing slows down. Work at the mill slows. Work in the gardens slows. Folks moves slower, too. Daddy had stayed on a drunk for close to two weeks. Me and Sammy had snuck up to see Alice at night, taking her to Cherrylog at least twice a week. Aunt Bessie was busy with her buggy and me with my quilt tops. Sammy had cut enough willow limbs to make two chairs, only to find out you need to cut them as you make the chairs or they git too dry. Also, Sammy was writing a story. It was about another Indian family. He said he might make it a long-enough story to be a book. I was real excited about it even though he wouldn't let me read one word.

What we'd decided to do with Alice was try to teach her words by talking to her a lot. We figgered nobody ever talked to her enough for her to learn to talk good. We spent ever minute of our time with her, yelling till we was hoarse nearly.

The funniest part was Alice's words. She simply made up words when she didn't know how to say what she wanted to say. It was hard not laughing, but we tried to be real serious. Like one time we was all three setting on a log and she picked a piece of bark off of it and said, "Hit make de set scrumplie." (She used a lot of "s" words.)

Me and Sammy looked at each other puzzled.

Sammy screamed, "SCRUMPLIE? THE SET SCRUMP-LIE?"

"Mmmmm."

"WHAT YOU MEAN, ALICE?"

She stood up and pointed to her behind. "Hit too scrumplie dare!"

"I think she means the log is too bumpie, huh?" I asked Sammy. He nodded.

"IS THE BARK TOO BUMPY?" he asked.

She set down on the ground and hugged her knees. "Mmmm. Hit scrumplie my butt."

We didn't laugh, but it was hard not to.

"Hit scrumplie yo' butt, Ellie?" she asked.

"YEAH, IT DOES." I got off the log and set beside her on the ground. Sammy didn't move.

Alice turned to look at him. Then she leaned close to me to whisper in my ear, though she didn't whisper low enough 'cause Sammy heard her.

"Men's stoggie butt, huh?"

I had no idea what she meant, but I giggled and nodded my head in agreement. Then she busted into giggles, too. Sammy didn't giggle.

Me and Sammy was visiting Alice two or three times a week. It was beginning to befuddle us that the Guthries never missed her when she was gone. Never checked on her in the night. Then one night when we was walking her back from Cherrylog, we seen a lantern light coming through the woods. It really scared us. We stopped in our tracks.

"Hit Ma-ma," Alice said. She pointed to a clump of sweet shrubs. Me and Sammy squatted behind them.

"Ma-ma?" Alice called.

The woman come running to her, lantern swinging. She stopped and helt the lantern up to see Alice's face. "YOU DON'T QUIT THIS RUNNING OFF, YO' DADDY'S GONNA FIND OUT! WHERE YOU BEEN? GIT ON UP THAT HILL!"

Alice started walking, following her Mama.

"YOU BY YOURSELF OR THEM PERKINS KIDS WITH YA?"

Me and Sammy nearly dropped our teeth, we was so shocked.

"She knows!" Sammy whispered. "My God, Ellie, she knows!"

We didn't hear what Alice said. Then her Mama hollered, "IF Y'ALL OUT THERE YA BETTER GIT ON HOME. IT'S PAST MIDNIGHT."

"She ain't mad!" I said. "My gosh, did you hear her? She ain't mad!"

We flopped down on the pine straw. I felt such a relief. We laid there talking a mile a minute, we was so excited. Now the whole problem was different. Now everthing was changed. But what did it mean? If Mrs. Guthrie knowed about us and wadn't mad, did it mean we could talk to her about Alice? Was Mr. Guthrie so mean she was scared to talk to anybody?

The next day I headed down the mountain on foot to tell Aunt Bessie. Sammy rode Poke to Doc Murphy's before going to the sawmill.

When I got there she was sweeping the front yard. When she seen me she leaned the brush broom against the porch and we set on the steps.

"Lordy mercy, youngun," she said grinning. "You walk down here?" She patted the step. "Set down and rest yore bones. I got some fresh tea and I got ice yesterday. You want a nice big glass?"

"I'll git it," I said, and pecked her on her cheek. "You

ain't gonna *believe* what happened. I can't wait to tell you."
I flew up the steps and into the house.

Aunt Bessie was as bumfuzzled as we was. She didn't
know what to make of it.

"Looks to me like," she said, taking a long sip of cold
tea, "that if the woman didn't approve of y'all visiting Alice, you'd know it by now. Looks to me like Mrs. Guthrie
might turn up with a heart after all. I always said ain't no
way a mama, no matter how no account she is, can treat her
youngun worse'n a dog 'less she's got something wrong.
'Less she's crazy. It ain't natural."

"Well, we know she's scared of Mr. Guthrie," I said.

"Can't blame her. I'd be scared of him, too. Looks to me
like if they was some way y'all could git to her, talk to her,
y'all might work out something about helping Alice more.
Surely to God Mrs. Guthrie could be made to see stuff like
Alice having a change of clothes, having some soap. I'll give
her all the soap she needs. We gonna have to give this a
lot of thought. Can't mess up now. Got to plan the best
way. Heck yeah. I could make the girl a dress or two if
that woman could figger a way to convince that no-good
drunk . . ."

I told Aunt Bessie about all the words we was trying to
git Alice to understand and how hard it was for her.

"Nothing worthwhile is easy, honey," she said. "Alice is
like a baby learning. It's gonna take a lot of time."

"You reckon she'll ever be like everbody else?"

"I hope not. If everbody was alike we'd all die of bore-
dom. My prayer is that she'll be like Alice. One of these
days y'all gonna have to sneak me up there to meet her.
Doc ever check up on that hearing aid?"

"He said he'd let us know."

"I decided I'm gonna donate two dollars."

"Oh, Aunt Bessie! Are you *really*?"

"The Lord's been pestering me. Reckon he don't want me

to spend so much fixin up my buggy. I might be able to donate a little over two, if I cut it close."

"But you gonna win the contest, ain't ya?"

She rolled her eyes and laughed.

"If them judges knows what's good for 'em, I will."

She stopped talking and set thinking. I was too wiggly to set. I got up and drawed hopscotch squares on the ground she hadn't swept yet. Then I found me a little flat rock and throwed it into the first square. Morgan come around the house and set with Aunt Bessie, so we had to quit talking.

"You finish cleaning the coops?" Aunt Bessie asked Morgan.

"Nah. I bumped against one and cut my shoulder on a nail. It was rusty." He pulled his shirt off his shoulder and showed her.

"It hurts bad," he said.

"Just a scratch," Aunt Bessie said. "Go git me some sut and rags and I'll fix it. Bring a pan of water and the soap."

When he got back Aunt Bessie washed the place good, then dabbed that black sut into the hole. She wrapped some tore rags under his arm and round his shoulder.

"It'll be all right," she said. "Yore daddy said come on down when you was done with the coops."

"But I can't lift no logs," he whined. "It hurts too bad."

"Then go on in and rest a while."

"I ain't tired."

He come over to my squares and walked through the lines, messing them up. I give him a mean look. Aunt Bessie fussed at him.

"What'd you do *that* for?" she said. "I swear, Morgan Perkins, seems like you take pride in messing. Now you draw them lines back, ya hear me!"

"Ellie's too old to be a-playing hopscotch," he muttered.

"What Ellie does ain't none of yore business. Now do what I tell ya." She stood up and reached for the broom.

He re-marked my lines in the sand with his big toe.

"Now git on down to the mill 'fore I make ya sweep this yard."

"I'm gonna take a nap."

"Well, take it then!"

He kicked my rock out of the block and went in the house.

"I love that youngun but he'll be the death of me yet," Aunt Bessie said. "I spoiled him so I only got myself to blame."

Chapter 18

*T*he next time me and Sammy sneaked Alice out of the shed Mrs. Guthrie was waiting.

She stepped out from behind the barn and scared the wits out of us.

"Where y'all taking Alice?" she asked.

We both jumped and neither one of us could answer.

"I know y'all been taking her off."

"Yessum, we have," Sammy said.

"Let's walk in the woods a ways. Can't risk Ormond hearin us."

We walked into the woods. It was a real dark night with no moon. I couldn't see her all that good but I could smell her. She stunk nearly as bad as Alice, 'cept different. Alice smelled more like pee. Mrs. Guthrie just smelled bad in general.

We all set down on the pine straw to talk. Sammy said, "We ain't doing nothing to harm Alice, Mrs. Guthrie. We want to be her friend."

"We want to help her if we can," I said quick.

"I reckon she needs friends. She ain't never had none. I need ta know if you'ns has told folks about her."

We didn't answer right away. I waited on Sammy to decide what to tell her. He decided to tell her the truth.

"Yessum," he said. "Pa knows and Aunt Bessie and Doc Murphy knows."

"I'se 'fraid of that. My husbin', he don't want nobody ta know. He ain't the kind of man that takes a liking ta nobody. He don't like folks around. Never has. He, well, I figgered I better tell you younguns. He can be mean. I don't want y'all gittin hurt."

"We try to be real careful," Sammy said. "We heard about Mr. Guthrie."

"He's bad ta drank."

"Yessum. So's our daddy. He gits mean, too, when he drinks."

"Ormond don't need a drank ta git mean. That's the way he is. He ain't never took a liking ta Alice here. She has spells. He says the devil done teched her."

"We seen her have 'em," Sammy said. "Doc says she's got epilepsy."

"Borned with it. I had the fever when I'se carrying her. She ain't never been right. 'Fore I met Ormond, I took her ta a doctor. He said warn't nothin ta do. Tried somethin called bromide. Didn't help."

Alice set beside her mama with her hand resting on her mama's knee. Mrs. Guthrie didn't touch Alice the whole time.

"I ain't never had no chance ta take her ta no doctor since I married Ormond. He don't believe in 'em. 'Sides that, he don't want nobody knowing he's got a stepgirl that's devilteched."

"How long has she been living in the shed?" I asked.

"'Fore we moved here, he kept her in a back room. Wouldn't let her come out."

"We'd sure like to help her if we can," I said. "Doc Murphy says they's such a thing as a hearing aid that can make her hear better."

"Tell him ta fergit it. Ormond can't never know nobody

112

knows. He'd beat us both. No tellin, he might kill us. I can't see as how they's anythang y'all can do that he wouldn't know about. Taking her out is mighty dangerous. He dranks ever night he has got it ta drank. Most times he's asleep, come eight or nine. He don't wake up, but if'en he ain't dranking he might catch ya'll if'en he goes to the toilet. I thought I ought ta warn ya. Hits only right."

"How do *you* feel about us taking Alice out?" Sammy asked.

"I git scared. The first time I seen ya, hit scared me bad. Ormond was still awake, roaming round in the dark, cussing. He does that sometimes."

"Does he ever go to the shed to check on Alice?"

"He don't never pay no 'tention ta her atall. Gits mad if I go out there fer anything 'cept ta feed 'er. I fixed her a way ta git out with a plank and a piece of iron. Trouble is, she can't put the latch back, but so far he ain't noticed."

"If you're so scared of him, why don't you and Alice run away?"

"Huh! I tried ta git shed of that man many a time. I recken that's why he hauled us up here in the middle of nowheres. I ain't got no family. Ma and Pa dead. Some sisters and brothers down in South Georgia, but shoot, they don't want us neither. Got they own troubles. One time I run ta my brother's place. Ormond come there waving that gun. Him and my brother got inta hit. Ormond busted his head, then ended up shooting at him. I never left him after that."

"Mrs. Guthrie," I said, "since Mr. Guthrie don't never check on Alice nohow, would you care if we got her a change of clothes, say another pair of overalls and shirt like she wears in case he *did* see her? He wouldn't know the difference nohow, would he?"

She thought about it a while. Then she said she reckoned it'd be all right.

"I'll bring her a comb and some soap," I said.

"What I been thinking about," Sammy said, "is a way that maybe you can let us know when it's safe to git Alice out. You reckon you could, say, lean a stick against the shed door when it's safe? Then when it ain't we'll know it."

"I recken I could do that, but what if the stick fell over?"

"I know!" I said. "What if you hung a rag over the log?"

"Good idea," Sammy said.

"That's the thang I'll do then," Mrs. Guthrie said.

I looked at Alice. She'd been setting quiet as a mouse. Of course she hadn't heard a word we said, but somehow I felt she liked us talking to her mama.

Then I remembered we hadn't even told Mrs. Guthrie our names, so I told her.

"Oh, my name's Ellie, and you know Sammy. Our daddy is Jack Perkins."

"I know yore names," she said. "I hear Alice calling 'em."

She didn't stay much longer, and she took Alice back with her. She said she'd put the rag on the log for us and she said when we come up on Saturdays to be sure to have Alice back before five to be on the safe side. They normally didn't git back from town till near dark, but no need taking chances. We said we'd do what she said.

Chapter 19

*M*e and Sammy never did learn how to make baskets. I had pieced together all my quilt scraps, but it wadn't near enough for a quilt. We was purty discouraged about raising twenty dollars. Aunt Bessie said she would talk to Doc and maybe her and him could give the money. She said she'd start saving up. She said she didn't see how Alice could ever really learn till she could hear. She said even if Alice couldn't take the hearing aid home, we would keep it and she could use it with us, which is the only time she needs to hear anyhow since her mama don't talk to her much.

Aunt Bessie give me a pair of Uncle Will's old overalls and a shirt for Alice. She cut off the overalls' legs and hemmed them up. She give me a comb, too, and three big round bars of sweet-smelling soap. She told me I ought to try to talk with Alice about keeping herself clean during her monthlies, and in the meantime she would make Alice three or four pair of bloomers.

The next time we went up, Mrs. Guthrie had the signal fixed. The rag was on the log. It was a nice warm night and we had all the stuff with us. When we got to Cherrylog, we showed everthing to Alice.

"NOW YOU CAN CHANGE YOUR CLOTHES

AND I CAN WASH THE DIRTY ONES," I said. "AND
LOOKA HERE. THIS COMB IS ALL YORES, AND
THIS SOAP IS, TOO."

She grabbed two bars of soap and pushed them against
her nose. We was setting with our feet in the creek. She
jumped up and helt the soap out to Sammy, who was setting on the log.

"Smell hit!" she said. "Hit smells mmmm. Hit mine! I
bath?"

"No, I don't think . . ."

She jerked the straps off her shoulders and started pulling
the overalls off.

"NO!" I screamed. "WAIT, ALICE!"

Sammy turned his head and covered his eyes with his
hands. Alice didn't wait. She got naked and waded into the
creek giggling and squealing. Sammy walked off not looking.

"I'll be back after a while," he said.

"Sam-my! Sam-my!" Alice called.

"HE'LL BE BACK AFTER WE BATHE," I said.

"Sam-my not dirt?"

"HE ALREADY HAD A BATH."

"Oooooh."

We had a wonderful time. Alice was in such a happy
mood. We splashed each other and pushed each other down
and she soaped herself so many times I was scared she'd
wash her skin off. I scrubbed her head.

When Sammy got back we yelled simple sentences to her
and told her to say them like we did.

Sammy pointed to the log.

"THIS IS A PINE LOG," he said.

She said, "Dis is a pint."

"NO, NO. THIS IS A PINE LOG. THIS. THIS. NOT
DIS."

"This?"

We both clapped and she beamed.

"I LIKE THE WATER."

"I lika."

"LIKE. LIKE."

"Like?"

"YEAAAA!" we yelled.

We knowed she wouldn't catch on to much stuff quick, but we had to start somewhere. We decided that by the next spring we might have her talking good. The trouble was all the words she didn't understand.

After we took her home, Sammy said he thought we ought to start playing games with her since she didn't never git to play none when she was little.

"We got to teach her fun, too," he said. Then he laughed. "Matter of fact, I reckon we'll have to teach her everthing."

On Saturday we decided to stay at the Guthries' and play games with Alice. I wanted to teach her to play hopscotch, and since the ground in the woods is covered up with pine straw and leaves, we thought we'd draw the squares right in their yard.

Alice set on the back porch steps and watched as I drawed the squares. Sammy looked for three little flat rocks.

"SEE, ALICE," I said, "WHAT YOU DO IS DRAW THREE SQUARES ON TOP OF EACH OTHER FIRST. THEN YOU DRAW TWO SIDE-BY-SIDE SQUARES. THEN ANOTHER SINGLE SQUARE. THEN TWO MORE SIDE-BY-SIDE. THEN ONE MORE SINGLE FOR HOME."

She smiled sweet as I hollered and drawed. It hit me that she don't know about numbers. While we waited on Sammy to find the rocks, which took him forever 'cause he has to have everthing perfect, I tried to show her what numbers meant. I helt up one finger.

"LOOK, ALICE. THAT'S ONE FINGER." Then I helt up two. "AND THAT'S TWO FINGERS."

Then I did three, and said three. Then I took two down.

"HOW MANY IS THAT?"

"Hummm?"

She didn't have no idea what I was talking about. I picked up a twig and broke it in three pieces and I told her I was showing her how to count.

"THAT'S ONE TWIG." I helt up one.

"One quig."

"TWIG."

"Twig."

"THAT'S TWO TWIGS."

She grinned. "Two twigs!" she said.

"GOOD. NOW THAT'S THREE TWIGS."

"Tree twigs."

"THREE."

"Three."

I did it over and over till Sammy come back. She was doing it purty good.

"LET'S SHOW SAMMY," I said, and helt up one finger. "NOW WHAT'S THAT?"

"One twig."

Sammy laughed.

"NO, NOT TWIG," I said.

"Hit finger?"

"IT."

"It."

"IT IS WHAT? HOW MANY?"

"It one finger."

Me and Sammy clapped and she did, too. Sammy showed her the rocks.

"HOW MANY ROCKS, ALICE?"

"Three rock."

"VERY GOOD!" He handed me one.

"HOW MANY NOW?"

"Two rock."

He started to tell her about plurals but decided he better not try. He helt up four fingers.

"THIS IS FOUR FINGERS."

We taught her up to six and thought that was enough for one day.

Sammy went first in hopscotch. He tossed his rock into the first square, then hopped over it into the second and third. He put both feet in the doubles, hopped in number six and so on. Then he throwed into number two and three and four. His rock rolled out of five so it was my turn. I got to four before I missed.

Alice's balance was gitting a lot better since we was taking her down that mountain so much, but I doubted she'd ever hopped.

"ALL RIGHT, ALICE. NOW FIRST WE BETTER SHOW YOU HOW TO HOP." I hopped around her and Sammy. She got her feet tangled a few times but she done it. She never did catch on to the rules of the game, but she done right good. We tried our best to let her win but we'd of been there all night. We clapped ever time she did something right, and she was so tickled she giggled half the morning. When we could see she was tired, we quit.

I had brought some biscuits with soggum and fried fatback for dinner. Alice eat like a hog. No manners. Me and Sammy give each other a look, like, oh nooo! Something *else* we got to teach her. Then we laughed.

When we was done I said maybe we could play tag. Alice never did understand the rules of that, so we quit and got a rope out of the barn and played jump rope. She loved that. I could tell she wanted real bad to do everthing we told her. She would look stunned when she messed up. The only thing we knowed to do about that was for us to mess up a lot and laugh about it. Sammy said that was to teach her it was all right not to do things perfect.

"Maybe you better learn that yoreself," I said, teasing him.

"Boys have to do things more perfect than girls," he said.

"How come?"

"'Cause."

"'Cause what?"

"'Cause we have to grow up and make a living and all."

"Yeah. I guess that's right."

Alice leaned her ear close to Sammy's mouth as we talked.

"Whaaa?" she finally asked. "Whaa say?"

"I SAID YOU ARE A GOOD ROPE-JUMPER."

She looked down at her dirty bare feet.

"WOULD YOU LIKE TO JUMP SOME MORE?"

She shook her head. Then she grabbed my hand and led me to the shed. She got a bar of soap from under the cot.

"We bath?"

We took her to Cherrylog. Sammy hunted arrowheads while we bathed but he didn't find none. When I heard his whistle I whistled back and he come running up.

"Come on!" he said, grabbing Alice's hand. "I wanna show y'all something." We run through the woods. That's the first time I'd seen Alice try to run. She wadn't as fast as us so we had to run slower. All of a sudden, Sammy stopped at a clearing and shushed us. Then we tiptoed over to a outcrop of rock. Two young deer laid beside a big rock sound asleep. They was too far away to see them real good, but we knowed we couldn't go closer.

Alice put both hands over her mouth and stared. I was sure she'd never seen one. We stood real still watching, and purty soon we heard the sound of something walking. It was a doe. When Alice seen her, she gasped. The doe heard her. She leaped toward the young deers and they jumped up. Then the three of them took off. A sight that'll take yore breath away. Deers don't run. They sail. They sailed through the clearing that was growed waist high in goldenrod. They flew in long leaps over them bright gold flowers and I helt my breath. Then they disappeared into the woods.

Alice stood like she was dazed. I was scared for a minute she was fixing to have a fit.

"Whaaaa? Whaaa dat?"

"THEY ARE DEER," Sammy said.

"Deer?"

"YES, DEER."

"Lika cow?"

"NO. LIKE A DEER."

"Yooouu hava deer?"

"NOBODY HAS A DEER AT THEIR HOUSE. THEY LIVE IN THE WOODS."

"Nobody hava at house?"

"NO."

She stared a long time toward the spot where the deer went in the woods. Then she turned and looked Sammy straight in the eyes.

"Nobody hava me," she whispered.

Sammy opened his mouth to say something but didn't. He give me a pained look and I turned away. What could we say to her? What in the world could we say? I couldn't think of nothing.

Chapter 20

*T*hat night when we was asleep Daddy come home drunk, fell off the steps, and broke his leg. We both heard him hollering. We run to him and then Sammy went to git Doc.

Doc said they wadn't no way he could tell how bad the break was. Sammy helt Daddy down while Doc set it and splint it. Then he told me and Sammy to git back to bed 'cause he wanted to talk to Daddy. I put my ear against the wall between mine and Daddy's room. I couldn't hear it all, but Doc give Daddy a talking to about liquor, then he told him he'd have to stay off the leg for several weeks and he wanted him to keep his leg up.

I was glad to hear it. Maybe if he couldn't go buy liquor for that long, maybe he'd quit.

The next morning I told Daddy to stay in bed and I'd bring him a good breakfast. I fried some fatback and made gravy. I made biscuits and eggs and lots of coffee. I could tell he was hurting but he didn't say nothing. He eat a big breakfast.

Sammy went on to the mill. While I cleaned the kitchen, I could hear Daddy moaning ever once in a while. I decided I'd go in and see if we could talk. I pulled a rocker up beside the bed.

"It hurt bad, Daddy?"

"I'm hurtin all over. My head's killing me, too."

"I'm sure sorry."

He didn't say nothing for ever so long. Then he said, "Ellie, I need a drink. Go out to the barn and look under . . ."

"No, Daddy," I said low.

"Did you say no?"

I nodded.

He sighed and looked around the room.

"Go git it, Ellie."

"No, sir. I ain't going. I ain't never gonna git it for you. I'm gonna pray about it so's maybe God'll stop you wanting it."

He pushed hisself up and tried to stand, then fell back on the bed groaning.

I bowed my head and closed my eyes, and prayed in my mind.

In a minute he said, "What you saying to God?"

I opened my eyes and looked at my daddy. I'd seen him hung over and hurting so many times I couldn't count. Now he was hurting double with his leg. He looked awful. Face red, puffed eyes.

"I asked God to keep you from drinking," I said.

He didn't say nothing.

"I'm believing you gonna quit drinking liquor, Daddy."

He hit his fist against the mattress and turned to look in my face.

"I can't quit!" he said.

"If you talked to God, well, if you told him you can't do it by yoreself, then . . ."

"What else was you saying to God?"

"Nothing."

"Say what you was saying. Say it out loud like yore mama use to do."

I got embarrassed. I ain't never prayed out loud in front of nobody. Daddy got calmer. In a minute he said, "Will you do it, honey?"

I bowed my head again and said in my mind, help me, God. Then I said out loud.

"Heavenly Father—I want—need—me and Sammy needs a daddy. We—we don't have one no more. I ask you, God, to please hurry and stop Daddy's drinking so's he'll be like he use to—so's he'll be like he use to be before Mama . . ."

I had to stop before I busted into tears. Daddy reached over and took both of my hands in his big one. I didn't look at him. Then he started sniffling and I knowed he was crying. I couldn't stand it. I hadn't seen him cry since Mama died. I laid my face against our hands.

In a little bit he took two big deep breaths. I still didn't look.

Then he said, "God, God help me." He choked on the words and pulled me over to the bed and throwed his arms around me and pulled my head down on his chest. He cried and I cried, and he kept saying, God help me, over and over and over.

It was a miracle.

Aunt Bessie come up in the afternoon. I told her about the praying. She said praise the Lord and we hugged.

"Now what you planning on cooking a sick man for supper?"

We went to the garden and picked some peas and squash and tomatoes. I made the cornbread after Aunt Bessie done everthing else. Sammy come in a little after six. I told him about the praying and he said that's nice. (Aunt Bessie says Sammy's still mad at God 'cause Mama died.) He changed the subject to Alice and told Aunt Bessie the latest news.

"But they's so much she don't know," he said. "She

don't know hardly nothing. She needs more than me and Ellie to teach her. If only she could hear."

"I seen Doc day before yesterday," Aunt Bessie said, handing Sammy a big glass of buttermilk. "He said they's a company that sends out salesmen to sell hearing aids. He don't know if any of 'em come to these mountains or not, but I don't see why they wouldn't go to towns like Ellijay or Bolton. We got a lot of folks round here that could use help hearing. He's gonna write to the company and see if and when they'll send somebody up this away."

"But we ain't got the money yet," Sammy said, "and the way it looks, we ain't gonna never have it."

She patted Sammy's shoulder. "I talked to Doc. I told him I'd pay half if he'd pay half. We gonna git that girl a hearing aid." Sammy grinned and hugged her, then he jumped over and hugged me. We was both so happy we danced around.

Then Aunt Bessie said, "You got enough sugar for me to make us some plum cobbler, Ellie?"

"I got enough," I said, and hugged her.

"Good. Let's go down the road a ways. I seen a plum bush with some ripe ones."

"I'd sure rather have blackberry," Sammy said. "You reckon they gone?"

"Honey, we canned enough for a bunch of cobblers. You want a blackberry, I'll make one. Now go talk to yore daddy."

After supper Uncle Will and Morgan come up. We helped Daddy to the front porch and we all set a while.

As it got dark the tree frogs filled up the night with their song. It was nice. Lightning bugs was blinking and they was a cool breeze.

Daddy and Uncle Will and Aunt Bessie talked about crops and rain. Stuff like that. Then about the sawmill. Under laid next to Daddy's rocker and snoozed. Daddy rubbed his head. Uncle Will and Morgan took a chaw of tobacco and set spitting off the porch. Uncle Will can spit real far. He come in second at the county fair one time.

"How about a chaw?" Uncle Will said to Daddy. Daddy never did care for tobacco.

"Think I'll try a little." Daddy reached for it. I looked at Sammy and he looked at me. We was surprised.

Uncle Will handed Daddy the plug. Daddy bit off a wad and started chewing. He coughed a little and we all laughed. Soon he was spitting.

"How far did that feller spit who won the contest?" Daddy asked Uncle Will.

"Thirty-eight foot," Uncle Will said.

Daddy snorted. "The hell you say!"

"I spit thirty-two myself."

"Why, that's downright impossible."

Daddy tried three times, but didn't spit over five or six feet.

"Can't beat Will," Aunt Bessie said. "One time I seen him hit a rock no bigger'n a plate at twenty foot. I got a name for him but I can't say it in front of these younguns."

"Ah, say it," Sammy grinned at Aunt Bessie.

"Nah. Can't do it."

"Doc calls him Cannon Mouth," Morgan said.

Daddy laughed.

After Uncle Will and them went home, Daddy called me and Sammy into the front room.

"Set down," he said and pointed to the chairs. He was on the bed with his leg propped up on a pillow. I glanced at Sammy and he had this stubborn look on his face, like here we go again, I ain't gonna listen. I leaned forward, looking at Daddy.

"Y'all know—well I reckon I've proved over and over I

can't quit drinking. I know it's killing me. I know what it's done to y'all. I reckon liquor is the worst curse of the devil. Gits ya weak. Works on yore mind so's ya can't think straight. Y'all never knowed my pa. He was a drinking man. Ruint his life. Messed us all up. Near killed Ma. Looks like I should of took a lesson but—I reckon I got his weakness. Can't think of nothing else. Yore mama hated liquor more'n she hated anything. She was a good woman. Best woman ever walked. I needed her like my own breath . . ."

Tears come in his eyes. I looked away. Sammy didn't. He looked straight in Daddy's eyes.

"Y'all fine younguns. Couldn't ask for no better. I made yore life hard. It's a wonder you're still here. It's a wonder you didn't run off. Will offered for y'all to live with them. It—it might be the best thing ever happened—I been thinking about it."

"I ain't leaving you!" I set up quick and straight. "I ain't never leaving you! Sammy ain't neither."

Daddy looked at Sammy.

"How you feel, son?"

Sammy stood up and put both hands into his overall pockets. He walked back and forth across the room, looking at the floor.

"Will you tell me?" Daddy's voice sounded tired.

"I thought I wouldn't, but one of these days I'm leaving, Daddy. I ain't going to live with Uncle Will. That ain't no answer. I want to *be* something. I can't stay in these mountains all my life, not being nothing. I been thinking on it a lot lately. I'd sure like to go to Atlanta, try to find a job so's I can study writing. Aunt Bessie said it's called journalism. When ya want to write for a paper that's what it's called. I'd like to write for a paper."

"That's a good thing, son."

Sammy stopped pacing, shook his head, and sighed.

"Ain't possible though, is it? How could I ever leave

knowing you might kill Ellie? Answer me that." Sammy caught holt of the back of my rocker.

"If I can't stop the liquor, the only thing is for *me* to leave. Only thing I can see."

"But Daddy," I said.

"Ain't no buts about it. Sammy's right. I know I'm dangerous. Can't remember, turn wild like my pa . . ."

"You gonna quit the liquor." I reached over and touched his hand. "I know it's the truth, Daddy, I *know* it. Why can't you think on quitting 'stead of thinking on what to do 'cause you can't quit?" I got up and got the Bible off the table.

"It's in here how to quit. Aunt Bessie . . ."

"Oh, good grief, Ellie," Sammy said, disgusted. Then he started talking about how Aunt Bessie didn't know everthing. He fussed at me 'cause I thought she did, and then he stomped around like a stupid bull, saying mean things.

After a while I got tired of the whole thing. Tired of worrying about Daddy. About Alice, who ain't never had a chance on account of a dadgummed man and his liquor. Tired of listening to Sammy's mouth. Scared to think of Daddy leaving us. I throwed the Bible on the bed.

"Go on!" I hollered at Daddy. "Why don't you just go on and run like a scared rabbit? Take yore liquor and run and hide. Don't ask God for nothing! Why don't you just lock me and Sammy in a shed so you won't have to *ever* be no daddy! Liquor! Liquor! Liquor! I'm gonna go git it for you right now!"

I took the lamp and left them staring with their mouths open. I left them in the dark and went to the barn and got the jug. Then I stomped back in the front room and helt it out to Daddy.

"Go on! Be a drunk. Don't be a daddy. Don't be nothing. Be a old sniveling, stumbling, puking sick weasel. Be one!"

I throwed the heavy jug at him. He caught it. Sammy stood there like a dummy not saying nothing, his head hung. I whirled around to him.

"Maybe I want to be something, too. Y'all ever think of that? Huh? Did ya?" Then I run out of the room and slammed the door.

Chapter 21

For a week we lived in such a strain I thought about running away, or just going to a highway and gitting a ride and going anywheres. I didn't even talk to Aunt Bessie. When she come I'd just mope around. She'd go from me to Daddy to Sammy, trying to find out what was wrong. I didn't even go see Alice, though Sammy did.

Saturday Sammy asked me if I wanted to go see Alice and I lit into him. I said, "Oh, you think you're such big stuff! You think you're gonna teach Alice to be a normal girl, don't you? You think me and you can go up there and undo all them years that crazy man mashed her mind into a blob. Drunk his damn liquor and slammed his wife around till she was too scared to pay 'tention to her chile, don't ya? You think the piddling stuff we do is gonna do a miracle and one of these days she's gonna bust out of that filthy shed and be normal, don't ya? Well, I'm done! I ain't doing it no more. You're so smart. You do it by yoreself, or you git yoreself on down to Atlanta and be a famous newspaper writer and leave me here to tend to Daddy the rest of my life. And leave me here to sneak up that mountain so's that crazy man can blow my guts out one of these days!"

Sammy didn't try to stop nothing I said the whole time.

He listened to ever word, staring right at me. Then he walked over to the water bucket, dipped out a dipperful and drunk it. Then he went out the back door, went to the barn, and got Poke and rode off. I set down in the kitchen chair, feeling whipped.

Then I got this guilty feeling 'cause I hadn't seen Alice in a week and 'cause of what I'd said. Then I stomped out of the house.

It takes a long time to walk to the Guthries. By the time I got there I was too tired to think. I stood in the woods, looking and listening a while, making sure they'd gone. Then I went to the shed. I could see before I got there the door was open a little. When I looked in, Alice wadn't there. I knowed Sammy must of come up and took her to Cherrylog. As I come out of the shed I looked toward the woods and got the shock of my life. There set that dern Morgan on his horse!

I already told you what he done, how he threatened me about telling if I didn't show him my bosoms. He started off by saying, "Ya looking for haints? What ya doing in that shed?"

"None of yore business!"

"What they keep in there?"

"Nothing!"

"How come you so interested in nothing? Maybe I ought to look, huh? Where's the Guthries? What's in that shed, Ellie?"

He turned the horse toward the shed. My heart dropped.

"They's baby chicks in there!" I said quick. "And me and you better git outa here 'cause the Guthries is due any second. You know how mean he is. He'll shoot us."

He turned the horse back.

"Uncle Jack know you come up here?"

I didn't answer. I started walking down the mountain. He

rode beside me. He kept talking about how Daddy would be mad if he knowed I had come up there. When we got nearly to my house is when he got off the horse and started poking at me. Finally I hit him and then's when he threatened me and I took off running and telling him I would shoot him with Daddy's shotgun if he ever tried to touch me or see my bosoms.

All in all it was a awful day!

I think Sammy and Daddy was as wore out with everthing as I was. We went about our own business like nothing happened. Sammy went up to Alice's by hisself and I went by myself, and I didn't ask him nothing about it. Aunt Bessie come up nearly ever day but I wadn't in the mood for talking. I walked in the woods a lot. Twice I went and set by Mama's grave and thought.

I quit praying. I didn't mention God to Daddy no more neither. I made up my mind if believing is the answer, then I was gonna rest a while and just believe. I reckon sometimes that's all we can do.

Before Mama died she did a needlepoint picture that hangs in a frame in my room. It's a blue background with white clouds and a peaceful scene of two trees and a little brook. Two bluebirds is setting on a tree branch and a baby deer is asleep beside the brook. Stitched under the picture are these words: *Be still and know that I am God.* Mama give it to me for Christmas the year after I told her about the deer birthing and all. Here I've had it all this time and didn't know what them words really meant. That week I looked at the picture a lot. That's how come it finally hit me to quit fussing in my heart and mind.

While Daddy was laid up with his leg, I think I growed up a little bit, not 'cause I turned fourteen on August 28, and not 'cause I got calmer about everthing, but I think the main thing was the difference in the way I felt about Daddy. Seemed like all of a sudden I seen that he was just a person who had fell apart when his wife died. Before she died he was strong and good and kind and I reckon I never could believe he could be nothing else.

Chapter 22

After a few times of me seeing Alice by myself and Sammy by hisself we just sort of started going together sometimes to see her. I reckon that's the way things happen. When life goes on being life and nothing don't change none, then I guess folks sort of forgit about fusses and fights and drift back into the same stuff.

I'd noticed Sammy was paying Bertha more attention at church and she was acting like a lovesick I don't know what. I told Aunt Bessie and she said when boys got Sammy's age they was itching in so many places they didn't know where to scratch, whatever *that* means. It was all gitting purty confusing.

Me and Sammy was working real hard trying to teach Alice. Gitting to go up there hadn't never been no problem when Daddy was drunk. Now that he'd been sober a while he noticed.

One day we was setting at the kitchen table and Daddy come hopping in and set down.

"I want ya to take me to Bolton, son," he said. "I got to git out of this house."

"You think it'd be all right?" Sammy asked. "Doc said stay off that leg."

"Go hitch up. I ain't gonna walk none. Maybe the ride'll do me good. You wanna go, Ellie?"

"Nah. Aunt Bessie's coming later on. She wants to show me what she's done to the buggy."

Daddy laughed. "Allembee's is gonna have to have another name. She paint it red?"

"No, wine."

"Same thing. Where'd you go this morning?"

"For a walk, that's all."

I knowed he knowed I was lying.

"That ain't so, is it?"

"No, sir."

"You go up to see that girl?"

I looked at Sammy. He looked scared.

"Yessir." I hung my head. "I didn't git to see her, though."

"You been goin up there a lot, ain't ya?"

"Yessir."

"I been going, too," Sammy said. Daddy looked from one of us to the other.

"Y'all find out what's wrong with her?" he asked.

Sammy had stood to leave and hitch up, but he set back down. We told Daddy everthing. It took nearly two hours.

At the end I said, "We both like her a lot, Daddy."

"She purty, son?"

"She's beautiful," Sammy said.

Daddy stood up.

"I'm gonna have to think on this a while. Now go hitch up. Ellie, git me my hat."

Sammy run out the door. I started to the front room.

"Ellie?"

"Yessir?"

"You're a fine girl."

That night I couldn't go to sleep to save my life. I don't know why. I twisted and turned till I thought I'd scream. I heard Daddy hopping around. Doc had said he'd bring him some crutches but hadn't brought 'em yet. I heard Daddy hop into the kitchen. I guessed he was making coffee. I wanted to git up and make it for him, but I was too tired. Finally I counted sheep. I remember counting past three hundred, then I went to sleep. If I'd of knowed what was gonna happen next, I'd of never slept.

The next night Sammy went to see Alice. I didn't go. Then for the next three days he acted like a crazy nervous wreck. Finally he told me he couldn't go see Alice no more.

"How come?" I asked.

"'Cause—well, 'cause she's a girl and, well, *you* know. Ellie, she don't understand why I won't take a bath with her. Once when I took her down there by myself she acted like we was gonna bathe. She started to take her clothes off. I had a awful time trying to explain."

"How *did* you? What did you tell her?"

He set down on the steps and put his head in his hands. Then he moaned and shook his head.

"Can you tell me?" I said.

"Oh, Ellie," he said, "the other night, oh, I can't. I just can't."

"Did something happen? I mean, did something . . ."

"I can't tell you."

I set down beside him. I didn't know what to say. My thoughts was racing with all kinds of stuff.

"You didn't . . . you didn't do . . . do nothing, did you?"

He jumped off the porch and paced back and forth in front of me a while. Then he set back down and put his head in his hands again.

"I think you better tell me," I whispered, and touched his shoulder. "I reckon I'm the only one you can tell." I was gitting scared. All the stuff Aunt Bessie told me about doing it and all filled up my mind.

He grabbed my hand and pulled me up.

"Let's go down to the valley," he said. "Let's go to the mill. I need to walk a while."

We crossed the road and went past the blackberry patch. Then we crossed the clearing and walked into the woods headed down the mountain. I said a few things about Daddy and then about the garden. He didn't talk, just grunted now and then.

When we got to the shoals we waded across and set on a rock. The gristmill was behind us. The old wheel squeaked and groaned and splashed water into the pond. I couldn't feel no breeze. The air was dry and still. The sun was setting behind the mountain, all pink and gold.

We didn't talk and I hated to pester him so I decided to tell him about Morgan. I had promised myself I wouldn't never tell nobody on account of him being our cousin and being Aunt Bessie's boy and all, but the more I thought about it, the more I thought that now was the time to tell.

"Sammy?" I said.

"Huh?"

"Morgan—he—Morgan tried to—touch me."

"Whatcha mean?"

I said it quick. "He tried to touch my bosoms."

He turned real slow to stare in my face. Then he shook his head and slid off the rock into the water. He waded to a sandbar and started kicking sand. I had expected him to git so mad he'd say he'd beat up Morgan. I expected him to scream and holler. He didn't do nothing. He just kicked the sand, clenching his fists.

Then he come back and set on the rock, and in a minute he said, "I ain't no better'n Morgan. I ain't no better'n that little no-account pipsqueak!" Then he turned and took my arm. "How come you didn't tell me before? How come you waited till now? You just trying to make *me* not feel so awful, ain't you? You told me now 'cause you know more than I think you know, about—me and Alice. Ain't that right? Tell me what you know, Ellie."

I looked in his face. "I don't know nothing," I said, "'cept that Alice likes you and I know you like her, and, well, I know what Aunt Bessie told me about boys and girls. That's all I know. That's why I think you ought to tell me. I worry about Alice, too. I worry all the time."

"Then Alice didn't tell you?"

I was gitting scareder. "She didn't say nothing. You just can't keep a secret on this. If you done something to Alice, well, then somebody's got to talk to her. Sammy, Aunt Bessie told me all about making babies!"

I set staring at our bare feet. A sick feeling come in my stomach. I watched Sammy's toes scrunch up and then relax and then scrunch up again. I'd never noticed Sammy's toes. They was long and strong looking. I'd never thought of toes being strong.

"I guess I better tell you," Sammy said, putting his head back into his hands.

"I guess so."

"It—it's this bathing business," he said finally. "I couldn't git her to understand. Like I told you, the first time when I told her I thought she understood, but it's for sure she didn't. I guess you and her was bathing a lot so she didn't mention it again. Then the other night—well, I was so tired. We unloaded four wagons at the mill. Had to git Mr. Attaway's siding cut and the edger saw kept messing up. It was trouble all day, it seemed like. When me and Alice got to Cherrylog I laid down and I bet it wadn't five minutes till I was asleep.

"Then a noise woke me. Something walking. Heavy

steps cracking some limbs. I raised up and looked toward the clearing where the noise come from. The moon was nearly full so I could see real good, and I seen Mohawk heading to the creek on up that way."

Then I gasped and started to say something, but he went on talking. "I reckons he got our scent 'cause she stopped and started looking around. I eased up to look for Alice. I didn't see her nowhere. Scared me half to death. Then I heard her splashing. I figured she was wading down close to the bend. I didn't think of her bathing 'cause she didn't bring her soap or nothing.

"Mohawk was standing still, sniffing. She hadn't seen me. I figgered it'd be better to wade to Alice rather than make noise walking on the leaves. I figgered Mohawk heard her splash, too, so I tried to hurry."

"But Sammy," I said, "You said Mohawk wouldn't bother nobody if they stayed out of her way or 'less they tried to mess with her cubs. Was any cubs with her?"

Sammy moved his hands away from his head and put one knee up and propped his arms on it. He clamped his fists shut.

"I didn't see no cubs. I figgered she was by herself. I couldn't take the chance of Alice doing something to git her attention, of maybe scaring her into attacking. Just 'cause she ain't never attacked nobody as we know of, don't mean she won't."

I shivered at the thought of that big bear attacking.

"Anyhow, I waded slow and easy down toward Alice. I didn't hear her splashing anymore and hoped she'd keep quiet and still till I got to her. I kept my eye on Mohawk. She had turned in our direction and was walking slow. I didn't think she knew we was there."

"Oh, Sammy! I bet you was scared. I'd of been scared crazy!"

"I thought my heart would pump out of my chest," he

said. "I couldn't think of nothing to do. Nowhere to take Alice. All I could think of was if Mohawk tried to git us, then either we'd have to outrun her or climb a tree. I was trying to think of a good climbing tree close by, but I was so scared I couldn't think."

"Then I got close to where Alice was, and Ellie, I saw her and she was setting on the bank slap naked. Oh, my God, Ellie, I was so shocked I guess I gawked at her and when I did, I bumped a log in the creek and knocked it up and back into the water. I just knew Mohawk heard the splash and— then—then I turned to see Mohawk stop and look around.

"I stood staring at that bear and she started walking toward us again. But she was still moving slow. I prayed she would keep walking slow. I prayed she would git distracted.

"Then Alice seen me and thank God she didn't say nothing. She just smiled. It was the damnedest thing I ever seen. You'd of thought she was fully dressed. She didn't even blink a eye. I put my finger to my lips so's she wouldn't speak and she didn't. Then I figgered the best thing to do was to walk on down the creek. I pointed to the bear and kept my other hand with my finger to my lips. Then I reached up and helped her into the water and we started walking."

Sammy rubbed his hand back and forth on his forehead. Then he went on. "I can't tell you—I can't explain how— how—strange it was with her being naked. She didn't know to be afraid of the bear. She might of even thought I was playing a game or something. It was crazy!" He brushed his hair off his forehead and stared into the water. I wanted to say something but I didn't know what to say.

"Then Mohawk started moving faster and we took off running. I knew we couldn't run fast in the creek on account of the slicky rocks, so I got her on the bank. Then we flew nearly. I didn't even look back. I pulled her and we run down the mountain and into the valley here. I figgered if I could git her to the mill we could climb up in the loft and be safe. When we got into the valley I turned to look but I couldn't see Mohawk. I guess we had left her and was safe a long time back but I couldn't of been sure. I took off my shirt and yelled at Alice to put it on. Then we went to the mill."

He stopped talking a while. He slid off the rock and stood in the water with his hands in his pockets, staring at the sunset. I couldn't set still neither. I slid off and waded to the sandbar and squished my toes in the wet sand. Something awful was happening to my stomach, something like knots pulling. Something you git when you dread the next thing you know's gonna happen. I didn't want to hear no more. I couldn't stand the thought of hearing about my brother doing it to a girl that didn't know nothing, who couldn't hear and couldn't understand and who was sick. I thought about the silly talk me and Lisa Mae had about lusting, then about what Aunt Bessie had told me about men gitting like animals sometime when they wanted to do it real bad and how that was *real* lusting.

The thought made me sick. My brother, who had always watched over me. I couldn't stand it. I turned to look at him. He looked like he was hanging there in the water from invisible wires or ropes. His whole body drooped. His head fell forward.

"Aunt Bessie told me about that stuff," I said low. "She said men git like animals. You done it, didn't you? You got like that with Alice. It makes me sick to my stomach. Sick like I ain't never been. I wish Mohawk had of caught you. I wish Alice would have run and Mohawk had of caught you." I bit my lip. Tears come in my eyes. "How *could* you have done it to somebody like Alice, Sammy! How? You're the last person in the whole world I would of thought!"

Then I got so flustered I bent down and got two handfuls

of wet sand. I wanted to throw them at him. I wanted to hit him. Pound him. I run at him with my muddy fists flying. He hung there limp, letting me hit his head, his shoulders, his chest and stomach. I was screaming at him the whole time. "Animal! Animal! You and that pukey Morgan is both animals. That's what!"

He let me hit him a while. Then he wrapped them big arms around me like he use to do Daddy, and pinned my arms to my sides. He lifted me onto the rock and helt me. He leaned against me.

"Hush up, Ellie," he said, the words choked out of his throat. "Hush up and I'll tell you the rest. You need to hear it."

I could feel his warm breath against my forehead. I could smell the sweet sharp pine smells from the sawdust in his hair and overalls. I quit struggling and leaned against him.

"I reckon you got to know about boys and men—know how it is. How it really is." He stopped to sigh heavy sighs. "I love Alice, Ellie. I've loved her for a long time. I don't reckon I know what grown-up lovin' is, but however it is I can love—then that's the way I love her. But it's all mixed up. It's mixed up with all kinds of scary feelings. It's mixed up 'cause she's like she is. 'Cause she's not like Bertha and you and anybody. So my mind tells me I can't love her. My mind's been hollering that at me since the first. I've tried to git my mind back on Bertha—I can't. I can't do it. Bertha's a nice girl. Purty. But, oh, Ellie, I look at Bertha and it's like Alice's face floats there and . . . oh, I don't know! I just don't know!"

He turned loose of me and leaned against the rock. I seen the little flecks of sawdust in his hair, some caught in the seam of his shirt collar. He turned his back to me and started talking again.

"When we got up in the loft we was both tired out. Alice set on a pile of cornshucks. She was out of breath. I was a mess. The whole day had been so bad I couldn't seem to git my mind to working again. I plopped down on the shucks to rest, too. I stared out the opening at the creek. At the rocks with the moon shining on them. I listened to the wheel groan and the water splash. I thought about Mohawk and how if it'd been just me, I'd of probably not panicked atall. I'd of stood quiet like I always done before when I seen her or some other bear, but on account of Alice I'd gone crazy. I . . ."

"You didn't have no choice, Sammy," I said. Now I was feeling sorry I'd hit him. "If Alice had of started hollering or making a commotion, then ain't no telling what Mohawk would of done."

He nodded. We set quiet a while. He sighed some more. I'd never heard him sigh so many times in my life, like breathing out the heavy thoughts.

"Well, Alice finally said something. She moved closer to me and said, 'Sammy, I run. Hit not run fast, huh? Hit a big dog, huh?'

"I looked in them eyes, staring into mine like I know everthing. Like I'm God, for gosh sake. Like I'm her big hero. She always looks at me like that, Ellie. There she set in my shirt that wadn't buttoned, with the shadows moving on her face and on one of her—her breasts—and on them legs and something popped in my head. All the thoughts, all the worries of saving her—helping her learn—teaching her—all them things seemed to clamp shut and I grabbed her and—and . . ." He covered his face with his hands and slumped forward and started sobbing.

I stared at his back, his wide shoulders, at the bones that showed through the top of his shirt. Feelings of love and hate all at the same time come over me. The awfulness of things—life—the sadness—that mashed out all the good— mashed it and squashed it. I slid off the rock to git into the clean cold water. Then I waded in little circles, staring at the water, not looking at Sammy.

He waded to me and stood looking down at me. He didn't try to touch me. He had quit sobbing. He just sniffed his nose.

"Aunt Bessie, she was right," I whispered.

"No, she wadn't right. It ain't all animal stuff." His voice helt the tears. "I don't think I would of really done it. You know I wouldn't hurt her. I *didn't* hurt her. I don't know how to explain it. Sometimes it ain't the animal. Sometimes it's—it's—a million fears and it's not knowing no answers. It's feeling like screaming and beating your head against a tree. Sometimes it's like this rock here is on your shoulders and you been toting it for years and years, knowing if you don't tote it, it'd come crashing down and finish off everybody. Oh, I don't know—I don't know—I didn't do it to her. I mean, I didn't really do it. I guess I was going to when I grabbed her 'cause at the same time I was trying to kiss her and feel of her, I was . . ." He stopped a minute, then went on. "She didn't even know what was happening. She wadn't scared at first—I mean, we've hugged her so much and—and Ellie, you might as well know. You ought to know on account of what I found out."

He took holt of my shoulders but I didn't look in his face.

"I—well, I got my—fly unbuttoned and got—and—and she seen it and started trying to git loose and she hollered—she hollered about her daddy's scrag. Another made-up word. She said, 'Daddy scrag, oh, hurta! Ma-ma come hit Daddy ona back wif fire poker. He screamin. I bloodin, I bloodin dare.' She pointed to herself. 'I cryin. Daddy hit, hit, hit me. We come dis place. Mama keepin me shed. She say she keepin Daddy drinka drunk. He not do no more. You—you not do, Sammy. You not do, huh?' She scooted away from me and huddled into the corner. Her words hit my brain finally. Ellie, the son-of-a-bitch had raped her!

144

That's the real reason she's in that shed. Her mama keeps her there and makes sure he's passed out ever night. It seemed like the world come down on me. Come down like a waterfall filled with nightmares—washing down and battering at my thinking. I just fell apart. I yelled at her to stay and I got out of there. I climbed down, went around the mill, and throwed myself into the pond and swum till my arms felt like they was falling off."

Sammy dropped his arms and moved away from me. He had rolled up the bottom of his overalls but now he waded into a deeper part and got them wet.

"I was gonna kill him, Ellie. I was gonna take her to our house and go up there and kill him with a ax or with Daddy's gun. Then like a hammer hit my head, I thought to myself—you nearly done the same thing! You gonna kill that drunk bastard and you nearly raped her yourself!"

Suddenly Sammy's voice sounded like he'd lost his breath. He stopped pacing in the water. Then his voice was so soft I nearly didn't hear.

"Then I got her and took her to git her clothes. I turned my head while she dressed. Then I took her to the shed. I ain't slept atall. I ain't slept none. I've thought till I can't think no more. I nearly done it to her but it's different. I ain't no animal, Ellie. It's different." His voice cracked and filled with tears again. "If ever you believed anything in yore life, you gotta believe me—you got to, Ellie."

Chapter 23

*T*he next few days I was a mess. It's awful to know something and have a hunderd mixed-up thoughts and questions and not have nobody to talk to. I'd promised Sammy I wouldn't tell. How can you tell something like that about your brother anyhow? I kept it a secret about Morgan wanting to see my bosoms all that time, and that ain't nothing when you think about what Sammy done.

I done a lot of thinking about boys and men. About what made them do things, like Daddy turning from good to bad with liquor and how I had thought myself that he couldn't help himself about drinking. About Sammy nearly raping Alice on account of being wore out with Daddy and on account of things piling up on him. I wondered if they was any men that you can count on no matter what. I thought of Aunt Bessie and how I could depend on her. I knowed in my heart that I could always depend on her, always trust her, just like I trusted my Mama.

On the fourth day I told Sammy me and him had to talk. He was moping around down at the barn, looking like somebody done told him he was dying from a bad disease. When I walked down, he was setting on a old nail keg whittling on a stick with his pocketknife.

"Sammy," I said, "I—I got to talk to you."

He glanced at me.

"Figgered we'd have to talk sooner or later," he mumbled.

I got the milking stool and set on it. I didn't know what to say to start it off, so I said, "The leg on this stool is wobbly."

"Yeah."

Then I set a while and said, "I—I kind of dread school startin, don't you?"

"Yeah."

"Aunt Bessie is gitting me new shoes. The othern's too little. Yores too little?"

"They all right."

I looked at Leety, who was eating fodder in her stall. Her sack was swole and heavy. I knowed Sammy hadn't milked her yet. She was swishing flies with her tail. I thought about how much stuff Sammy had had to do in the past two years. Stuff that Daddy used to do. The milking, the plowing, the garden and all the chores and fixing things that broke, and working at the mill. I looked at him slumped over with his elbows on his knees.

"I ain't real mad at you," I said quick. He didn't say nothing.

"It's just that, well, I reckon I just don't understand. I don't know how you could of even thought of doing it. I mean, well, I mean no matter how tired you was. No matter how bad everthing is. Sammy, you *got* to tell me about men. You *got* to. I ain't got nobody to ask. I been thinking till it's got me crazy. You—you all I got, Sammy."

He looked at my face a second, then looked at the whittled stick. I thought he'd never speak. I set twisting my shirt. Finally he throwed the stick to the ground.

"I don't know how to tell you, Ellie," he said, shaking his head. "I just don't know. It ain't something I can tell 'cause I don't understand it myself." He closed the knife and slumped farther down till his head was hanging between his arms.

"Does boys—ah—men, do they do it 'cause they *have* to? I mean, is it like they ain't got no control atall? Is that it?"

"That ain't it."

"Well, say, when I git older and when I, say, maybe have a sweetheart and say we are off by ourselves and all and we kiss, and then he gits to lusting, what if that happens and I don't know what to do, and what if he was to rape me? Aunt Bessie says I can't never let a boy kiss on me and touch me and all on account of if I let them do all that, they might rape me, and then I'd git all swole up and have a baby, and I wouldn't even be married. And I'd have to go way off somewheres 'cause I'd be a disgrace. What about that? What if you'd of gone on and raped pore Alice? She didn't even do nothing to cause it. If she didn't do nothing, then how come you got to lusting? Sammy, you got to tell me. How will I know if you don't tell me?"

He looked miserable setting there. I didn't want to make him miserabler but I was so upset I thought that if he didn't tell me *something* I'd scream. In a minute he got up and he breathed deep breaths. He stuck his hands in his pockets and stood there with his shoulders hunched. Then he said, "You think I ain't been going crazy myself? You think I can lay down and sleep when I'm thinking about it ever minute?" He kicked at the ground. "I told you I love Alice. I *do*, Ellie. I know it's hard to believe that I'd hurt her if I loved her. If anybody hurt you I'd want to kill 'em. That's the way I feel about her. I feel it even more on account of how she is. When I think about it I reckon I think the same as you do, that if *I* can hurt her—or even think about hurting her, then what the hell's wrong with me! But it ain't animal. Ellie, it *ain't*. I don't know what it is, but it *ain't* animal."

He jerked his hands out of his pockets and yanked at his own hair, twisting his hands through it. He was like a caged squirrel I seen once, jerking and frantic. All of a sudden he rushed at the barn gate and slammed his fist into the post. I jumped up. He done it again and I could see blood on his knuckles. I didn't move to him. In a way I wanted to and in another way I wanted to hit him like I did that day. I *never* felt so mixed-up.

He twirled around to face me, his fist showing blood.

"How can *I* tell you anything! I can't! All these months I been treating Alice just like you treated her. I told myself I was her friend—that was all. I bet you never knew how I felt, did you? There I was being her—damned *hero* friend, for God's sake, and look what I done! I ain't gonna see her no more, Ellie. It's too crazy. She ain't like us. She's like a baby. It don't make sense, me loving a baby like that! It's plumb crazy! Don't ask me no more questions. *I* don't know nothing. I can't do a simple thing like be her friend, and I *sure* can't be her hero friend or yore hero brother neither!"

He slumped onto the gate.

"Oh, Ellie. Oh, God."

I went to him to touch his shoulder, but he twisted away. My stomach felt like I'd swallowed vinegar. He pushed past me and run through the pasture headed to the woods. As I watched him disappear into the trees, the awfulest thought flashed like lightning across my mind. The most sickening thought I reckon I ever had. Over and over it flashed till my stomach churned with it. "He tried to rape her. It's a good dadgummed thing he loves her so much, or no telling what he'd of done to her."

While I was trying to go to sleep that night I come to know something I hated to know. I hated it worse'n I ever hated anything. I had kept loving my daddy through all the drinking, but I knowed now I didn't like him. Same with Sammy. I listened to his story and though I still loved him, I knowed that right then I didn't like him atall. It made me cry. Then after bawling a while and twisting and turning I started gitting mad. The more I twisted the madder I got.

The next morning I didn't fix their breakfast. I got up early and I got Poke and thought to myself, let Sammy *walk* to the mill! I rode down the mountain to the valley. Then I rode back up the mountain and then rode down toward Aunt Bessie's. I passed Aunt Bessie's and headed toward the school. All that riding didn't do me no good atall. It didn't solve nothing. Here I thought I had growed up a little. I thought I understood about Daddy at least, but now I knowed I didn't understand a thing. I rode to the school. Then to the church. Then back to the valley. I set there till dark. Then I thought about letting *them* worry for a change and the more I thought of it, the better I liked the idea. I rode Poke into a clump of willows and tied her. I was real hungry. I went into the Hudson's garden and got four carrots and two 'maters and a sweet 'tater. I eat them all, then I curled up in the willow clump.

I heard them calling me. Sammy—then Uncle Will and Morgan. I laid there grinning, thinking about making three men worry and hunt me. Poke didn't make a noise, thank goodness. One time Morgan passed not ten foot from me. I had to cover my mouth so's not to laugh out loud. Even though I got scared and didn't sleep for worrying about snakes and bears I stayed till nearly dawn.

Then I rode up that mountain and busted through the kitchen door to see them all setting there baggy-eyed, drinking coffee. Even Aunt Bessie. They all started saying stuff. Everbody talking at once. I stood there a minute glaring at the men. Then I stomped into my room and slammed the door and locked it. I ain't never done nothing so wonderful in my whole life!

The next day I told Aunt Bessie that I was done with doing for Sammy and Daddy. They could cook their food, they could clean their rooms and wash their clothes! And I told her that by cracky I was plumb sick of hearing excuses for boys and men. I said how come men can do awful things and whimper that they "just can't help theyselves." What I wanted to know was why *couldn't* they help theyselves! Then I had another crying fit. And then she tried to tell me stuff but what she ended up with was more excuses, the biggest one being that men was just big babies anyhow.

But at least I got it all out.

And that night I went to face Alice.

She was glad to see me, but the first thing she asked was, "Where Sam-my?" It was like nothing hadn't happened. She wadn't upset. She wadn't hurt or mad or nothing as I could see. She was the same as always. All the way to Cherrylog I thought of how to git her to talk about it. I felt like we had to talk. Here her friend Sammy had gone and nearly done what her daddy done and I couldn't see how she wadn't just destroyed.

I decided to act like nothing hadn't changed. I thought I'd give her time to bring it up. I was going to try to explain why she couldn't bathe with boys, about how they are different, so's maybe she'd talk about it. I told her I needed to tell her something before we bathed.

"Whaaa?" She leaned close to my mouth.

"IT'S ABOUT YOU BEING A GIRL, AND, WELL, ABOUT SAMMY BEING A BOY."

"Mmmm."

"WELL, SEE, THE THING IS GIRLS DON'T BATHE WITH BOYS, AH, IT AIN'T NICE AND . . ."

"Whaaa nite?"

"NICE," I said, correcting her.

"Nice."

"WELL, NICE IS—NICE IS SORTA LIKE—IT'S LIKE

151

RIGHT. YOU KNOW. RIGHT AND WRONG." How can you explain nice?

"NICE IS THE RIGHT THING TO DO," I said.

She helt up her right hand. We had taught her her right hand from her left. "Dis right."

"NO, WELL—YEAH."

She smiled big. Clapped. I never been so frustrated. I thought I'd try another way. "HAVE YOU EVER SEEN A BOY, OR A MAN NAKED?"

"Nooooo—you seen?"

"NO. BUT SEE, IT AIN'T NICE—AH—RIGHT TO SEE A BOY NAKED. BOYS AND GIRLS ARE DIFFERENT. BOYS HAVE THINGS DIFFERENT THAN GIRLS."

She nodded. I was getting somewhere. I pointed to myself. "THEY ARE DIFFERENT THERE. THEY ARE NOT LIKE US."

She nodded and lowered her eyes.

"Sam-my show hit—hit lika Daddy. I tell Sam-my no, no—not put hit dare. I tell him not. He not do hit."

"YORE DADDY—HE PUT IT THERE?"

"Mmmm. Hit hurta. I bloodin'. I tell Sam-my not."

She said it all so casual, like rape was just another everday kind of a thing. Like when you go through so much, then what's one more thing. Like it was all just the way life is. The whole thing made me cringe.

She started to undress and I watched her, shivering. The nights was too cold now to be bathing in the creek, but she never mentioned the cold. The cold was just another thing to bear, I decided. I remembered Aunt Bessie telling me about a woman who lost three younguns in four years and a bunch of other troubles she'd had. She said the woman was strong. A rock. She said she helt up 'cause she knowed she had to, then one time she broke like a piece of glass over a little thing.

After we bathed, we walked around. A hoot owl high over us made its spooky noise. She didn't hear. She wanted to run and we run a while. Then we set on the log and I combed the tangles out of that long hair. While I was combing, she said, "El-lie?"

"HUH?"

"Tell 'bout boys."

"I CAN'T. IT'S HARD TO TELL."

"Sam-my come back?"

"HE'LL COME."

"Sam-my hava hurt?"

"NO. HE'S FINE."

She touched her stomach high under her bosoms. "Hit hurta."

"YOU GOT A STOMACHACHE?"

"Nooo. Wif Sam-my. Sam-my hurta hit."

"HE HURT YOUR STOMACH?"

"Mmmm."

"HOW?"

"I not cry."

"YOU DIDN'T CRY?"

"I not."

"IT'S ALL RIGHT IF YOU CRY."

"I not cry."

"BUT YOUR STOMACH HURT? DID HE BUMP YOUR STOMACH?"

"Noooo."

I didn't know what she meant. I set thinking. Then I thought of the knots I get in my stomach when I get upset. Maybe that was it. It was so hard to figger.

Chapter 24

*M*onday was the first day of school. Me and Sammy rode Poke down and didn't speak a word. I had fixed breakfast. I had helt out on cooking and all, but the sight of Sammy and especially Daddy, with his cast, fumbling around doing woman's stuff got me feeling sorry for them. Sammy didn't mention that he was glad I made breakfast but Daddy did. Daddy had been patting me and hugging me a lot since that night I'd stayed out. It was like I'd done something that left him mixed-up that he didn't know how to handle.

When I slid off Poke, I said, "You *really* ain't never going back to see Alice?"

"I can't, Ellie," he said, tying the horse to a tree.

"She needs you, you know."

He didn't say nothing.

When we separated to go to our different rooms, I said the word that had been pestering my mind the last few days. "Coward!"

That night I didn't git to Alice's till late on account of Daddy didn't go to bed as soon as he had been doing, so I couldn't sneak out.

She asked about Sammy the minute we got far enough

away from the house. She'd learned not to ask us nothing too close 'cause she knowed we couldn't yell the answer.

"HE'S GOT A LOT OF HOMEWORK," I said.

"Whaaa dat?"

"IT'S SCHOOLWORK. IT'S WRITING DOWN STUFF AND READING STUFF."

"Wha reading?"

"YOU EVER SEEN A BOOK?"

She shook her head no. I thought a while, trying to think of how to tell her. I couldn't.

"I'LL BRING ONE NEXT TIME AND SHOW YOU," I said.

We didn't bathe. We walked to the clearing so's we could see the stars better. Alice loves the stars. She counted ten and then ten more.

"Wha after ten?" she asked.

"'LEVEN."

"Wha after 'leven?"

I taught her up to fifteen. She counted fifteen stars six times. I clapped and clapped. Lately I'd noticed Alice gitting more and more flustrated 'cause of not knowing things, and I got more and more flustrated not knowing how to tell her.

"Ellie?" Alice poked my shoulder.

"HUH?"

"You dotta Daddy?"

"YEAH, I GOT A DADDY."

"He tum ta see?"

"HE COME TO SEE WHAT?"

"You."

The question was strange. Then I thought that she must think I live out of the house, too.

"I LIVE IN THE HOUSE WITH DADDY AND SAMMY," I said. "I SEE DADDY EVER DAY."

"You lika?"

"YEAH. I LIKE DADDY."

"You lika Mama?"

"I AIN'T GOT A MAMA. SHE DIED." I wondered if she knew about dying.

"DO YOU KNOW ABOUT PEOPLE DYING?"

"Seena rats die," she said. "Oooooh, dey gitta scrimped."

"SHOW ME. SHOW ME WHAT SCRIMPED LOOKS LIKE."

She laid back and spread out her arms and legs real stiff.

"THAT'S *STIFF,* ALICE."

"They gitta stifft?"

"STIFF. WHEN *PEOPLE* DIE, WELL, THEN YOU PUT THEM IN A BIG WOOD BOX. THEN YOU DIG A BIG HOLE IN THE GROUND AND PUT THEM IN THE HOLE."

She made a face.

"Ooooh, ina hole? Dey cry ina hole?"

Here I was again in a spot I knowed I couldn't git out of. I changed the subject.

"HOW'S YORE MAMA, ALICE? HOW IS SHE DOING? IS SHE ALL RIGHT?"

"Mmmm, she giva me beans. Piece-a schicken too!"

"HEY. THAT'S NICE. YOU LIKE BEANS AND CHICKEN?"

"Mmmm."

"SHE EVER GIVE YOU SQUASH?"

"Mmmm. She giva biscuit. One day she giva milk. She not giva sugar."

"YOU LIKE SUGAR?"

"Mmmm."

I had never seen anything but the remains of a pan of mush. Biscuits and coffee or cornbread and milk. Me and Sammy called it soaky.

"WHAT DO YOU EAT EVERY DAY—MOST OF THE TIME?"

"Scrangish."

"IS SCRANGISH BREAD AND MILK OR COFFEE?"

"Mmmm."

"DO YOU EVER EAT APPLES?"

"Mmmm."

"DO YOU EAT NUTS? PEECANS OR WALNUTS?"

"Whaaa dat?"

"DO YOU EAT BERRIES?"

"Nooooo."

"ALICE, SAY *WHAT*, NOT *WHA*, AND SAY *THAT*, NOT *DAT*. SAY IT."

"Whattt dat?"

"WHAT THAT. *THAT*."

"What that?"

I clapped.

I went up the next night but I forgot the book. I brought her a little sack with peaches, apples, and peecans. (I showed her how to crack them and eat them.) I told her to hide them under her cot. I needn't have bothered telling her. She took them with us into the woods and ate them all.

That night, when I sneaked in, Daddy was up and waiting on me. I was scared. I just knowed he'd tell me I couldn't go no more.

"Let's set on the porch, Ellie," he said. We went out and set on the rockers. Under followed us and laid beside Daddy. I wondered for a minute if dogs had memories. Could Under remember Daddy throwing the chair at him? He had never acted like he remembered.

"How is the girl?" Daddy asked.

"She's all right."

"What you reckon that man would do if he caught you in that shed with that girl?"

"Ain't no tellin. Prob'ly shoot me, but Daddy, I ain't never seen him even once. Mrs. Guthrie leaves us a signal if he's passed out on liquor. We ain't never been there but two times when the signal wadn't on the door. We come back home them times—honest."

Daddy propped his bad leg on the other rocker. "Ellie, it's past midnight. It's close to one o'clock. I don't like this atall."

I didn't say nothing.

"Y'all really like Alice, don't ya?"

"Can't nobody help but like her, she's so sweet. I don't reckon she'd even know how to be no other way. I sure wish you could see her . . . and you know something . . . she's hungry. I mean, for good stuff. Mostly she gits soaky. Tonight I took her some peaches and apples and peecans and she eat 'em like a hog. I bet she ain't never had, say, had a piece of cake or pie in her whole life. It's awful. And she don't know words. She don't know what words mean. We've been helping her. If we don't help her, won't nobody . . ."

"You can't go by yoreself no more," Daddy said. "If Sammy don't go, I don't want you going. A man's family is his own business. I always said that, and looks like Guthrie don't take no interest, but I don't like it. I don't like you up there. Neither one of you—and I sure ain't gonna put up with you going by yoreself, ya hear?"

"But Sammy won't go no more. He's scared to go on account, ah—on account of her being so purty and all. Please, Daddy. *Please* let me go," I begged.

"We gonna all set down and talk about this," he said. "I've give it lots of thought. I've talked to Bessie. She said maybe we ought to git Doc up here and all of us make some kind of plan to help that girl. What you think of that?"

Chapter 25

Doc come up Sunday afternoon. I rode Poke down and got Aunt Bessie. She come back in her buggy with a chocolate cake and a gallon of tea. She brought some ice, too, wrapped up in a sack in a bucket. We ain't never had a ice box. Uncle Will bought them one two years before and Aunt Bessie loves it. Uncle Will has to go to the ice house in Bolton to get ice, though, 'cause the ice man don't come out as far as their house. Twice she talked Mr. Lambert, who is the peddler, into bringing some on his wagon, but too much of it melted 'fore he got there.

Doc was real interested to hear about how Alice was doing. I told him everthing.

"Seems to me like," he said, waving a forkful of cake, "that maybe I need to have a talk with Mrs. Guthrie, or maybe you could, Jack," he said to Daddy. "I'm thinking the woman ain't too ignorant to understand about feeding the girl better. I know they're pore and Guthrie can't make much on them chickens. A man that ain't got a big enough chicken house can't make a living. Rusty Cofield told me Guthrie sold some syrup to Harold Fountain. You younguns seen any cane Guthrie's growing?"

"I ain't," Sammy said.

"Me neither." I poured Doc some more tea.

159

"They surviving on something 'sides chicken. Reckon he's making liquor?"

I looked at Daddy.

"You know where he buys his liquor, Jack?" Doc asked.

"Never seen him on Sohee Ridge," Daddy said.

"Sohee where the Blanchard boys got their still now?"

Daddy nodded.

"Figgered it was up thataway somewheres. How long's it been since you had a drink? You're looking a hell of a lot better. Think you gonna stay off it?"

"I been off it over a month."

"That's 'cause you can't git it. Think you'll head up to Sohee first chance you git?" Doc leaned toward Daddy across the kitchen table and looked in his face.

Daddy looked back at Doc. "I hope I can stay quit," he said.

"Jack," Aunt Bessie leaned toward Daddy, "I been thinking. Me and Will's both been thinking about how—about how you've had so much trouble since Mary died. Will says a man ought to have a woman. We think you ought to think about gitting yoreself another wife. Me and Will . . ."

"Hush up, Bessie," Daddy said, looking at me and Sammy.

"No, I ain't hushing. It's time we got all this out. Ya'll been living up here ever since Mary died, playing like things is gonna git better, that you gonna quit drinking any day, when we all know good and well you ain't. I want to ask you just one question, Jack Perkins. Do you love yore younguns or not? Answer me that!"

Daddy sighed. "You know I love 'em, but that ain't got nothing to do with gitting them a new mama. Couldn't nobody take Mary's place and you know it."

"We ain't talking about nobody taking Mary's place. We talking about starting a new life, of gitting yoreself back like you use to be. I tell you, Jack, *I'm* sick of it! Will is, too, but he ain't got the guts to tell ya!"

Aunt Bessie was gitting mad. Me and Sammy set staring at her, shocked. She ain't never talked to Daddy like that. She even slapped the table and nearly spilt the tea. Before Daddy could say anything, Doc said, "Bessie's right, Jack. We all been walking on eggshells, talking to you like you was a youngun, 'cause we know what you went through. But I'm on Bessie and Will's side here. I think it's time we all face up. Time might come when these younguns will have to go somewheres else to live, go to Bessie's, if you pick up that jug again. Me and you's known each other for over twenty years and I feel like I got a right to tell ya."

Daddy set with his head down. He didn't say a word.

"How do you feel, Sam?" Doc asked. "You feel like going through more years of this?"

"I ain't gonna leave him, Doc. I wanted to, but I thought about it. I ain't leaving." I looked at Sammy. He turned away.

"How about you, Ellie?" Aunt Bessie asked.

"I'm staying with Sammy and Daddy."

Doc reached over and touched Daddy's shoulder.

"They love you more than you deserve, Jack," Doc said.

"I know," Daddy said. "All I can say is I'm gonna try!"

"We're all rooting for you," Doc said.

The plan was for me to tell Alice to tell her mama to sneak out on Thursday night after Mr. Guthrie was asleep and meet us in the woods where we seen her before. Then Doc would try to talk some sense into her. Doc said he would go ahead and buy Alice a hearing aid in Atlanta. I could of kissed him! I looked at Sammy and his eyes clouded up. Doc said Mr. McClung was driving his old Ford into Atlanta sometime next month and he'd ride with him to git Alice a hearing aid.

"I'll git it myself. Me and Bessie'll pay for it, and I'll tell the folks there the problem. If it don't help the girl, maybe they'll let me send it back."

"Tell Mrs. Guthrie," Aunt Bessie said, "that I'll be glad to send up food for Alice to keep in the shed. If the old man don't never go out there I don't see what it'll hurt."

"Won't hurt to try," Doc stood up. "I'm gonna have to get on now. Ya'll let me know if we can talk to Mrs. Guthrie on Thursday."

"I'll come tell you," I said.

After Doc and Aunt Bessie left, Daddy come in and set at the table. His face was so sad looking I couldn't hardly stand it. Sammy went out on the porch.

Daddy didn't look at me. Under whined to go out and Daddy got up and opened the screen door. When he set back down he reached up and run his hand through his hair and said, "I'm gonna do better, honey."

I nodded, gitting choked up.

"I promise I'll try."

I didn't want to talk about it. I didn't want to hear no more about him trying. I nodded again.

"This time I'll make it." He put his hand on my arm. I looked up at him but I still couldn't say nothing. I nodded again and looked away.

Mrs. Guthrie met me and Doc on Thursday night. Sammy made a big excuse about homework and didn't go. I could tell she was scared and nervous. I could see her lots better than before 'cause the moon was nearly full. She had on the same old housedress. Before Doc started talking to her, he tried to test Alice's hearing. He had two funny-looking prong things that he hit together next to each ear. I could tell by his face he was discouraged. Then he yelled at her from different spots and all. Alice liked him. She touched him lots of times. It was something to see. She'd just reach out and touch his arm or shoulder. One time she touched his big nose and we laughed.

He started out by telling Mrs. Guthrie that he was gonna see about gitting a hearing aid for Alice. Mrs. Guthrie looked at him suspicious.

He explained. "It's a little boxlike thing that we will put in Alice's ear and hopefully it will make her hear better," he said. "I can't guarantee it. There are different kinds of hearing problems. I think it will help her, but then if she has noises, roaring, in her ears, she might not can stand to wear it. It might make her too nervous. These aids work a little like eyeglasses that magnify. They make the sounds she hears louder. Do you understand?"

"I ain't got the money fer it," she said.

"I will buy it for her. I'd like for you to see that she wears it."

"Ormond won't have it!" She snorted and turned to walk off.

"Wait!" Doc said. "Please, Mrs. Guthrie, we need to talk about this. If Mr. Guthrie is against it, then I'm sure we can work out a way to keep it a secret. I can tell you're a fine woman who wants to help her youngun and . . ."

"Can't help nobody's teched by the devil."

"Alice is not teched, she . . ."

"She was borned teched, been crazy since she was borned. I had the fever. I ain't against these here younguns coming and taking her outa the shed now and again. I recken everbody needs ta be with folks sometimes. Ormond, he don't let me stay with her none and he won't let the other younguns near her 'cause he says them devils might jump on them. Life ain't been easy, Doc, I can shore tell ya that much."

Doc patted her shoulder and big tears rolled down her cheeks. When Alice seen the tears she tried to touch her mama's cheek, but her mama moved away. I was setting on the pine straw and when Mrs. Guthrie done that, Alice set down with her face blank, looking, staring straight ahead. I patted her arm but she didn't notice.

"I can see your life ain't been easy," Doc was saying. "Life is hard for a lot of folks. Hard on Alice here. What I'd like to do is try to make it a little bit easier on her. I'm sure it'd help you, too, if you didn't have to yell at her."

Mrs. Guthrie stood fiddling with the front of her dress over her stomach.

"She's a right good girl," she said.

"She's a fine girl," Doc said and patted Mrs. Guthrie's shoulder again. "And I don't believe there's a thing wrong with her mind. I don't believe she's teched. She can learn. If she could hear and could go to school she could learn like anybody else. Your girl ain't crazy, ma'am, she just don't know nothing."

Mrs. Guthrie didn't answer him.

"I'm gonna be going into Atlanta next month. I'll git an aid. Now I want to ask you something and I'd appreciate it if you'd listen careful. If it's all right with you I'd like to see if Alice can be put in a—well, a school of some kind, a place where she can learn. I don't even know if there is one. And if there is, if it's a state facility or not. If there's such a place with free help, how would you feel about it?"

"Ya mean take her off?"

"Yes, ma'am."

Mrs. Guthrie pointed her finger at Doc.

"Ain't nobody takin my youngun! I'm keeping my youngun. Wouldn't nobody but me have her no way. You ain't takin her nowhere, Doc!"

"But Mrs. . . . ."

Mrs. Guthrie grabbed Alice by the arm and pulled her up.

"COME ON," she screamed. Then she pulled Alice through the woods. Doc didn't try to stop her. He sighed and set down beside me on the ground. After a while he said, "Sad case."

"We can't give up," I said. "Doc, we can't give up. You still gonna help her, ain't you?"

"That woman might be so upset she'll start guarding the shed," Doc said. "None of us might never see Alice again."

"They ought to be a law," I said. "Ain't they no kind of a law?"

"I'm afraid not, Ellie. I ain't never heard of one."

I ain't never felt so helpless. I set thinking awhile, then I said, "I think Mrs. Guthrie'll git over it. I believe she will. Maybe she'll keep hanging that rag on the door so's I can git Alice out."

Doc put his arm around my shoulder."

"Alice is a mighty purty little thing," he said. "Your Daddy said Sammy was right took with her. I feel like it's my duty to warn Sammy. He better be mighty careful. I can't see nothing but heartbreak there."

Chapter 26

"*H*ow old was you when you married Uncle Will?" I asked Aunt Bessie on Saturday.

"Mighty young, honey. I was fifteen. How come?"

"How old was Mama when her and Daddy married?"

"Humm. Yore mama was, less see now, I think she was prob'ly eighteen. How come all these questions?"

"How old was Uncle Will and Daddy?"

"Will was nineteen two days 'fore we tied the knot. Jack was yore Mama's age, younger'n Will. He must of been eighteen or nineteen. Folks ought not marry that young, I always say. Shoot, when we was growing up, you was a old maid if ya wadn't married by seventeen—eighteen. I had a cousin over on Sand Mountain, Alabama, married when she was thirteen. Had two younguns by fifteen. Mighty young. Ain't no sense . . ."

"I was thinking," I said, "Alice is prob'ly sixteen, Sammy's nearly eighteen. You think him and Alice could marry so's she could git outa that shed?"

Aunt Bessie stopped the horse. We was in the buggy going to Bolton to git some stuff she needed.

"Louellen Perkins!" she said. "I'd be ashamed of myself. Now you know you don't want Sammy taking a wife that ain't nowheres near normal. His life would be a misery.

How come you even thought of such a thing? Now I'm for helping that girl all we can, but I ain't for Sammy messin up his whole life. Why, y'all told me she don't even understand plain words. Has them fits. Can't hear. You know she don't know how to keep a house. Who'd cook yore brother's meals? And Lord forbid if she had younguns in her condition. Ain't no telling what'd happen. Who thought this up? You or Sammy?"

I hung my head.

"Well . . . me," I said.

"I thought so. Sammy's got more sense than that." She flipped the reign and started us going. "And you ought to know better'n such crazy talk."

"It might be the only way she'll ever git out," I said. "I told ya what her mama said. She won't let her do nothing."

Just then Aunt Bessie's horse (she calls him Will Two 'cause she says he's as persnickety as Uncle Will) started doing his business. Aunt Bessie screwed up her nose.

"Pheew!" she said. "I swear, Ellie, if that horse messes up my carriage I'm gonna shoot him!"

She brought the horse to a stop till he was done. I just kept on talking.

"Anyhow," I said, "I thought you cared about Alice. I know you ain't never seen her but we've told you how sweet she is and all."

"I love the pore thing. I love everbody. But that ain't got nothing to do with it. Honey, *something* can be done besides Sammy marrying her. You quit ya worrying. Now what you need at the store?"

Sammy had finished up two willow chairs. They was right purty, and since we didn't have to sell them to git money for the hearing aid, we set them on the front porch along with the two rockers Daddy made years ago. When me and Aunt Bessie got back from Bolton, Sammy was setting in one of the willow chairs writing on his story. Under was laying under a rocker. Aunt Bessie hollered at Sammy, then went on home. I took the sack of stuff in and put it away. I didn't see Daddy. I asked Sammy where he was.

"He rode Poke to Bolton," Sammy said. "I reckon it's time he got out some."

"You wanna go up and see if we can see Alice tonight? *Please,* Sammy. I told Daddy I wouldn't go without you. He said I couldn't go by myself no more and sneaking out after he's asleep is dangerous."

He waited a long time, then he said, "Yeah, I'll go."

I flopped down in a rocker. I felt such a relief but I tried not to show it.

"How's the story coming? Can I read it yet?"

Sammy looked up. "I told ya you couldn't read it."

"I bet you write better'n Bertha. You still going with her to the Founder's Day picnic?"

He folded up his tablet, then he stuck his pencil behind his ear.

"Yeah, I am."

I could of just cried.

"What's for supper?" he asked.

"Whatcha want?" I said.

"I'd sure like some chicken, or rabbit. Maybe I'll git Daddy's gun and go hunt us a rabbit or squirrel. Some meat would taste good, don't you think?"

"I think we ought to of raised us some chickens. We ought not to eat Uncle Will's. Maybe Daddy will buy us some next spring. Reckon we can git some next spring?"

Just then Under raised his head and started growling. Me and Sammy glanced around but didn't see nothing. Under got up and run down the steps and headed to the woods at the side of the house.

"Wonder what he hears?" Sammy said. "Maybe it's a rabbit." Sammy headed to git Daddy's gun. Under started barking like crazy. I left the porch and walked toward the woods as Sammy run up with the rifle. Me and him walked quiet into the trees. Under's barking was way off to the right, on up the mountain. We headed that way. When we seen Under he was barking at something that was either hid behind a big oak or up in it.

"He's treed a squirrel," Sammy whispered as we snuck closer, looking up into the tree. Then I seen a hand and arm, clinging to the trunk. Sammy seen it, too, and sucked in his breath. We run up and there was Alice, scared outa her senses with her back pressed against the oak.

"ALICE! ALICE!" I screamed.

She looked awful. The whole side of her face was bruised, her eye red and swole. Sammy shushed Under and I grabbed her.

"WHAT YOU DOING DOWN HERE? WHAT HAPPENED? WHAT'S HAPPENED TO YORE FACE? DID YA FALL? TALK TO US, HONEY! PLEASE!"

I set her down so's she could lean against the tree. She set staring at Under. Sammy was staring at Alice's face, horrified. He squatted down to hold Under. It hit me she ain't never seen him in all this time.

"HE WON'T HURT YOU. HE'S OUR DOG. HIS NAME IS UNDER."

Sammy rubbed Under. Then I did, too, to show Alice he wouldn't hurt us. Her face relaxed a little. Sammy's face looked hard as rocks. He closed his eyes like he didn't want to see her. Then he opened them and let Under go and moved to her side. He took her hand and yelled, "TALK TO US. TELL US HOW YOU HURT YOUR FACE."

She touched her cheek and winced. I did, too.

"Daddy hurta," she said. "Hurta Mama, run strooped, hit, strooped ina yard. I run. Mama head bloods. Hit dark. *It* dark. I glip unner house."

"HE *BEAT* YA'LL?" Sammy looked so upset I thought he'd cry.

"Mmmm. He strooped, he hit Mama. Me. I not cry. I not."

"YOU DIDN'T CRY?" I was so horrified I started shaking.

"I not cry."

Sammy sagged against the tree, his fists clenched up tight.

"Why don't she cry, Ellie?" He choked the words out. "Why don't she *ever* cry?"

I hugged Alice to me. She was stiff as when she gits with them fits, 'cept she wadn't having a fit.

"What can we do, Sammy? Oh, what's to do?"

He set up straight.

"WHERE'S YORE MAMA AND DADDY NOW?" he asked. "ARE THEY HOME?"

She shook her head no.

"THEY GONE?"

"Mmmmm."

"What time you reckon it is, Ellie?"

"I don't know. Maybe after two."

He got up and pulled Alice to her feet. She slumped against him.

"We'll take her to the house," he said, putting his arm around her. I put my arm around her, too, and we helped her walk. She was real weak. I prayed she wouldn't have a fit.

We got her to the house and up on the porch, then we set her in a willow chair.

"THIS IS OUR HOUSE," I said. "ARE YOU HUNGRY? YOU SIT STILL NOW. I'LL GET SOME COLD CLOTHS FOR YOUR FACE. ARE YOU HUNGRY?"

She nodded.

Sammy pulled a rocker close to her chair and set down. He took her hand.

"YOU GONNA BE ALL RIGHT. WE GONNA HELP YOU. WE GONNA FIX YOUR FACE. DOES IT HURT BAD?"

I run in and got a pan of cold water and two rags and took them to Sammy. Then I run to the spring and got the milk and butter. I got some biscuits out of the warmer and put butter and scuppernong preserves on them. I took the biscuits and milk to the porch. Sammy helt a rag against her eye and cheek while I fed her. She eat ever bite.

"I'll git her some apples," I said. I run out back and picked four nice ripe ones and run back. She gobbled them right up.

I was gonna git more but Sammy said no. Said she might git sick eating so much so fast.

"YOU WANT TO LAY DOWN?" Sammy asked. "YOU CAN LAY DOWN ON ELLIE' BED IF YOU WANT TO. YOU WANT TO?"

"Nooooo."

"YOUR FACE FEEL BETTER?"

"Mmmm."

"HOW COME YORE DADDY HIT YOU?"

"He splabbed—he drinka drunk."

Sammy give me a helpless look.

"WHEN DID HE HIT YOU?"

"Ina dark."

"You reckon he saw you and Doc with them?" Sammy asked me. "You reckon he followed y'all?"

"DID YORE DADDY KNOW YOU AND YORE MAMA COME OUT TO SEE DOC AND ELLIE?"

"We dit dare he come out. He strooped ina yard. He strooped ina porch."

"What you reckon *strooped* is?" I asked Sammy.

171

"No telling."

"HE HIT YOU IN THE YARD? ON THE PORCH?"

"Ina my house."

"IN THE SHED?"

"Mmmm. He hit ina dark. He hit now, too."

"HE HIT YOU TODAY?" Sammy yelled.

"Mmmm. He strooped ina yard."

"Maybe *strooped* means walking or running," I said.

"DID HE RUN?"

"Nooo, he run, he strooped."

"DID HE STUMBLE?" Sammy asked, then jumped up and staggered and stumbled across the porch.

"Mmmmm."

"That's *it*! He staggered!" Sammy exclaimed.

"THAT'S *STAGGER*, ALICE. STAGGER."

"Slagger?"

"*STAGGER.*"

"Stagger."

Sammy helt her hand a long time. When she got to feeling better we walked her around the yard. Under followed us ever step, but Alice didn't act scared. When we took her back to the front porch, up rode Daddy. Me and Sammy both panicked for a minute till we seen he was sober.

Daddy rode Poke to the steps so's he could git off easier, all the time staring at Alice. Sammy helped him off and got his crutches. Then he helped him up the steps to his rocker.

"It's Alice," Sammy said. "Her daddy beat her and her mama. We found her in the woods." Daddy's face looked pained.

Alice's big eyes stared at Daddy. He smiled at her.

"Hey, Alice. Nice to see ya."

"She can't hear you," Sammy said. "Talk louder."

Daddy yelled. Alice nodded.

"Tell me about it, son." Daddy pulled a willow chair closer and lifted his leg onto it. I knowed the cast had been gitting on his nerves for a long time. I took Alice down to the barn and showed her everthing while Sammy told Daddy what happened.

I hugged Alice and patted her a lot. She was calm. It's the same old thing, I thought. What's a little beating? Just one of those things. Another one of those things. I took her back to the front and helped her onto Poke. I had to git her back to the shed before the Guthries got home. Sammy and Daddy told her 'bye. Both their faces looked sad and helpless. Sammy took Alice's hand a minute, then we rode off. When we got to the shed the signal was there. The rag was on the limb. We could keep seeing Alice!

Chapter 27

*B*y the first of October Aunt Bessie's buggy was finished. It was beautiful. Daddy still hadn't had a drink and me and Sammy was gitting Alice when we could. I was just like somebody had put all the bad stuff in a box and hid it so's nobody could find it. It seemed like I was the only one who remembered it ever happened.

We was pleased that Alice was making a little headway with words. Also, Mr. McClung had canceled his trip to Atlanta, so Doc didn't go git her hearing aid. He sent money to the company and asked them to send one. And they did, but it didn't work right, so he sent it back and they was gonna send another one. We was real excited about that. And another thing I was excited about was that the leaves was turning.

You should see them mountains in October. You never would breathe right again. Across Yager Valley the fall colors rise up to meet the sky. Bright reds and yellows and golds and oranges and rusts all mixed up together like God dropped his watercolor jars from Heaven. It's a sight that knocks the breath right out of you. Ever year I forgit how purty it is, and when it happens again I can't hardly do nothing but look. Aunt Bessie is the same way. She loves fall better'n spring. She says spring means summer's next, and she suffers from the heat too much in summer.

Daddy says in fall you better watch out for Bessie 'cause she gits a second wind. Sets into house cleaning. Airing pillows and mattresses. Scrubbing floors and windows and wears Morgan flat out. It tickles me to death the way she makes him work come fall. He moans and groans like he's dying.

Sammy likes fall, too. He got into all sorts of things. He'd write on his story a while, then he built a box for his newest arrowheads. Then he'd clear the garden and haul manure to rot for spring planting. It seemed like he was trying to stay busy ever minute of his life so as to not think of what happened. I don't git like Aunt Bessie. I do my best stuff in the spring. In the fall I look and look, and I walk in the woods till my legs hurt. One Saturday when I had Alice walking, I seen Mohawk, like a huge black furry ball, walking up the mountain. I couldn't tell Alice. I didn't want to remind her of that night.

Also by October we had taught Alice to print her name. Aunt Bessie bought her a tablet and pencil and she kept it hid under her cot. After she finally learned how, she printed her name on ever page in big block letters that run off the side.

Aunt Bessie had made Alice three pair of bloomers and two camisoles. Two pair of the bloomers was white, but one was pink with lace and it matched a camisole. When Aunt Bessie give them to me she give me a box of talcum powder to take to Alice, saying a girl her age ought to start smelling good. She give me one, too.

It was gitting too cold to take Alice to the creek to bathe at night. We still bathed on Saturdays but we done it mighty quick. The day I took her the new things she was a

175

little bit foggy 'cause she'd had fits the night before. I got to where I could always tell.

Sammy was with me and he left us so's we could bathe. After we was done I showed her the presents and told her Aunt Bessie sent them. In my life I don't reckon I ever seen such a look as come on her. I thought for sure her face would break from her trying not to cry. She set down naked on the ground and examined each pair of bloomers, turning them this way and thataway. She must of smelled the powder twenty times. She was so quiet I got worried. Then she pushed herself up and brushed the pine needles off her bottom. She helt out the powder.

"Whaa do it?" she whispered.

I took it and powdered her back and shoulders.

"NOW YOU PUT IT ON YOUR FRONT."

She took the box and dipped the puff in. She powdered her face, hair, neck, chest, hands, stomach, her you know, her legs, knees, and feet. It was all I could do to keep from busting into giggles. She looked like she'd fell into a sack of flour.

I kept a straight face. She wanted to put on the pink bloomers and camisole so I helped her. When we had them straight she stared down at herself, grinning.

"I purty?" she turned around twice. She looked real funny with all that powder, but 'course I didn't tell her.

"YOU LOOK BEAUTIFUL!"

"Sam-my see?"

"NO—WELL, YEAH." I didn't see why not. She was plenty covered up. I finished dressing and we waited on Sammy. I wanted to wipe some of the powder off but I didn't. When he come up, he gasped. He said later he thought something awful was wrong. Alice turned round and round for him to git a good look.

"I purty?" she asked, beaming.

"Don't say a word," I whispered. "It's talcum powder."
His face relaxed.

"YOU'RE REAL PURTY," he said, and I could tell he
was holding back a grin.

"I noob it?"

I looked at Sammy.

"WHAT IS *NOOB?*" Sammy asked.

Alice thought a minute, then she clutched the bloomers
and camisole.

"DO YOU MEAN CAN YOU KEEP IT?" I asked.

"Mmmm."

"IT'S YOURS. ALL YOURS."

She grabbed the powder off the ground.

"Dis mine?"

"THAT'S YOURS, TOO."

She opened the box and got a puff full of powder. She
powdered Sammy's face. He let her. She powdered his shirt
and the bib of his overalls. He stood grinning.

Alice was leaning toward him trying to hear his words.
He brushed some of the powder off her cheek with his fingers. Then he tried to brush it off her eyelashes and she
jumped. She started rubbing her eye.

"GET SOME IN YOUR EYE?" he asked.

"Mmmmm."

"OPEN IT. I'LL GIT IT OUT."

She opened her eyes wide. Sammy asked me to hand him
her other camisole. He took it and screwed up the end to
make a tiny swab.

"OPEN WIDER," he said, and she did.

"I SEE IT. NOW BE REAL STILL."

Alice stared into Sammy's eyes as he leaned toward her,
looking at the speck. He touched the speck with the cloth.
He had got it.

"I GOT IT," he said. "FEEL BETTER?"

Alice blinked her eyes several times. "Mmmm."

He patted her shoulder. "GOOD!"

She patted his shoulder. "Wha good?"

"GOOD IS LIKE NICE."

She nodded. "I know nice," she said.

"YOU KNOW NICE? THAT'S GREAT. Ain't that great, Ellie? WHAT'S NICE, ALICE? CAN YOU TELL ME WHAT NICE IS?"

"Mmmm. Nice Sam-my."

Chapter 28

*T*he day before the Founder's Day picnic I couldn't keep my mind off of Alice and kept gitting madder that Sammy was taking Bertha to the picnic. I thought about all the worrying I'd done about Sammy and girls when he hadn't never done no worrying about me and boys. The more I thought about it the madder I got. I decided it was time I made him worry for a change. I decided to tell him I was claiming somebody special. The problem was who to claim. I thought about claiming Randolph, but Randolph was claiming Karen, although that don't mean nothing. I ain't never seen them talking, but just 'cause you claim somebody don't mean you talk to them. Finally, I decided Randolph was it, because after all, he has looked at me and spoke and all.

At lunchtime I strolled by where the boys was playing horseshoe. Randolph didn't look my way, but Richard and Michael did. Michael even grinned a little and I think his eyes got wider, though I'm not sure. It got me feeling purty good, so I decided to go on and stroll over to where some of the other boys was playing jackknife. That ended up being the best idea I'd had all day. *Four* boys looked! David looked but you can't count him. That stupid elephant ears looked. Then Grant Campbell, who's too young, looked, but best of all was John Frazier, who is only the handsomest boy ever walked on two feet! I thought my heart would jump out of my chest when he looked, but better'n that, he winked! Honest! Never mind I heard he winks at ever girl in school and one time even winked at Miss Hutchins, who teaches third, fourth, and fifth. Sammy is gonna die when I tell him all *this,* I thought!

I couldn't hardly do my schoolwork for thinking about telling it. I planned ever word. I decided to wait till we'd rode about halfway home, maybe past Uncle Will's and Aunt Bessie's, then I would say, Sammy. And he'd say, huh. And I'd say, I'll bet you a purty you won't guess in a million years who I'm claiming, and he'd say, who. And I'd say, oh no, you gotta guess. I'll give you three guesses. So then he'd say, elephant ears, and I'd hit him. Then he'd say somebody else and I'd act like that guess was as dumb as elephant ears. And he'd keep guessing and git madder and madder till I told him who.

I got so carried away with the plan that I couldn't set still. Then I thought, hey, wait a minute here, why should I tell him I was claiming somebody like Randolph when I could just as easy tell him I'm claiming John!

I thought that bell wouldn't never ring. Finally, when we was on Poke, I told him right off. I said, "Sammy?"

And he said, "Huh?"

"I'll bet you a purty you can't guess in a million years who I'm claiming."

"Didn't know you was claiming anybody."

"I wadn't. I just started. Now guess! Guess who it is. You won't *never* guess! I'll give you twenty guesses."

"Ain't twenty boys in the whole county."

"Well, I'll give you ten guesses. Five."

"Elephant ears."

I hit him.

"David."

"Nope."

"Richard."

"Nope," I giggled. He'd *never* guess.

"John."

I could of just puked.

"How come you guessed him?"

"Everbody else claims him. You might as well git in line."

"Oh, shut up!" I said.

"I think you'd better claim elephant ears or Randolph," he said.

Oh goodie, I thought, he don't know Randolph is claiming Karen.

"Well," I said. "I was sorta thinking of claiming Randolph on account of . . ."

"Won't do you no good. He's claiming Karen."

"Would you stop this horse and let me off!"

He laughed.

"Nope," he said.

"Whoa! Whoa, Poke," I hollered. "Poke, I mean *stop!*" Poke didn't stop. I pounded Sammy's back. He laughed.

When we got home I talked Sammy into us going and gitting Alice and taking her on a picnic that night so's she could see what a picnic was like (and so's he could see Alice and maybe that would put her in his mind before he seen Bertha the next day). I fixed biscuits and preserves and corn-on-the-cob and tea, but when we got there the rag wadn't on the log. We was real disappointed. Here we had all the stuff.

"The old man must be sober," Sammy said as I nodded.

"Dadgum shame."

"Yeah," I said, then I giggled. "Never thought I'd call it a shame when a man's sober."

Sammy grinned and we walked back to Poke. When we got home Daddy was up reading the almanac.

Sammy went on in. I said hey from the kitchen.

"Couldn't see her?" Daddy asked.

Sammy shook his head. "Reckon Guthrie's sober."

"Too bad," Daddy said, and me and Sammy laughed. I put the biscuits in the warmer.

"You hungry?" I peeped around the door.

Daddy put the almanac on the table.

"I might be. Whatcha got?"

"Biscuits and corn. Some fatback."

"No cake or pie?"

"Nope, but I'll bring ya some from the picnic tomorrow. Aunt Bessie's making four pies. Three apples and a pumpkin."

"Sure would like something tonight. How about you, Sam? Think we could put together something? How would fried pies taste to ya?"

"Sounds good to me," Sammy said. "Ain't it a little late to start a fire and cook?"

"Ain't much past nine. Whatcha say, Ellie?"

"I sure ain't sleepy," I said. "Maybe *we* could have a picnic."

"Us?" Sammy made a face.

"Why not?" Daddy pushed hisself off the bed. "I haven't been on a picnic since—in a coon's age. Where'll we have it, Ellie? What time y'all leaving tomorrow?"

"Uncle Will's gitting us about nine. I got to roll my hair tonight."

"Tell ya what. You do that, and me and Sammy'll fry the pies. Go pick us nine or ten apples, Sam. I'll start a fire."

I washed my hair and rolled it. They peeled and cored and sliced the apples. I boiled them a few minutes and Daddy made a crust. Then Sammy cut out squares and I dropped the apples onto them and sprinkled lots of sugar.

Daddy put little hunks of butter on, and folded them. We fried them slow till they was gold brown. It was now past eleven.

"Where ya wanta have the picnic?" I asked Daddy. "In the pasture? Think you can git there on your crutches?"

Daddy smiled big. "Think what we'll do is have it at the branch. I can make it there."

Me and Sammy looked at each other.

"At Mama's *grave?*" Sammy looked stunned.

"Dadgummed right!" Daddy said. "I been sober, what now, over six weeks. I think Mary'd like us doing something, ah—I think she'd like . . ."

"Well, okay," Sammy said, but still looked funny. "I'll git the tea, Ellie. You git the pies. Should we take the biscuits and corn?"

"Might as well," I said. "I'm starving."

That night me and Sammy and my daddy had us a picnic. We set on the quilt beside Mama's grave, surrounded by what was left of the petunias, and talked about lots of things. Aunt Bessie's buggy. Alice. And last of all, Mama. We talked about all her good and happy stuff. Didn't nobody cry once. We didn't git to bed till nearly two. It was sweeter'n any Founder's Day picnic could ever be.

Chapter 29

*T*he next morning I woke smelling coffee. I jumped up, thinking it must be late if Daddy was already up. I run in the kitchen.

"What time is it?" I asked him.

"You're early," he said. "It's not seven."

"What you doing up?" I slumped into a chair.

"Thought I'd go with y'all."

I perked up. "You mean it?" Daddy hadn't been to a Founder's Day picnic since Mama died. "You think you can hold out?"

"Might run in the sack race," he teased, pouring me a cup of coffee.

"Ah, Daddy."

"Think I could pitch a little horseshoe at least. Maybe do some calling for the dance."

"You ain't never called a square dance in yore life," I said, and poked his stomach.

"Called 'em ever Saturday night right after yore Mama and me married."

"I didn't know that."

He poured hisself some coffee and set down. He told me about taking Mama to Dahlonega in a wagon and what a good dancer she was and how jealous he was when some-body twirled her too long or helt her too tight. I could just picture her all fixed up, dancing and laughing.

Uncle Will was surprised to see Daddy was going, but he was glad. They bet on who'd win at horseshoes. Sammy combed his hair over and over. I made fun of him till we got to Aunt Bessie's, then Daddy told me to hush up. Aunt Bessie had croker sacks and sheets covering up ever part of the carriage she could cover. I jumped down and rode with her. We followed Uncle Will's wagon. She was so excited and nervous I thought she'd pop.

When we got into town Aunt Bessie pulled the buggy into the alley behind the post office. Sammy jumped off the wagon to go hunt Bertha. Uncle Will pulled the wagon into the picnic grounds in the pasture behind Mr. Hudson's house. Me and Aunt Bessie unloaded the food and then he took it and parked it in the field with everbody else.

Bertha looked like a harlot sure enough that day. I never seen the like. Her dress was white with dark blue stripes. It didn't have no sleeves and the neck was too low. Aunt Bessie gasped. Bertha's hair was combed into bangs and cut short in the back. She looked boogerish. Sammy looked a little nervous. I just had to look the other way.

I thought about Alice a lot that day. Her up there in that shed. Us down here having a good time. Made me mad. Even madder at Sammy and Bertha. Lisa Mae run over to help spread out the food. I never seen as much good stuff in my life. Lots more than was at the school party in the spring. Everybody bragged on Aunt Bessie's outfit. (They didn't know—yet—that it matched her carriage.) She had made a pale rose blouse with crocheted collar and cuffs. Her skirt was wine and flared out at the bottom. She didn't make a bonnet like she said. She took her big brim straw hat and wrapped a wine band around it with crocheted edges. Then she took the pale rose material and made rosebuds and put a big bunch of them in the front. It was real purty.

When the food was spread and covered, me and Lisa Mae walked around looking at everbody. I asked her had she seen Bertha and she said she thought she looked like a floozy. David walked by and Lisa Mae nearly swooned. He grinned at us and went on. By the time we spoke to everbody and gossiped it was time to eat. They don't have a bidding for baskets on Founder's Day. What they do is give all the girls a number and all the boys a number. I hadn't never had a number before 'cause I was too scared, but Aunt Bessie insisted I was taking one this year.

Me and Lisa Mae was nervous wrecks. Mr. Attaway got up on the homemade platform and made announcements before Rachel Campbell and Flossie Moore give out the numbers. My hands was shaking when I reached in Miss Flossie's basket. My number was eight. Lisa Mae's was twelve. When everbody had a number all the girls got up on the platform and called out their number one at a time. Then the boy with the same number would walk up and git her and take her to the table and when they'd filled their plates they'd go set and eat. Bertha and Sammy didn't take numbers.

I thought I'd faint up on that platform. Lisa Mae kept fidgeting and whispering and I couldn't hear a word she said. Me and her was close to the end of the line so it took longer. When she sqeaked out twelve, Grant Campbell helt up his number and yelled out, me! Then I sputtered out eight and Mark Hudson come running up waving his number. I was so glad to git off that platform I could of kissed him. David got Karen's number. Randolph wadn't there. He was sick. I can't remember who got who else.

Me and Mark set under a big hickory tree with Lisa Mae

and Grant. Mark's sister Elaine and her beau Phillip come up and eat with us. Mark talked my head off and he's real cute. He's got dimples. I finally got relaxed and was talking, too. Lisa Mae spilled lemonade all over Grant's new shirt but he didn't git mad. Sammy and Bertha eat with a bunch down past the pasture by Burn's Creek.

Grant and Mark hung around us all afternoon. Mark won the sack race again. Sammy come in third and Bertha carried on so I thought I'd git sick. Squealing and jumping up and down and hugging him just like he'd won first. Lisa Mae come in second jumping rope. She jumped 573 times before she missed. Alecia Robertson won with 603. Alecia's little brother Daryll won at marbles. We all had a good time.

The buggy contest was at five o'clock. They was nine buggies in the contest, and rumors was going around that Ruth Ellis had a buggy that'd knock yore eyes out. I said two prayers that Aunt Bessie would win, till Lisa Mae told me she'd said three that her mama would win. So I hurried up and said two more, just in case.

Harold Fountain, who runs the drugstore, made a speech before the contest started. All about how Calvin Bolton had come to these mountains in the early 1800s and settled in Yager Valley. How he'd built his house and a trading post and all. I'd heard the story a hundred times, it seemed like.

After that he introduced the judges, six women. Florine Attaway, Jessie Miller, Aurora Lancaster, Sally Sims, Mattie Hill, and Christine Whitley. They come up on the stand and waved at everbody.

The buggies was drove out in alphabetical order according to the ladies' names, and when the first one come out I knowed everbody else was in trouble. It was Ruth Ellis' and I never seen nothing like it in my life. I was standing beside

187

Aunt Bessie (they was all lined up on the road nearest the pasture) and me and her both gasped.

"Mercy Heavens alive!" Aunt Bessie sputtered. "Ellie, would you l-look at that!"

"Oh, my gosh!" I said. "Oh, my goodness, ain't that purty? Aunt Bessie, how'd she *do* all that?"

"It's that girl of her'n!" Aunt Bessie snorted. "It don't seem hardly fair. You ever know Emily? She married Marie Keever's fiancé's brother, Robert somebody. They live down in Tucker. He's rich. Emily sent her mama all that velvet. Hardly seems fair."

Mrs. Ellis and Emily was both in the buggy. It was painted cream-colored all over—the seat, wheels, spokes, tongue, everthing. Then on the hub of the wheel was painted lavender violets. It had cream velvet cushions with lavender crocheted lace, and the whole top was lavender crocheted lace that hung down in scollops. It took my breath away. It took everbody else's, too, I reckon, 'cause you could of heard a pin drop, then all this oohing and ahhhing. I looked up at Aunt Bessie and she set there biting her lip.

The next one was Judy Lemming. Aunt Bessie said she ought not be allowed in the contest 'cause she don't even live close to Bolton. She lives close to Mineral Bluff. Her carriage was a shocker, all black and white, and she was dressed to match.

"She looks like a twenties flapper," Aunt Bessie said. "Lookit that dress! It don't even cover her knees."

The next carriage was blue and pink. The next red, white, and blue. The next wine and blue. The next was Mrs. McClung's, yellow and green.

Then it was Aunt Bessie's time to pull out into the pasture. Each carriage circled the judges' stand. People clapped and whistled and hollered at each one, but when Aunt Bessie pulled out they did it the loudest 'cause decorating buggies was her idea.

"Now, ladies and gentlemen," Mr. Fountain hollered. "We have the lady who started all this buggy fun. Mrs. William Perkins, our very own Bessie!"

I had a little hope that 'cause they clapped so long she'd win. She smiled big and waved and bowed like a real queen.

After her was two more. One red and white, and one brown and yellow.

The judges made a big to-do over the judging. They walked around inspecting all the buggies till I thought my stomach would bust if they didn't hurry. Me and Mark and Lisa Mae had run up to the judges' stand to be close.

"Mama and yore Aunt Bessie don't have a chance," Lisa Mae said. "Why, I just think it's plain awful that Ellis woman sent her mama all that fancy stuff. *Anybody* could win with velvet! It ain't fair, is it?" She was twisting and fidgeting.

Sammy and Bertha come up and stood with us, the first time I'd got close to him all day.

"Everbody thinks Mrs. Ellis is gonna win," I said to Sammy.

"Ah, she might not," he said.

"She cheated with all that velvet," Lisa Mae said. "I bet Mama's fit to be tied!"

"Aunt Bessie's buggy is real purty," Bertha cooed. I give her a dirty look.

We stood waiting for the judges to git back to the stand. When they did, Mr. Fountain yelled.

"Everybody quiet now! I think the ladies have come to the big decision." He leaned down and Florine Attaway whispered in his ear.

"As you know," he shouted, "there will be but one winner. No second or third place. Quiet! Quiet now! I have the name of the talented winner." He stopped a minute to make us go crazy, then yelled, "Ladies and gentlemen, it gives me great honor to announce the winner of the Beautiful Buggy Contest is none other than—are you ready? None other than Ruth Ellis."

I could of just throwed up.

Me and Sammy run over to Aunt Bessie. Will and Morgan was beside the buggy and Daddy hobbled up, too.

I was proud of her. She didn't shed one tear and she was smiling. We was raving on about how she should of won and all. Uncle Will helped her down and we all hugged her.

"Just wait till next year," she said. "Y'all ain't never seen nothing like I'm gonna do next year. I'm gonna fix me a buggy that'll make them judges cry, it'll be so purty."

The square dance was helt in the street in front of the post office 'cause it's smoother there than in front of the store. In Bolton they ain't too much asphalt, mostly dirt, and they ain't no sidewalks 'cept a little stretch between the drugstore and the post office. The women had decorated by hanging crepe paper streamers onto everthing that stuck up, like posts and trees. Lanterns hung all around. Dan Snyder and his Blue Ridge Mountain Boys was gonna play, and his wife Lynn would sing. They was always plenty of liquor that the men kept in their wagons or cars that made me real nervous. I counted nine cars, the most I ever seen at one time.

Me and Lisa Mae and Mark and Grant walked over early to see if we could help with anything and to pick the best spot to set. Everbody always sets on the grassy spots that's on both sides of the street, but I like to set close to the sidewalk where the band is set up. Lots of the women bring a kitchen chair to set in. Aunt Bessie always brings a rocker. The men don't set much, they wander around.

Everthing looked real purty. The women had outdone theyselves. The streamers, in red, orange, yellow, and brown, was blowing in the breezes, and they had put fall leaves everwhere. Baskets full of ever color was setting around the bandstand (on the sidewalk). Big cotton basketfuls was setting here and there where folks would set. A stand for lemonade and tea was set up close to the sidewalk. Fruit jars full of yellow, purple, white, and pink mums was setting on the stand and on the table where the cakes and stuff would be.

Aunt Bessie was spreading a big white cloth over the table to keep the bugs off the cakes when we walked up.

"Y'all younguns wore out yet?" Aunt Bessie asked. "Where's yore mama, Mark? I told Will just last week that Roylene Hudson had the purtiest smile in these mountains. Sweet woman, yore mama. Where'd she go?"

"Last time I seen her," Mark said, "she was walking toward the Hoods, prob'ly gonna see the new baby."

Aunt Bessie give me one of them roll-eyed looks when Mark looked away. She thinks he's cute and thinks I ought to claim him.

Me and Mark went to git a bucket of water for the women and when we got back, folks started wandering up from the pasture. Dan Snyder and his boys was on the stand plunking their guitars and banjos and fiddles, gitting them tuned. Daddy was setting on the sidewalk talking to them. I crossed my fingers that he'd git to call some of the dances. I could see he was nervous. He kept fooling with his crutches. When we walked over, he winked at me, and I knowed the wink was because of Mark, just like Aunt Bessie's eye rolling.

By the time everbody wandered up, the lanterns was lit and the Snyder boys was ready to start. Dan hollered out to git everbody's attention. He made a little speech about how much fun everbody had had and about the purty buggies and good food. While he was talking, Mark's hand sort of bumped into mine.

"Now y'all git yore partners," Dan hollered. "Grab 'em purty girls and circle up. I got a little surprise for ya."

When we was all circled up in a long skinny circle that went from the edge of the post office on past the drugstore, he told us Daddy was gonna call a few sets. Uncle Will and Aunt Bessie yelled and clapped—then others did, too. After we clapped and everbody helt hands and Mark took mine, I thought my heart was gonna pop.

They started playing "Alabama Jubilee." Daddy stood up and started calling. I could of just busted, I was so proud. He was real good.

"Swing yo' partner, do si do, swing that gal to and fro. Swing 'er to the left and swing 'er to the right. Tell her she's a purty sight."

Mark wadn't the best dancer in the world but he was sure the bounciest. I thought he was gonna jar my teeth out. Doc and Mrs. Murphy danced past us and Doc winked. I giggled 'cause all these grown folks and their eye doings was gitting funny.

"Circle up four," Daddy yelled.

We circled up with Marie, and Tony what's his name, who is a giant. I bet we hadn't took ten steps before some woman screamed and then you never seen such a commotion. Everbody run over to where the scream come from, which was where all the women had their chairs set. We couldn't see nothing over everbody's heads. Then I heard Aunt Bessie holler for Morgan. What happened was, he'd put a dead snake under Mrs. Upshaw's chair and scared her half to death. Us kids thought it was right funny 'cause she's such a old grouch, but Aunt Bessie didn't. She made

Morgan go set in the wagon for the rest of the events, after she made him tell Mrs. Upshaw he was sorry.

After that things went fine for, oh, a hour or so. Then Lisa Mae got a cramp in her foot so we all went and set on the grass.

When Lynn sung "Careless Love" so everbody could dance a slow dance, Lisa Mae got tears in her eyes on account of David, and after that we square-danced some more.

When me and Lisa Mae went to use Mr. Hood's toilet, I told her I had decided to go ahead and claim Mark. She got real excited.

"Oh, that's just about the wonderfulest thing I *ever* heard!" She was inside the closet and I was waiting outside. "You think he'll claim you?"

"He squeezed my hands two times."

"He did! Oh, Ellie, oh, he's cute, don't you think so, them dimples and all? And he's tall, too. I like tall, don't you? And so what if his voice is funny. He ain't got no pimples and his hair lays down nice. You think he'll claim you? Oh, good gracious. They ain't no paper in here. The catalog is used up."

Wylie Frazier was calling the dances when we got back, and Daddy wadn't nowhere in sight. I told Lisa Mae I'd be right back and took off looking for him. I seen Sammy and Bertha and asked Sammy where Daddy was, but he said he didn't know. I made a face so's he would know I was worried about Daddy drinking, so he said he'd help look for him.

By the time the dance was over we knowed Daddy had got some liquor. He wadn't nowhere to be found. It just made me sick. I rode on home with Aunt Bessie and Morgan. Uncle Will and Sammy stayed to wait on him. At close to one he still hadn't showed up, so they come on. Aunt

Bessie said for us to stay at their house that night, so we did.

The next morning up drove Harold Fountain in his wagon with Daddy passed out in the back. He said Lamar Williams had come up on him when he went out to milk his cow. Daddy was asleep in his barn. Me and Aunt Bessie both cried and Morgan even got tears in his eyes.

Chapter 30

Sunday night me and Sammy both was still real upset about Daddy. We had moped around all day, so when night come I asked Sammy if we could go to git Alice. Maybe she'd cheer us up.

When we got there Alice was asleep. She woke up the minute we opened the door. She'd done that before and we couldn't figger it out 'cause she couldn't hear the door opening.

She was real peppy, so we knowed she hadn't had a fit in a day or two. The nights had got purty chilly, so Sammy had brought her a old jacket of his.

We didn't go to Cherrylog. We went to the clearing.

By the time we set down, she started pointing and counting stars. She counted to twenty seven times and we clapped each time. Then we asked her numbers.

"HOW MANY BROTHERS YOU GOT?"

She helt up two fingers. "Two," she said.

"HOW MANY SISTERS?"

She helt up one finger. "One."

"HOLD OLD ARE YOU?"

"Sisteen."

"HOW MANY WINDOWS IN YOUR SHED?"

"Two."

"WHEN IS YOUR BIRTHDAY?" We'd never asked her that before.

"Huh?"

I yelled the question again.

"Wha dat?"

"WHAT'S THAT?" Sammy corrected her.

"What that?"

"WHAT DAY OF THE YEAR WERE YOU BORN?" She shook her head. Sammy changed the subject.

"HOW MANY FINGERS DO YOU HAVE?"

"Ten."

"TOES?"

"Ten." She helt up her bare feet and giggled.

"I dot ten toes. Ten fingggers. I dot twooo eye, twooo ear, I dot . . ." She pointed to her teeth.

"How many teef?"

I thought quick. I didn't know. Sammy didn't neither.

We laid quiet a while staring up at the sky, the sounds of night creatures all around us. Ever once in a while Alice would ask us something she had asked us before. How old Ellie? How old Sam-my? Then she said the strangest thing.

"Daddy do Mama ona tomach, kick ina barn."

Sammy set up and looked down at her.

"SAY IT AGAIN, ALICE."

She said it just like before.

"I think her daddy kicked her mama in the stomach," he said.

"Sounded like it."

"IS SHE HURT?" I yelled.

"Mmmm. Her holler, her dit sick ina barn. I ditta polt outa. I run ina barn. Mama scrimble ona ground sick. She cry. She taka polt hitta Daddy polt. Hitta, hitta." Alice set up quick and swung her arms like she helt something and

196

was swinging it. "Mama hitta head polt. Daddy scrimble. He dead."

Me and Sammy both gasped. Sammy grabbed Alice's arm.

"DID YOU SAY YORE DADDY IS DEAD?" Sammy screamed.

"Mmmm. He dead ina barn. Den he gitta bloodin. Mama washt Daddy dit up. Mama . . ."

"HE GOT UP?"

"Mmmm. He falla, dit up, falla."

"THEN HE AIN'T DEAD," I yelled.

"Mmmm, head bloodin, he falla."

"YOU MEAN HE GOT UP, THEN FELL—THEN DIED?"

"Mmmm."

"Oh, my God! Oh, Ellie, oh my God!" Sammy said.

I just set there staring at Alice. I couldn't believe what I was hearing.

"WHAT—WHAT DID SHE HIT HIM WITH, ALICE? WHAT IS A POLT?" Sammy was shaking Alice.

"Door open ita polt."

"THE IRON POLE?"

"Mmmm."

"Oh, God," Sammy cried again. He stood up and pulled Alice to her feet.

"We're gonna see. Come on, Ellie."

We started running, Sammy yelling questions. "WHEN DID SHE KILL—HIT HIM?"

"Ina barn."

"NOT WHERE. WHEN? WAS IT TODAY?"

She shook her head no.

"THE DAY BEFORE TODAY?"

"Mmmm."

"IS HE STILL IN THE BARN?"

"He ina house. Me—Mama pulla ina house."

"IN THE HOUSE? IS YORE MAMA ALL RIGHT? HOW'S YORE MAMA?"

"Mama washt, Mama nobered rag ona head."

"Why would she wash him if he was dead?" I grabbed Sammy's arm.

"Maybe he ain't dead. Maybe she don't know what dead means."

"I think she does. We talked about it one time. She'd seen a dead rat."

Alice give out of breath so we set down for a few minutes. Sammy said what we'd do is put Alice back in the shed, then we'd sneak and see if we could see in the windows of the house. Or, if they wadn't no light, if everbody was in bed, then we'd just have to figger something else.

We figgered it was too late but it wadn't. We could see lamplight in one room. We told Alice 'bye and hugged her. After we locked her in, we tiptoed to the window where the light was. Sure enough, it was the front room. The window was too high for us to look in, so Sammy helt his two hands and I stepped one foot in them and he hoisted me up so's I could see.

Mr. Guthrie wadn't dead. He laid on the bed with the boys, sleeping. His head was wrapped with rags. Mrs. Guthrie was setting in a chair shucking corn. Two cotton basketfuls set close by.

The next day Mrs. Guthrie went in their wagon to git Doc Murphy. Doc said Mr. Guthrie had a bad concussion and two gashes that he sewed up. He said he should be in the hospital. Mr. Guthrie was still only half-conscious, talking crazy. Doc said wadn't no telling what kind of damage was done. He tried to talk Mr. Guthrie into letting him take him to the hospital in Atlanta, but he wouldn't. Kept ranting and raving for Doc to leave.

"It's a wonder he ain't dead," he told us later. "She hit him don't know how many times. His eyes don't focus. His speech ain't right, and he can't move his legs. Could be paralyzed the rest of his life. Damn fool come at her drunk. I wouldn't blame her if she had killed him."

Chapter 31

W ell, Daddy sobered up again, with the same promises, and saying he was sorry. He set in to reading the Bible at night. I didn't say nothing to him and Sammy didn't neither, and Aunt Bessie hadn't mentioned gitting him a woman since that first time.

Sammy turned the garden under and I cleared off Mama's grave. He cut firewood and I gathered bucketfuls of twig kindling and stored it under the porch for winter. We both dreaded winter more than ever, on account of Alice. We couldn't take her to the creek in winter and set around. Our trips outside wouldn't be long enough to keep teaching her stuff.

We explained to Alice as best we could about her daddy. How he wadn't dead and how he couldn't walk yet 'cause his head was hurt. She couldn't understand what his head being hurt had to do with his legs. Mrs. Guthrie come out one night and told us we could git Alice anytime, even daytime, cause Mr. Guthrie couldn't see the shed door from his window.

Me and Sammy talked a long time about how we could bring Alice to our house now. We was excited about that.

"If Daddy'll stay sober we can help her lots at the house," Sammy said. "Maybe Miss Flossie could lend us some picture books to show Alice. Maybe some first-level readers or something."

I asked Daddy if it would be all right for us to bring Alice to the house on Saturday and he said that'd be fine. Him and Sammy went into town to git some stuff, so I went and got her. I give her a nice warm bath in the washtub and washed her hair. I let her put on my pink skirt and a white blouse, and I tied her hair back with a pink ribbon. She looked beautiful. I had it all planned to git her fixed, then let her see herself in my dresser mirror. I didn't think she'd ever looked in a mirror in her life, and sure enough she hadn't.

I led her to the dresser and watched her face. At first she looked shocked, like another girl was in the room. Then her eyes got bigger and bigger as she moved closer to the mirror. She touched it with her hand.

"Whooo dat? Whooo dat? Dat me? Dat me ina sky?" She turned and twisted to see each side.

"THAT'S YOU, ALICE. YOU LOOK PURTY. AIN'T YOU PURTY, THOUGH." I touched the glass. "THAT IS CALLED A *MIRROR*."

"Mirror?"

"YES."

She leaned across the dresser and pressed her cheek against the glass.

"Hit nice, hit showa."

"IT, NOT HIT."

"It nice."

Then she stood up real straight and stared at herself a long time.

"I not looka fits, I looka you, Sam-my."

She must have meant she looked normal.

"JUST LIKE US," I said. I set down on my bed to watch her.

"I dot night hair."

201

"BLACK HAIR."

She touched her white cheek. She turned to look at me. "You dot—not me."

"I GOT DARKER SKIN. I GOT FRECKLES, TOO. THAT'S 'CAUSE I GIT IN THE SUN ALL THE TIME."

She leaned toward the glass again and opened her eyes wide.

"BROWN EYES," I said, "DARK BROWN, THE TIE, THE RIBBON. IT'S PINK."

I could tell she liked the ribbon. She felt it over and over.

"Pink," she whispered, and I saw tears gather in her eyes. She stood up straight again fast. I could see she was fighting so's not to cry. Then her eyes stared at the eyes in the mirror. I wanted to know what she was thinking so bad I couldn't hardly stand it. I looked at the reflection of them sad wet eyes and my heart fell, such a sadness come on me. She stared wide-eyed, unblinking, at the stranger in the mirror. I got up and stood beside her and she looked at both of us.

"MY HAIR IS RED, AUBURN," I yelled.

She pointed to my eyes.

"GREEN."

She would not leave the eyes in the mirror. Finally I took her hand and led her from the room to the front porch.

When Sammy and Daddy come up in the wagon, Daddy didn't know her.

"Is that Alice?" He grinned.

Sammy helped him down from the wagon and handed him his crutches. He helped him up on the porch and into his rocker.

"She's a purty girl," Daddy said. "YOU ARE A MIGHTY PURTY GIRL, ALICE." Sammy just stared.

Alice hung her head and her cheeks turned red. She twisted her hands in her lap.

"WE—I'M GLAD YOU COME TO VISIT US," Daddy said. "CAN YOU STAY FOR SUPPER?"

She looked at me. She looked confused, scared.

"SUPPER. DADDY WANTS YOU TO EAT WITH US."

"Mmmm."

"WOULD YOU LIKE TO STAY?"

"Mmmm."

Sammy set down on the steps, still staring. Alice wouldn't look his way.

"She's timid," Daddy said. "She always that timid?"

"She gits timid in a dress," I said.

"She ain't got a dress?" Daddy was surprised.

"No, she ain't."

"Damn shame." Then in a minute, he asked, "How's her daddy?"

"I don't know."

"I been thinking, honey. As long as he's stuck in the house, why don't you ask Mrs. Guthrie if Alice could come down more often. She might could spend the weekends. He'd never know it. Y'all might could take her to church."

"Mrs. Guthrie wouldn't let her go nowhere like church," Sammy said. "Ain't nobody suppose to know she exists."

A pained look come on Daddy's face. "Something ought to be done," he said.

"We been saying that for all these months," Sammy said and set down on the steps. "Doc says ain't nothing nobody can do, but as long as Mr. Guthrie is stuck in his room we can at least bring her here."

"Y'all should have seen her looking at herself in the mirror." I patted Alice's knee. "She ain't never looked in a mirror before."

Daddy looked at Alice and smiled. Then we set a while

not talking. Finally Daddy asked, "How bad off is Guthrie?"

Sammy shrugged. "Doc don't really know. Says he can't move his legs. Don't know if he'll ever walk again. I just can't think of what Mrs. Guthrie is gonna do. How will they eat? How'll she take care of everbody? She's kind of— ah, backward. Her family won't help her none."

Alice set looking in her lap at her hands. She picked at her nails. I knowed she knowed we was talking about her. All of a sudden it didn't seem right.

"ALICE, ARE YOU HUNGRY?" I touched her knee. She shook her head no.

"ARE YOU THIRSTY? I GOT SOME COLD MILK." She didn't say nothing. Daddy leaned toward her and shouted, "HOW'S YORE MAMA, ALICE? WILL YOU TELL US ABOUT YORE MAMA?"

"Mmmm. Mama fine. Daddy narvith." She had used the word before.

"She means he's hurt," I said.

Daddy nodded. He studied Alice's face.

"COULD YOU—WOULD YOU TELL ME ABOUT YORESELF, TELL ME ABOUT ALICE? DO YOU LIKE COMING TO VISIT US? WOULD YOU LIKE TO COME BACK?"

She touched the pink ribbon.

"DO YOU LIKE THE RIBBON?"

She nodded.

"WHAT ELSE DO YOU LIKE? DO YOU LIKE—TO PLAY? PLAY GAMES? WHAT DO YOU LIKE TO DO?"

She didn't answer. Kept picking her nails. Sammy moved from the steps and set at her feet. He wrapped his arms around his legs and stared up at her. She wouldn't look at him.

Clouds had gathered over the valley and hung low and

dark, hiding the sun. A sudden breeze rustled the brown leaves of the old oaks beside the porch. Alice didn't notice. Under ambled up from the barn and laid under Daddy's rocker.

He started whining and Daddy reached down and rubbed his head. I watched Sammy's face as he studied Alice. He chewed his top lip. I could see she was real uncomfortable. She squeezed her eyes shut and took deep breaths.

I wanted to stop her being uncomfortable. I wanted to help her. Offer to play games. Anything.

I could see Sammy was gitting uncomfortable, too, watching her. Daddy was now rocking slow, back and forth, back and forth, barely missing Under's tail. Sammy glanced at me, looking desperate.

The breeze was stronger now, picking up leaves and sending them fluttering across the yard. Heat lightning flashed behind the clouds, and in a few seconds, low rolls of thunder echoed across the valley. Alice didn't notice.

"We could use a good rain," Daddy said, his voice dull and flat.

"Yeah," Sammy said.

"She don't never try to talk? Carry on a conversation?" Daddy asked.

"She don't know how," I said.

"Should we ask her questions? Try to . . ."

"I think she's embarrassed, Daddy. Let's leave her alone."

"I better put Poke in the barn." Sammy got up and jumped off the porch. He led Poke through the yard, the wagon squeaking and groaning. Alice still didn't open her eyes. Now she had her fingers laced together so tight they was purple red. I moved my chair closer to hers and touched her arm. She didn't look up.

"ARE YOU FEELING ALL RIGHT?" I yelled.

She nodded.

"Maybe she's fixing to have a seizure," Daddy said. "She git like this when she's fixin to have one?"

"Can't never tell," I said. "They ain't no real warning."

"Damnedest thing I ever seen." He shook his head. "Reckon she's scared of storms?"

"Nah, she ain't, as I know of."

"Maybe she's scared of me."

"That ain't it. She wadn't scared of Doc."

In a few minutes Sammy come back. He set on the steps. Alice didn't move. She kept her eyes squeezed shut. The heat lightning changed to jagged streaks in the far distance over the mountains. Claps of thunder followed. A few fat raindrops hit the tin roof. Under whined some more.

Daddy struggled to stand. "Let's take her inside," he said.

Me and Sammy stood and Sammy took Alice's arm.

"LET'S GO IN, ALICE," he said.

She didn't stand. She didn't look up. I looked at her hands. They were shaking.

"She's shaking," Sammy said and patted her shoulder. Soon her whole body was shaking. I jumped toward her but she wadn't having a fit. I squatted and was going to put my arms around her but all of a sudden she bolted from the chair, her eyes panicked, and before we could grab her, she flew down the steps and across the yard. Me and Sammy took off after her. The rain was falling faster now and the wind blew harder.

Alice crossed the road and run down the bank where the blackberry patch is. We both yelled but she run right into it like it wadn't there, the tangling mess of briars ripping the skirt and scratching her arms and legs. She didn't scream out. Sammy jumped through it with long leaps but it tore my legs up.

My legs hurt as we chased her into the woods and down the mountain. Now the rain was pounding us, soaking us.

The lightning flashed like arrows across the valley. Sammy screamed Alice's name over and over.

I couldn't believe we couldn't catch her. I couldn't believe she could run like that, a white and pink soaking wet streak down that hill. The ribbon had come off, her hair clung to her shoulders and down her back.

I finally give out. I had to slow down and git my breath, but Sammy kept running. He caught her about halfway down. He grabbed her and they fell onto the soggy pine straw, breathless. When I got to them, Sammy was laying across her chest, holding her arms out to each side.

Alice twisted beneath him, throwing her head from side to side like a pinned wild animal. Awful sounds come from her and a choking whine, low and sad. Her eyes was again squeezed shut.

"Oh God, oh God, oh God!" I cried. "Help us. Oh, what's wrong with her? Help us, help us!"

Rain run off both their faces like rushing streams. Sammy helt her fast.

"Please don't let her go into a fit!" I begged.

She twisted and fought till she was finally wore out. Then she laid there limp, white, beaten. The sight broke my heart. A silly thought come in my mind of the morning glories that covered our garden, before Sammy plowed them under. Their vines twirling and winding and covering the sagging vegetable plants, but with sweet fragile flowers, blue and pink and white that raised their heads in the early mornings to cover their world with color. By noontime they closed, with the heat of the sun, into sagging buds, lifeless and wilted, their show ended.

Alice looked like that. Like a fragile pink and white flower that was ended.

Sammy turned loose of her arms but she didn't move

them. He pushed hisself up and set staring down at her, his red hair washing over his face.

My mind raced, searching for words. Something, anything to say to her. I couldn't think of none. I leaned close to her ear and shouted, "I LOVE YOU, ALICE," but she didn't move. Didn't open her eyes.

"Why don't she cry?" Sammy whispered. "Oh, I wish she'd cry." He choked up.

When the storm ended, we still set. I was beginning to think Alice was in some kind of a scary coma or something. I said prayers in my mind.

Then her eyes opened, them big eyes, liquid and haunted and dead. She stared into the trees. Sammy took one of her hands and I took the other. We patted her.

Then she said words, words that will stay with me for the rest of my life. She looked in Sammy's eyes and with a voice, whipped and tired, and whispering, she said, "I want be real girl."

The words stunned us so bad we didn't move, them whispered words like sledgehammers in our stomachs. Words as plain as we'd ever heard her say. For a minute we sagged against each other. Then Sammy straightened up, wiped the tears and rain off his cheeks with his fists, and grabbed Alice. He pulled her up against him and helt her tight. He rocked her back and forth like he done when we sung "Jesus Loves Me" to her. He said words in her ear under that wet hair that I didn't hear and I knowed she didn't. Words, talking, humming.

I stared at them, so tired myself, so wet and tired and lonely. I got up and walked back up the mountain. I went in the house. Daddy was in the kitchen making coffee. He took one look at me and helt out his big arms. I fell into them.

When Sammy brought Alice back to the house and I got her into some dry clothes, we decided not to try to git her to talk. Daddy said he thought we ought not push too much on the girl at one time. Seeing herself in the mirror had been enough for one day.

The rain had left a cool fresh smell, and Sammy took Alice back out on the porch while I fixed supper. Daddy helped me. He peeled the 'taters while I made some cornbread and heated up some black-eyed peas. Once Daddy went and peeped out the front window and come and got me to let me look. Sammy was setting in one rocker and Alice the other. The rockers was side-by-side, and Sammy was holding Alice's hand as they rocked back and forth. She was finally gitting relaxed and was looking calm.

She eat purty good. After supper we talked to her a long time, telling her how much we liked her, how purty she was. She finally smiled. Sammy whispered to me that maybe we should play a game with her. Then he told her he sure would like to play a game of hopscotch if only he had someone to play with him. He asked her if she would play and she nodded. Daddy set on the porch and watched as we played on the wet ground. We played four games and she was understanding it real good. Sammy won two and me two.

"One more," Sammy said when we was done, and this time I knowed he was throwing the rock wild on purpose so's Alice would win, so I did, too.

When I throwed it way past the fourth square, Alice eyed me like she was suspicious. "Whaa do dat? That? Twit do that!"

"DO WHAT?" I asked, trying to look innocent.

She grabbed my rock and plopped it into my open hand. "Do ina! Twit doit outa!"

Daddy laughed from the porch.

"She's got y'all figgered," he said. "Now don't go insulting her no more. She'll win one sooner or later. Give her time."

She did. We played three more games till my right leg was tired of hopping. She won the third. Me and Sammy and Daddy clapped and whooped. She beamed.

Later while we was resting, the mist rose off the creek and made Yager Valley look like a huge blue lake. Then a gold moon rose over the mountains behind. We all set quiet watching the whole thing like if we talked it'd go away. Daddy and Sammy set in the rockers and me and Alice set in the willow chairs.

I was sort of in a dreamy daze thinking of the good nights like this when Mama was alive and Daddy would hold me on his lap and rock me to sleep. I looked at Alice, wondering if her real daddy ever rocked her before he died.

Sammy went in and made coffee and brought him and Daddy a cup and me and Alice some buttermilk. Under heard something at the edge of the yard and run over to sniff. In a distance the whoooo of a owl echoed over the valley. We set till we all got sleepy. Finally, Sammy got Poke and helped Alice on him. He got on and she wrapped her arms around his back and he took her home.

Chapter 32

Doc Murphy brought the hearing aid to our house the next Wednesday. Me and Sammy got so excited we couldn't hardly stand it. Sammy rode up and got Alice. By the time he got back with her, Daddy and Doc was pacing back and forth.

The hearing aid was a funny-looking thing with wires that hung down to a box that was suppose to be wore under yore blouse or dress. In Alice's case it went under her daddy's shirt and overall bib.

Doc set Alice down at the kitchen table with us hanging over it watching. He tried to explain what he was doing.

"THIS THING HERE IS GONNA HELP YOU HEAR BETTER, ALICE. NOW, IT WON'T HURT YOU. IT WON'T HURT A BIT." He showed her the aid.

"I believe," he said to us, "that she has what's called conduction deafness, which is caused by different things. Most likely hers was caused by the fever her mama had when she was carrying her, or she might have some blockage in the eustachian tube, maybe in the adenoid tissue, can't tell."

He put one little part behind her ear. It hooked over the front. Then he let her hold the box with the batteries. He twisted and fixed and watched Alice's face. Then he turned a nob on the box.

"Ooooooo, wha dat?" Alice's eyes popped wide. He put his fingers to his lips so we wouldn't talk. He moved behind her back so she couldn't see him.

"Alice," he said, lower than a yell.

"Huh?" Her eyes darted around the room. Her mouth hung open.

"Can you hear me?" His voice was normal.

"Mmmm."

"Say what I say, Alice. Will you do that?"

She was froze in the chair, staring straight ahead.

"Say—my name is Alice Guthrie."

"Mmmy name, hits Al-ice Guth-rie."

Me and Sammy and Daddy stood staring, amazed.

Doc stepped back. "I can hear what Doc is saying," he said.

"I tan hear whaa Doc sayeeeee."

He moved another step backward. "I live on top of the mountain."

"I live ona top de mountain."

We was about to bust, we was so happy. I wanted to say something but Doc shushed me. He moved to the stove. He opened the oven door and closed it easy. It made a little clunk. Alice jumped. He lifted the dipper out of the water bucket and tapped it against the warming oven. A soft ting. Alice heard it. He took her hand and led her to the front porch. We followed. He set her in a rocker and stood beside her. He started the rocker moving, a little rumble of wood against wood. The rocker had a squeak. She heard it.

Her face was still froze. Her eyes wide and unbelieving. It was like she was afraid to breathe. She rocked back and forth listening to the squeak like it was the purtiest song ever sung. Rocking slow and listening.

Finally we set down and Doc talked to her, telling her about the hearing aid. Telling her silly stuff, too, but she never did smile. Doc said she was too stunned to realize what was happening. He said it'd take a while.

After a while Doc stood up and looked at Alice a few seconds, then he let out a big sigh. He patted the top of my head and said, "Take her in the woods, Ellie. Let her hear the birds." Then Sammy stood and took her hand.

"Let's take a walk, Alice," he said soft.

She got up from the rocker. They went down the steps. I followed, then Under did, too.

"I could use a good cup of coffee," Doc said to Daddy. Daddy put his arm around Doc's shoulder.

"You can have anything I got," he said.

Sammy walked slow. She heard the dead leaves crackle when she stepped on them. She heard the crickets in the tall grass at the edge of the woods. A woodpecker tapped into a hickory. She heard it. She heard the squawk of a bluejay high over our heads. Her head and eyes flew in all directions looking for the sounds. Sammy named them all. She never said a word. It was like the time I seen the doe birthing the fawn. It was like God was walking with us, smiling.

I think I had expected her to squeal out with each new sound, but she never did. Sammy didn't talk except to name the sounds, and he never turned loose of her hand. Me and Under followed them up the mountain.

We walked to Cherrylog. It took nearly two hours. Up the mountain past her house and halfway down again. Sammy speeded up when we got close to Cherrylog. He led us to our usual spot and we all set down.

"Listen to the water, Alice," he said.

She set stiff and staring. The stream gurgled and splashed over the stones. She heard it for the very first time. Her face changed. She quit staring and tears come in her eyes.

"Hit wat-ter?"

"It's water," Sammy said.

Two tears spilled out and run down her cheeks. Me and Sammy watched them tears. I was happy and sad and overcome. I knowed he was, too. The tears dropped onto the bib of her overalls, then two more followed. Then two more. They was the purtiest tears I ever seen in my whole life.

I don't think she knowed she was crying for a few seconds, but then she quick wiped the tears off her face.

"I not cry," she said, looking at Sammy. She touched the hearing aid. "Hit maka hear."

He hugged her, then helt her away from him.

"The word is it, not hit," he said, smiling and looking in her eyes. "The word is it."

"Th-the word is it," she whispered. I started to clap but changed my mind.

We hadn't been there but a few minutes when Doc rode up on Poke.

"Anything wrong?" Sammy asked, helping him off.

"Nothing wrong. Thought y'all would be here. I forgot to tell you that Alice ought not to wear the hearing aid too long at first. She needs to git use to it a little at a time."

"How do you feel, hon?" he asked Alice.

She nodded.

"Do you hear any roaring? Any noise?"

"Whaaa?"

He made a roaring noise in his throat.

"Do you have sounds in your ears?"

She nodded.

"I thought you might. That's why you need to take the aid off—well, for today."

"Take off?"

"Just for today. You can wear it again tomorrow."

Her face clouded.

"I—I keep?"

"You sure do, honey. You keep it. It's all yours."

"Hit mine—ah—it mine?"

"It's a present from Doc and Aunt Bessie," Sammy said.

"Present?"

"Gift—er—a present is something somebody gives you 'cause they like you."

She lowered her head.

Sammy took the hearing air off her ear and handed it to Doc. We shouted at Alice the rest of the day.

Chapter 33

*T*hat next night when we took Alice home, Daddy
went with us. We rode up in the wagon. He wanted
to talk to Mrs. Guthrie. We decided the best thing to do was
for Alice to call her out, so we put Alice in the shed and she
screamed for her mama.

Mrs. Guthrie was nice enough when she seen us and
walked with us into the woods where Daddy was in the
wagon. I told her it was my daddy. She said howdy do.

"Howdy, ma'am," Daddy said.

Sammy helped him out of the wagon. He leaned against
the wheel.

"Doc tell ya about Ormond?" Mrs. Guthrie asked.

"He told us everything," Daddy said. "We understand
Mr. Guthrie's been beating up on you and Alice. You had
to protect yoreself."

"Hit the fool with a iron rod," she said. "He's in a bad
way. Can't walk. Don't talk too good, neither."

"We could git him to a hospital in Atlanta if he'd go." Me
and Alice and Sammy set on the pine straw. Mrs. Guthrie
kept standing.

"He won't go nowhere. Hates doctors." She looked at
Alice. "Hates her *worsen* doctors. He's gittin' meaner,
crazier iffen ye ask me. I don't know how much more I can

take. The little 'uns is scared of him, too, but I ain't gonna leave." Her shoulders sagged.

"They's ways we can help you," Daddy said. "They's some nice folks in this county, ma'am. Ain't nobody rich as I know of, but they good God-fearing folks. Help each other out. We'd like to help you. Help Alice. You got a fine youngun here. She could learn. She could learn just like anybody else if you'll let us help."

"Ain't got nothing to pay with." Mrs. Guthrie didn't raise her head. She kept looking in her lap.

"We know you ain't. We know yore troubles. We ain't expecting nothing. We just want to help. Them little 'uns need schooling. Alice here needs schooling. She . . ."

"Ain't no help for her," Mrs. Guthrie whispered. "She's teched. Can't hear. It's a punishment. The Lord's punishin me, lettin the devil tech her. Hit's hard living with it, tell ye that."

Daddy started to say something but I spoke first.

"The Lord don't have nothing to do with giving you troubles, Mrs. Guthrie, and he wants to help ya just like we do. Alice ain't no more teched than I am. She's got a sickness, that's all. Doc said so."

Daddy told Alice to stand up.

"I want to show ya something, ma'am," he said. He reached in the bib of his overalls and got the hearing aid. He put it on Alice and turned the nob. Mrs. Guthrie stared.

"Talk to yore girl. Say something, but don't yell," Daddy said. Mrs. Guthrie was quiet a minute and then yelled.

"ALICE."

"No, don't yell. Speak to her normal."

"That thang make her hear?"

"Yeah. Yeah, it does."

She leaned toward Alice. She stared at her a minute, then said, "You hear me, Alice?"

Alice smiled.

"I—I hear ya, Ma-ma."

Mrs. Guthrie stared at Alice like she was seeing a freak.

"Talka more, Ma-ma. Talka me more."

"That there—ah—that there thang hurt? Hurt ye ear?"

"Hit—it don't hurta. It don't."

Mrs. Guthrie put her hands over her face and started bawling.

Daddy touched Mrs. Guthrie's shoulder. Alice patted her mama's back.

"You cry, Ma-ma? I not cry. I not cry, Ma-ma."

It took her a long time to quit. She wiped her face on her dress sleeve.

"Yore girl can hear as good as we can," Daddy said.

When she got calm, Sammy asked her why didn't Alice never cry. He told her how Alice had finally started to cry when she heard the water, but it seemed like she was scared to.

"He beat her when she was a little 'un. He beat her iffen she cried."

"I kind of figgered that," Sammy said.

"He's a mean 'un. Hit's been hard."

We talked to Mrs. Guthrie till past midnight. Daddy and Sammy told her lots of plans, but when they talked about helping her git a place to live so's she could leave Mr. Guthrie, she said no.

"Ain't never leavin. Hit's till death, I say. Hit's the way the Lord tells us. I hurt 'im. I made 'im lak this. I'll tend to 'im."

It was decided that since Mr. Guthrie couldn't hurt Alice no more, couldn't hit her, couldn't walk around, that we'd keep gitting Alice. Mrs. Guthrie said we could try to teach her. She said she'd give some thought about putting the seven-year-old in school.

218

Chapter 34

*T*he next week we had a bad rainy spell and it got cold enough for a fire. Sammy went into Bolton and got a bunch of pasteboard boxes and covered the inside walls of Alice's shed. Then me and him went up the day after he done that and scrubbed it out good. Aunt Bessie sent two sheets and a pillow and a pillowcase. When the weather cleared we washed the quilts. Alice helped us do everthing and wore her hearing aid. We talked ever minute, even if we didn't have nothing to say. Alice had two fits while we was doing all that, but one of them wadn't real bad.

Then on Sunday after church Doc and Mrs. Murphy and Aunt Bessie and Uncle Will come. They left Morgan at home.

I never seen Daddy git so carried away. He did most of the talking. He said he thought that with time he could talk some sense into Mrs. Guthrie's head about sending her younguns to school and about leaving Mr. Guthrie. He said in the meantime he wanted Aunt Bessie to talk to Preacher McKay about asking folks to give stuff to keep the family going.

"I wish you'd of been here to see that girl when Doc put that hearing aid on her," he said to Aunt Bessie. "Ain't nothing got to me like that in a long time. Alice is a smart youngun, I can tell, and if you'd of seen her face and them eyes, well, it was a sight. A real sight."

"When I git this thing off my leg I got me a plan. Talked to Sam Tilson about it coupla days ago. He sells more chickens than anybody in these parts. Figger if that idiot Guthrie can keep a family alive on the few he raises, I could make purty good with a good-size chicken house. Me and Sammy could git one up before spring and this is my idea. See whatcha think. I start making us some good money and I could take care of that woman and her younguns and mine, too. Raise a bigger garden. Git me some pigs, maybe another cow. She's a right pitiful ignernt woman. Can't see what kind of a chance she's got if somebody don't help her."

We was all setting staring at Daddy. I don't think none of us could believe what we was hearing.

"Well?" Daddy said grinning. "Whatcha think?"

Aunt Bessie stood up and pushed her chair aside and headed to the coffeepot.

"I think I'm in the wrong house. I thought I'd come to the house of a old drunk crippled-up fart."

Uncle Will and Doc laughed. Mrs. Murphy tittered behind her hand.

"Whatcha think, Doc?" Daddy nudged Doc's arm with his elbow.

"I think it's a damn good idee," Uncle Will said. "I'll lay you ten to one you fall on yore a—on yore face."

Doc set and studied his cup. Daddy helt his out for Aunt Bessie to pour him more coffee.

"Tell ya what, Jack," Doc said, "you stay sober long enough to git that chicken house built and I'll lend ya the money for your equipment. That a deal?"

"I can see you'd make a helluva gambling man," Uncle

Will said. "I'll lay you ten to one he don't git the foundation laid."

Me and Sammy looked at Daddy. All Uncle Will's insults didn't seem to phase him. He helt out his hand to Doc.

"How much interest ya charge?"

"I thought you was saving up fer a vehicle, one of them fine Packards," Uncle Will said to Doc.

"Changed my mind, Will. McClung told me about a good '34 Ford a man wants to sell over past Sohee."

"How much ya paying?"

My head was a-spinning with all this big talk. Sammy was looking at Daddy like he ain't never seen him before and Aunt Bessie was snorting. Mrs. Murphy, who hardly don't never talk nohow, was not talking again.

In a little bit Sammy went outside and I followed him. We walked down the road. He said he was worried about Daddy's big talk and I said I was, too.

"One thing at least," he said, "we ain't neither one seen him interested in nothing in a long time."

That day Doc Murphy finally took the cast off of Daddy's leg and put a brace on it. Daddy walked right good, though one leg looked littler than the other'n. He started going to the sawmill ever day even before we left for school. He'd work there if they had work and if they didn't, he went on over to McClung's and helped him build this truck bed he was working on. Daddy's working at the sawmill instead of Sammy give Sammy time to finish up his writing.

One day Daddy and Mr. McClung come up in the truck with a big load of lumber. I run out when I seen the truck chugging up. Sammy was riding on top of the lumber grinning like a possum.

"He's gonna do it?" I screamed at Sammy. He jumped down.

"I reckon he is," he said. "I reckon we just might be going into the chicken business, Ellie girl."

Then I seen Lisa Mae up front with Daddy and Mr. Mc-Clung. They all got out and she was even excited.

"Why, for goodness' sake, Ellie, ain't it something! Why, one of these days y'all might even be rich! Daddy says they's good money in chickens. Yore daddy'll buy you all these new clothes and you can git some real makeup and all. . . . I seen a movie magazine in the drugstore that had them different shades of pancake, you know, little squares of different colors to see which ones you is best suited for and all. You ought to git one of them Tangees, too, maybe a orangish . . . oh, ain't it all exciting?"

Sammy laughed and pulled her hair. "Don't go spending his money before he makes it. I can see Ellie in orange lipstick. Ugh! She'll look like a sick pig."

"Oh, hush up, smarty," Lisa Mae said. "You'll be sorry when Mark Hudson comes driving up one of these days to take her on a date. I'm thinking he's claiming her already. Wait till she gits all fixed up cute, you'll be sorry. I bet he'll drive up in his daddy's *car*."

"It'll be a cold day in July when I see *that*," Sammy said.

"Little you know, just little you know." She stuck out her tongue at him. He grabbed at it. Then he run across the road to where Daddy was showing Mr. McClung where he was gonna build the chicken house. We run over, too. Down past the blackberry patch the land runs purty even for a little ways before it starts dropping toward the valley.

"Got a little over half a acre to work with here," Daddy said, then spit some tobacco into the blackberry patch. He'd took up tobacco since the spitting contest. "Figger with the grade, won't need but, say, oh, three, four foot higher that end, maybe five. Ain't too much."

The three of them walked on down, stepping high in the briars.

"Looks ta me like," Mr. McClung said, "the best way to head off water troubles is do yore trench so's it'll empty on both ends. Head most of it thataway." He pointed.

We followed them down, pushing the briars aside with sticks. I love to listen to men plan and talk things. Lisa Mae was all ears herself.

Sammy hunted up some sticks for stobs and Mr. Mc-Clung pulled a roll of string out of his jacket. They walked this way and that, dodging scrub pines, counting their steps, then starting all over again. Sammy run and got a hammer and drove the stobs where they said.

"Startin off thisaway is good," Mr. McClung said. "You can always add on. After you git it squared up, measured up right, you'll have, oh, whatcha think, thirty by sixty? Sixty-five? Still got plenty flat enough land left. How far away is the spring?"

"Long ways." Daddy pointed in the direction. "Prob'ly four to five hundred."

"Lotta pipe." Mr. McClung shook his head.

"Don't figger on using pipe," Daddy said. "All the land slopes thisaway. The spring heads down over yonder past that clump of rhodos. Figgered I'd di-vert 'er. Oughta be easy enough. Figger we'll git the place cleared by Wednesday. Git the rocks laid." He spit again. "Let's unload next to the blackberry patch. Figger I'll git Dan Haney to grade me down a road if his dozer's still working."

Chapter 35

You never seen such carrying on as when Daddy started his chicken house. I reckon men can't stand it when things is being built and they can't give advice or help. We had helpers all over the place. Mr. McClung and Uncle Will and Mr. Hudson and Mr. Keever. Even Morgan toted some rocks and shoveled some dirt out for the gully for the spring to run in. Sammy was so busy what with between school and working a little at the sawmill and building the chicken house, me and him didn't hardly ever git to talk. He fell in bed wore out ever night. Daddy, too.

I was in half a daze myself. Aunt Bessie helped me cook for them all, but my schoolwork was gitting harder so's I had to spend more time with it. We tried to go git Alice when they wadn't nobody extra around. It was a lot to do but I don't reckon I'd been as happy in a long, long time, seeing Daddy like his old self and all.

Doc Murphy had been up to look things over and help a little, and poke around with the men. I could tell he was proud of Daddy. He come once when Alice was there and couldn't believe it was her. She looked so different, he said, so much better, and real clean. Him and her walked down to watch Daddy saw some planks, and he was real happy about how much better she was talking. He told her he wanted her to try to wear the hearing aid all day now till she went to bed, and she told him she was already doing it. He was tickled about that.

Sammy come back from the sawmill with a wagon load of stuff while Doc and Alice was with Daddy. I put aside the 'taters I was cooking and run down there. Me and her come on back to the house and I helped her with her ABC's. She could print 'em up to P, even though some of them didn't look too good. I didn't clap no more when she got things right on account of Daddy told me not to. He said we ought not act like she was a little kid. He thought a hug would be better. He said Alice could use all the hugs she could git to make up for all them years when nobody touched her. Daddy hugged her all the time. Doc did, too. We all walked around with a arm around her. Sammy more than any of us.

She was gitting more like a reg'lar girl all the time, 'cept she was still so timid. Wouldn't never speak first or ask for nothing. I think she'd of starved before she asked for a bite or a drink of water.

She'd got to where she never did stink and was so clean she nearly glowed. She used up all of the talcum powder Aunt Bessie give her, so I give her my box.

Aunt Bessie and Uncle Will finally got to meet her. I went and got her after church one Sunday. They come up in the buggy, and Aunt Bessie took me and Alice for a little ride. When I brung Alice up to the buggy I thought Aunt Bessie was gonna drop her teeth.

"Why—why, my Lord, Ellie, this child is a living beauty!" She helt her hand out to Alice. "Honey, you are just the purtiest little thing I reckon I ever seen. How come you didn't tell me, Ellie? Lookit that chile, Will. You ever seen one as purty?"

Alice looked at the ground.

"We all told ya," I said, feeling so proud of Alice I could of busted. "We told ya she's purty."

"Raise that head up, honey. Let me see that face."

Alice peeped up.

"Lookit them eyes. Mercy in Heaven, the good Lord done blessed this chile with the eyes of a angel. We got us a dark-eyed angel here. No wonder yore daddy loves her so much, Ellie. You ever rode in a fancy buggy, chile?"

"Nome."

"Then it's about time. Get up here, girls. Will, you go on in and talk to Jack." Uncle Will climbed out smiling at Alice. "Alice, you set in the middle. Me and Ellie don't want you falling out. I can see now we gonna have to git you out of them overalls." We climbed in the buggy. "I got me some leftover eyelet the color of fresh cream. I'm gonna make you a blouse. A ruffeldy blouse. Got some twill, Ellie. Make her a little skirt, maybe pleats. Won't she be a doll, though? You like hair bows, honey?"

Alice nodded.

"Maybe I'll stitch you up a eyelet streamer. Make a bow for that hair. Lookit that hair. Goes past her waist."

We rode down the road a ways and turned and come back. Aunt Bessie talked all the way. Said she'd git some nice heavy flannel for a gown for Alice and she'd cut down her old gray coat, and if Sammy would git her some rabbit fur, she'd make a nice collar. Alice set with her hands in her lap like she was scared to move.

When we got back to the house Aunt Bessie asked Alice what she thought of all her ideas. Alice couldn't do nothing but nod. I made up for Alice's nod. I give Aunt Bessie a big kiss on the cheek.

During the next week Aunt Bessie got together with the church ladies and got six sacks of used clothes for the Guthries, and four boxes of food. Canned stuff and cornflakes and sugar and coffee. Sammy took it up in the wagon and give it to Mrs. Guthrie. He told her Aunt Bessie wanted to meet with her and talk, but she got real scared looking and said no. The days was gitting cold now so he cut her up a bunch of firewood. He said Alice didn't come out of the shed while he was there. He asked about Mr. Guthrie. Mrs. Guthrie said he still couldn't move his legs but he could see all right and he'd got his voice back good enough to cuss half the time, ordering her around.

"Does he hit you, ma'am?" Sammy asked.

"Tries to," she said, wiping one of the little kids' noses. "I dodge. He can't git to me no more."

"Is Alice okay? I don't see her around."

"She's all right. Had a fit this morning. She's all right now."

"This wood ought to last a few days. I'll come back."

She give him a half smile and went on in the house. When he got back home he told us about it.

Then Daddy said to me, "Go up and check on Alice, why don't you."

"How come?"

"She had a fit. She might of fell."

"Mrs. Guthrie *said* she was all right. I got to study. I got to cook supper. She's all right if her mama said so. Don't worry."

"You trust Mrs. Guthrie, honey?"

"Well, well, I reckon so. How come you ask that?"

He sipped his coffee, not saying nothing.

"She wouldn't say Alice was fine if she wadn't," I said. "I don't see why she would."

He stood up and took his hat off the nail beside the door.

"I'll go see about her," he said. "How long till supper?"

"Not long. I could keep it warm."

He kissed me on the head.

Chapter 36

By the middle of December the chicken house was nearly done. The tin roof shined like silver in the sun. It had a door at each end and four windows (or openings) on each long side with little door things that you could close up in winter or when it rained. Daddy was so proud he couldn't set still or shut up. He showed me and Alice ever new thing that was done. The trench at the top side that carried the rain water away from the building, the new gully to bring the spring water, the inside partitions made out of wire.

We had already had some bad weather that slowed 'em down some and one snow that stayed on the ground for three days. During the first real cold spell Daddy went to Alice's shed to make sure it was warm enough. The pasteboard Sammy had nailed on the walls helped, but Daddy worried that it would catch fire too easy, so he took it off. He chinked ever crack with whitewash clay. He cut the pasteboard to put in between the studs as a insulation, then he covered up the whole thing with scrap lumber.

He moved her cot farther away from the little potbellied stove and set the stove on a big piece of tin in case any sparks fell out. Then he come home and told us our Alice was safe from fire and snug as a bug.

Sammy was helping Alice with her words. Miss Flossie give him two first-level readers and Alice could read most of the words.

I had started teaching Alice to cook. She just loved to cook. One time she cooked the whole supper while I done my schoolwork. Biscuits and tenderloin and gravy and beans. It was real good. Also, ever time she come she wanted to help me sweep or dust or wash clothes. I hate washday worse than the devil hisself (well, nearly), but Alice didn't seem to mind it atall. Fact is, if I didn't know in my heart that *no*body could really like washday, I would of swore she liked it.

The first time she helped me wash was a purty sunny day though it was cold and windy. She helped me carry the sheets full of dirty clothes out to the wellhouse.

"I draw wa-ter?" she asked after we set the clothes next to the tubs on the washshelf.

"Well, sure, if you want to. I'll make the fire."

I set some kindling and a few short logs up under the washpot, but ever time I struck a match the wind blowed it out. She poured the first bucket of water into the pot, then squatted to help me. Under was sniffling the wood.

"I do," she said, and took the box of matches. "Hola dress out."

I got on my knees with my back to the wind and helt out the skirt of my dress to block the breeze. She struck a match and helt it to the kindling. It caught. She went back to the well while I stayed till the fire was going good.

"Bring me the soap chips, Alice," I said. She brought the box and poured about a cupful into the pot.

"Four more buckets wa-ter, huh?"

"That might do it. We'll boil the whites first."

She drew the buckets while I put sheets, towels, and white socks into the pot.

"Doze Sam-my's?" I was dropping in Sammy's socks.

229

"Uh-huh."

"I do."

I let her put them in. She was as careful as if she was holding eggs.

"Sam-my read me Jesus today?" He had read her a Bible story from a Sunday school lesson the day before.

"Jesus helpa children. He come helpa me?"

I stood a minute holding the wash stick, wiping the sut off with a clean rag.

"Jesus, he won't come in person to help you—he—well—he helps you—he helps us inside." I touched my chest. "He talks to our hearts. We hear him—we listen by our mind. I guess you'd say. It's not out loud. It's inside. You see?"

She looked down at her chest.

"I not see."

"Jesus makes us think good thoughts. That's how he talks."

"I thinka dit washin clean. I thinka dat."

"That's a good thought. What else do you think?"

She closed her eyes and screwed up her face.

"I thinka you. I thinka Sam-my. I thinka purty dress Aunt Bessie do. I thinka learna read, learna cook. I thinka he be Daddy—not he be—that good?"

"That's all good. Whatcha mean he be Daddy, not he?"

"My daddy not be—you daddy be. Ma-ma say my daddy not be. My daddy dead ago, my real daddy."

She covered her face with her hands. I couldn't understand what was happening. Her mama must of told her Mr. Guthrie wadn't her real daddy. I looked at her standing straight as a stick in them big overalls with that hair blowing like a cloud around her. She looked like the wind might blow her away.

"Yore daddy ain't yore real daddy," I said. "I already knowed that. I bet yore real daddy was—was fine. I bet he

230

loved you a lot." I took a step toward her but she stepped back.

"My daddy loves you a lot, too," I said. I wished she'd take her hands off her face.

"He—he thinka I tapaka he, Sam-my, he think I tapaka."

She had not invented a word for a long time. I didn't understand at all.

"*Tapaka*? Tell me about tapaka. Try to tell me, Alice." Under rubbed against Alice's legs. She didn't reach down to pet him.

She shook her head.

"I not. I not."

"Is tapaka—is it sick?"

She kept shaking her head.

"Does it mean—does it mean that Daddy and Sammy think you are—are different—not like, well, not like us?"

"I not. I not a real girl, I not!" She stamped her feet on the ground and scared Under. He run off.

"Sam-my, Sam-my, he know I not!"

She slumped for a minute, then twirled and took off running.

"Oh, dear God," I cried. I throwed the washpot stick on the ground and took off after her, my mind racing like my feet, remembering when we chased her down the mountain in the rain, the day she first seen herself in the mirror. Now she run past the house toward the chicken house. Daddy was up on the roof nailing down a piece of tin that was rattling in the wind.

"Alice!" he screamed. "Whatsa matter? Alice!" He come down the ladder so slow on account of his leg, that she was already heading down the mountain. Then the most amazing thing happened. All of a sudden she stopped. I was running toward her. She turned and started running back. Now she passed me going the other direction. She run straight to

Daddy before she stopped. He put his arms around her and set her down on a nail keg.

"Honey, what is it? What's wrong?" He squatted on his good knee in front of her.

"What is it, baby? Tell me."

She hung her head. "I—I not runna." She pointed to his bad leg. "You hurta. I not runna."

Daddy looked at me to see if I understood. I did.

"She don't want you to have to chase her on account of your leg, so she decided not to run away from us."

He looked at Alice. He put his hand under her chin and lifted her face. He looked at her face.

"Why did ya run? Please tell me. Why did ya run?"

She didn't answer. She covered her face with her hands again. I squatted down.

"Can I tell him, Alice?" I said. "Do you mind if I tell him what you said?"

She shook her head. She uncovered her face. Then she stood up and looked down at me. A new look come on her face. Stubborn. She mashed her lips together and shook her head again.

"We washa. I draw wa-ter. I washa. I want washa, too. I washa good. I do it!"

She stood at the washboard scrubbing them clothes till it's a wonder she didn't scrub them apart. She ordered me to sit. I couldn't believe it. Like a order! She washed, and dipped scalding, dripping clothes from the washpot and toted them to the tubs on that stick. She scrubbed them and rinsed them and wrung them, and she hung them out. All the wash. All by herself. When the last piece was hung on the line and flapping in the breeze, she stomped over to where I was setting on the well base watching the whole thing. The front of her overalls was soaking. She pointed at the clothesline.

232

"Dey clean?"

"They look *real* clean. They look cleaner than they ever looked, honest. You're a real good washer. You're better'n me."

I relaxed against the well. It might take a long time for her to understand and I might not know how to tell her stuff, but all of a sudden they wadn't a doubt in my mind that one day she would understand it all. Ever single bit.

Things changed in my mind about Alice that day. Any other time I would of told Daddy and Sammy anything she said. I would of told about her saying that tapaka word, but she had not wanted me to, and for the first time I give her credit for enough sense to know what she wanted. I can't explain the feeling, but it seemed like I had thought about Alice more like a—well, I'll have to say it. She said it, and she was right. I hadn't thought of her as nothing like a normal girl. I remembered Mama reading me a Bible story one time, and one of the lines said "and a child shall lead them." I never forgot it 'cause it was so strange thinking of a child leading grown-ups.

The night of the washday I had laid in my bed thinking about that line. I thought about how things had changed—how we had changed since we had met Alice. It kind of give me goose bumps.

Chapter 37

January the thirtieth Sammy got a letter from the *Atlanta Journal*. They had read his story and said it showed great promise, the same as the other letter said. They said his poems was even more promising. We didn't have no idea he had sent poems, that he'd ever wrote a poem in his life. Me and Daddy begged him for nearly a hour to let us at least read his poems. He said he throwed them away. He didn't have none. He blushed and said poems was girl stuff. Anyhow, finally he got so upset, Daddy let him be and told me to let him be.

The people at the paper said Sammy ought to study and keep writing and go to college. Sammy nearly cried. He already knowed what he *ought* to do. Doing it was a different thing. Daddy told him not to worry. By the time he was ready to go, the money would be there. He set me and Sammy down and told us about how the world was changing. About how Adolf Hitler was gitting Europe into war. About how President Roosevelt had tried to help pore folks in the Depression, and if they was a big war, how it would change everbody's lives.

"We got a good man in Washington," he said. "If they is a war, they'll be new jobs, lots of jobs. Money will start flowing, you wait and see. This country will need ever bit of food we can git, too. Chickens will sell 'fore you can raise 'em. You got no worries about schooling, son. Thing is, you're the right age to be called up. If that happens schooling will have to wait."

"Sammy might have to go to a war?" My heart sunk. I couldn't stand the thought.

"He might. All the boys might." He got up and poured hisself more coffee and set back down to talk some more.

"I'm thinking the whole world is in trouble. Things is gonna change."

My head was just a-swimming with Daddy's talk. We had heard a little before. Our teachers told us stuff, but I never paid no 'tention.

"Would *you* have to go, Daddy?"

"Doubt it. Too old. Got this leg."

I looked at Sammy. I'd never thought of him gitting to be a man. I sure never thought of him going to no war. Fact is, as I set at that kitchen table looking at my brother and my daddy, I got scared thinking about all the stuff I never thought about. The stuff I didn't know about and never heard of. I didn't want nothing to change. I hated the thought. I wanted me and Sammy and Daddy and Alice and everybody else to stay like we was.

I reckon if I would of admitted it, I knowed for a long time that Sammy was changing, gitting restless. Aunt Bessie said if he tried to keep on at our school, he never would amount to nothing. Her and Uncle Will and Daddy set at our table with Sammy one night till midnight trying to come up with a answer for him.

"The service is the best idea," Uncle Will said. "Learn a lot, travel. I can't see as how he could do better. He could write about what he sees."

"Hogwash!" Aunt Bessie said. "If we git into the war, then he'll be obliged to go, but I think he ought to finish as much schooling as he can before that happens. I was talking to Flossie. Ain't no reason he can't go to Rabun Gap Nacoochee. That's what it's for, to help mountain young-uns git a education. Gits 'em ready for college. Fine school. Won't cost a cent. They live at school. He works his way through. The boys work in the dairy or do the farming. Flossie says it's a good school."

Sammy said that he hated to go in the middle of the term, and hated for them to know he was in the ninth grade at eighteen years old, but he would be glad for the chance at a decent school.

The thought of Sammy going off and leaving me to do everthing and leaving me to handle Daddy if he got drunk again scared me bad. We talked about it and he said he wouldn't go but I said no. I said I reckon he had to. Aunt Bessie said she'd help me all she could, that she'd try to come up two or three times a week.

That Saturday Mr. McClung drove Sammy and Miss Flossie and Daddy over the mountains to Rabun Gap and that night when they got back I learned my brother really would be going away. I didn't cry in front of Sammy and Daddy. We all hugged and set talking about how lucky Sammy was while my stomach knotted up and my heart hurt with feeling lonely.

When we went to bed I laid there staring out my window into the starlit night. Crying and thinking about how life ain't fair. How it seemed like nothing is forever. I thought about how close me and Sammy had got after Mama died. At first close like two children hanging on to a log in a river that was rushing over rocks going fast to nowhere. Scared and mixed up and clinging for dear life.

I remembered the day we buried her. How I screamed out at God. Running through the woods with Under at my heels, screaming and pitching the biggest temper tantrum I could pitch. Then finally falling to grab Under to me and hold him like if I didn't hold him my breathing would stop and I would die. And I had set there holding him to me with him licking the tears off my face and then I started saying Jesus, Jesus, Jesus, over and over and over. Just whispering his name into Under's furry neck. Jesus, Jesus, oh, Jesus. Over and over and over, till I got so limp I sagged into the pine straw with Under in my arms. Then a, well, a softness come on me. That's the only way I can explain it. A softness like laying in a big pile of fresh picked cotton. Fluffy and white and pure and warm like sunshine. Then I slept, and while I slept I dreamed I saw him, clear and plain as day. I saw Jesus setting on the mossy bank down at Cherrylog, and he was holding me and Sammy on his lap and all around us for miles and on to forever was children . . . and each one come and he would hold them, too. All of us. Hundreds or thousands and it seemed like his lap had space for more and more.

I woke to hear Sammy and Daddy calling my name. Then they found me and Daddy picked me up and toted me back to the house. We set on the front steps and I told them my dream and Sammy and Daddy cried.

Now Sammy was going away and I knowed that nothing would ever be the same again. He'd be gone for two years, maybe three. My brother. My best friend. Mama had always wanted more children. Oh, how I wished there had been more so I wouldn't be alone. The tears started again. I thought of wrapping my quilt around me and going to Mama's grave, but I didn't. I slipped out of bed and tiptoed into Sammy's room. He wadn't asleep.

"Can't you sleep either?" he whispered.

I couldn't answer. I sniffled.

"Come here," he said and helt out his arms. I set on the bed and he hugged me and helt me for a long time, till I got to feeling silly. Then I give him a punch in the chest and pulled his hair and he wrestled me down and goosed me on my ribs and we felt better.

Me and Sammy and Daddy talked about how to tell Alice about Sammy going away. Daddy finally decided it would be better not to tell her right away. Sammy brung her down the last night and told her as best he could. I was sure she didn't really understand. She set with us at the table like a mummy. I knowed she understood he was going away, but that was all, and that was enough. She set froze and quiet and holding her hands in her lap. It scared me. Daddy, too.

Sammy said he didn't think he could take her back. He didn't want to remember her for the last time at the shed. Daddy got Poke and brung him to the steps. Sammy put his arm around Alice.

"Daddy'll take you. Now you be my good girl. Be good and take care of yoreself. Will ya do that for Sammy? Will ya?"

She stared straight ahead.

"I'm gonna be back for a visit in four weeks. That ain't long. It really ain't long."

On the porch he hugged her to him and kissed the top of her head. She didn't hug him back. He helped her on the horse. She helt her back stiff, her chin high. I couldn't watch. I turned my head, tears coming.

"'Bye, hon," Sammy said. I heard Daddy sniffling.

"'Bye, Sam-my," Alice whispered. That was all.

Chapter 38

After Sammy left, I thought me and Alice was gonna die. I got her ever day after school and kept her till bedtime. She had more fits. Doc said it was because of Sammy. She quit trying to read or write. She was nice and smiled and helped me with the housework, but it was like she was forcing herself. Daddy petted us both and brought us candy bars. One time he brought us a movie magazine with Clark Gable and Bing Crosby and John Garfield and Carole Lombard and Hedy Lamarr and Alice Faye. I spent a long time telling Alice about movie stars and picture shows (though I hadn't ever seen one).

She liked the purty clothes but she didn't understand about picture shows. I told her she was as purty as any of them and was prob'ly named after Alice Faye. She just blushed.

The chicken house was done and ready for chickens by February. Daddy was gonna git his first baby chicks, a whole five hunderd. I couldn't wait. I wrote Sammy all about it.

Dear Sammy,

I am fine. I cut my hair in front to look like Alice Faye with waves and all but it don't. Daddy says hey and he will write tomorrow but he's busy. The chicken house is all done. He will get 500 baby chicks before you come to visit.

Alice is all right. *(I hated to tell him she wadn't all right.)* I git her ever day. She misses you as much as me and Daddy does. She had 2 fits day before yesterday.

Aunt Bessie lost 7 pounds but I can't tell. Daddy said if she lost 67 we could tell. He's kidding. Under misses you too and Poke. Leety is gonna have a calf.

Love,
Your Sister
Ellie

P.S.—I made 82 on English.
P.P.S.—If they have Moroco red lipstick at Rabun Gap, git me one to bring home when you come and I will kiss you with it on. Ha.
P.P.P.S.—Uncle Will bought a real radio.

In March we got the chicks. They was just three weeks old. Oh, they was the sweetest things you ever seen, but Lord, was they lots of work. Kept me and Alice and Daddy busy all the time. Keeping fires in the heater to make sure they didn't git too cold at night. Feeding them. Cleaning the pens, having to watch where you was stepping ever second. Alice worked as hard as we did. I asked Mrs. Guthrie and she said Alice could spend some nights with us. That was good on account of all we had to do.

The wonderfulest thing that happened was Doc brought Alice some medicine. A new thing called Dilantin. He showed her how much to take and told her when to take it. It was a true miracle. She stopped having them fits 'cept ever once in a while. Even when she had one, it wasn't as bad. Daddy said we ought to thank the Lord.

One night I thanked God for all the miracles. For the chicken house. For Sammy gitting good schooling even though I missed him. For Daddy not drinking and for Alice having medicine. I got so carried away and got so happy, I couldn't sleep, so I wrapped a quilt around me and tiptoed out of the house and went to Mama's grave to tell her.

Telling Mama all that good news got me even more awake and excited, so I run into the woods with Under at my heels, and with the quilt a-flying around me, I run and run, and I squealed and I sung. If anybody would of seen me they'd of thought I was plumb crazy, but the only one seen me was God and it felt like he was running and singing right beside me.

The medicine made Alice so much better I couldn't hardly believe it. Seemed like before, so much of her life was wasted on gitting over the effects of the fits. For all the good days, when her mind was clear, they was the bad days when it wadn't. Now she mostly had good days, days when she was so bright and smart it was amazing. I had talked to her about Sammy and how good it was that he was gitting good schooling so's one of these days he could make a good living for his wife and younguns. I didn't tell her how scared I was he'd marry some new stranger from the school. He wrote us about how many purty girls they was.

Alice got over the moping and being sad after we talked. It was like she got a new spirit. She went back to studying her words and all. She even got to where she'd pick up Daddy's almanac or the Bible and ask us to read to her and explain the words. Also, she got to where she giggled more. Most times she'd cover her mouth with her hand like she had a big secret, but then sometimes she'd just giggle or laugh like anybody.

Aunt Bessie got to where she come up every day nearly. Her and Daddy talked and talked about how to git Alice some schooling. Daddy had asked Mrs. Guthrie three different times about letting Alice go to school. He told her she could live with us now that Sammy was gone, but she wouldn't hear of it. She said she wadn't sending no sixteen-year-old sick girl to the first grade. All Daddy's talking done some good, though. Mrs. Guthrie let the two boys start. One was nearly eight and the other'n six. Daddy went up and got 'em ever morning and drove us all in the wagon. The boys is right cute. The oldest is Gus and the youngest is Aldon.

Sammy didn't come for a visit at four weeks. He wrote and said he was taking more subjects to try to catch up and he wouldn't have no time to be coming home. I missed him so bad I couldn't hardly stand it, but Daddy said we was both gonna have to accept it for Sammy's sake.

Alice was studying more than me. Ever afternoon after we got the chores done she set at the table with a pencil and tablet and practiced writing. I got her two more readers and, with Daddy's help, she learned the words.

Then one day she showed me her first letter to Sammy. Aunt Bessie had helped her with it. Aunt Bessie don't spell too good. She just went to the fourth grade. The letters covered up two lines and some of them was backward and she didn't have no periods, but we bragged on her just the same.

Dar Sammy

How ar you I am fine The chikens are fine I hep care of chikens Ant Bessie say I sew good to and cook I larn to be a good clener Ellie say I mak a dres so you see you come you rite me to

Love
Alice

Sammy loved the school. He raved on about it in ever letter. How it set up on a hill. How the other buildings set around it and how nice the dairy was and what good grades he was making, except in algebra. He didn't answer Alice's letter right away. It took three weeks. I had to read it to her. He told her all the same stuff but also told her how proud of her he was of her cooking and sewing and cleaning and all. She just beamed all over herself.

The best part was he wadn't writing Bertha. She'd wrote him, no telling how many times, and never got but two letters. Daddy said boys are not letter writers like girls, but I hoped it was for a different reason.

Daddy was working real hard. He worked at the sawmill and him and Mr. McClung was building a cabin over close to Sohee for this man from Atlanta. He said by the time they was done he'd have enough to pay Doc Murphy back all he owed him, and even pay a little bit on what he owed Uncle Will. Me and Alice was tending to the chickens by ourselves nearly.

The middle of May Daddy sold his first batch of chickens and we would of felt like a celebration 'cept that we got a letter from Sammy asking Daddy if he could stay at Rabun Gap when it come time for summer vacation. He said one of the teachers, a Mr. Graves, said if Sammy would help him on his farm that he'd tutor him. We hated the thought of not seeing Sammy, but Daddy wrote back that he thought it was a good idea. Then Sammy wrote that if Daddy could git somebody to come and git him when school was out that he could stay at least a week at home. We was glad of that.

That night I read that letter to Alice. We had cooked a right good supper. When Daddy got home he washed up and come on to the table. He said the blessing (he'd got to where he always said it) and Alice squeezed her eyes shut tight. Then he said how good everthing looked. Me and

Daddy started eating, but Alice didn't touch her food. She just stared at us.

"Why ain't you eating, honey?" Daddy asked. "You feeling all right?"

She lowered her head. "I fine," she said.

"It's, I'm fine or I *am* fine," Daddy said and took a big bite of chicken.

"I *am* fine," Alice said, still not looking up. We kept on eating, not paying her no mind. In a minute or two I looked at her and she had picked up her fork and was eating with it instead of a spoon. She was doing purty good, too.

After supper me and Alice set on the porch steps. The moon was rising over the mountains and the night creatures was singing. The mist in the valley rose and the air was cool.

Alice tugged on the cords of her hearing aid and pulled the little box out of her dress top. She helt it, looking at it.

"Real girls not hava this, huh? This ugly coming out. Sammy think it ugly. Sammy lika girl not hava ugly." She took the part that goes behind her ear off and helt it in her hand, too. I had to yell.

"SAMMY IS HAPPY YOU GOT THAT HEARING AID. HE'S REAL HAPPY. HE DON'T THINK IT'S UGLY."

She set a while staring at the hearing aid, twisting the cord around her thumb.

"ALICE?"

"Huh?"

"WE ALL LOVE YOU A LOT. DON'T YOU KNOW THAT? WE GLAD YOU GOT THE AID."

She didn't answer.

"YOU ARE LIKE OUR FAMILY. WE LOVE YOU LIKE OUR FAMILY."

She laid the hearing aid on the steps and stood up. She walked slow toward the road. I got up and caught up with

244

her. We stood looking past the chicken house into the misty valley.

"My mama lova me?" she whispered.

"I'M SURE SHE LOVES YOU LOTS."

"My daddy, he not lova me. He hate me. He usta say I slobber animal. He say I a crazy. He hit me. I not cry."

"HE AIN'T YORE REAL DADDY. HE'S A MEAN MAN. IT DON'T MATTER WHAT HE SAID, IT DON'T MATTER NONE."

"Real girls live ina house. Go schoolin. Go schoolin an go church an go store. Real girls go alla 'em. I not go."

I didn't know what to say. I got a lump in my throat. I put my arm around her but she moved away.

"I thinka I not doin no more hearin aid. I thinka I never be's a real girl if I doin hearin aid alla my time on an on. I thinka I be's no more'n a slobber animal, a crazy, huh? What I doin it for, huh? What? I be in shed alla my time, on an on. You be's in house. You go schoolin, church. You do, I not, never alla my time till I dying dead ina ground like yore mama ina flowers."

She shivered and walked off toward her house with her arms wrapped around herself. I felt awful. I followed her.

"ALICE, THAT AIN'T TRUE. ONE OF THESE DAYS YOU GONNA GIT OUT OF THAT SHED. YOU GONNA LIVE IN A HOUSE. I KNOW YOU WILL."

She whirled to face me.

"How I do it, huh? How I git out? How I go schoolin, huh? How?"

"I DON'T—I DON'T KNOW YET, BUT . . ."

"They laughin. The peoples laughin if I go schoolin. They say I slobber crazy. I have fit, they say it. You not have fit. You not wearin hearin aid. What you know, Ellie, huh? You and Sammy laughing me? Alla time you laughing, huh?"

"OF COURSE NOT! YOU KNOW WE AIN'T *NEVER* LAUGHED AT YOU . . ."

"I goin shed. I goin. You not go. I go by self." She walked off. I watched a minute, then I caught up.

"LET ME WALK YOU HOME, ALICE."

I looked at her face. It was shining with tears. I was afraid to mention them. She didn't speak. Then she started sniffling. Then she started sobbing.

She was doing it! She was crying. I walked a step or two behind her. I wondered how many years it had been since she'd let herself cry. Her back was straight. Her arms hung by her side. Sometimes her shoulders shook. The sight of her tore me apart. Tears run down my face.

We walked a few minutes with her sobbing. I wanted to hug her. Help her. I decided not to. I don't know why. Then she stopped crying. She said without turning, "Go home, Ellie. You goin home. I want you goin."

I stopped. I watched her a few seconds.

"GOOD NIGHT, ALICE," I screamed. I knowed she didn't hear me.

Chapter 39

*D*oc Murphy fiddled with his coffee cup, turning it round and round in his hands as he listened to Daddy talk. Aunt Bessie and Uncle Will set at both ends of the table and I set beside Daddy.

"And that's the way I see it," Daddy said. "We been fooling around too long. Some way or another we gotta git Alice out of that shed and we gotta do it quick. It was different when she didn't know no better."

"But nothing's changed, Jack," Doc said. "We ain't got no right atall here. Her mama's got all the rights. She can do anything she wants to and she's let us know in no uncertain terms that she ain't gonna let that girl go nowhere. Alice is only sixteen years old. We can't do nothing."

"Looks to me like," Aunt Bessie leaned her elbow on the table and propped her chin in her hand, "that we've tried everthing they is to try. She won't let Alice go to school. She won't let her move down here with y'all. What else is they?"

Daddy slid his chair back. I got up and poured everbody more coffee.

"The woman's ignernt," Uncle Will said. "We all know that. She's pore and she's pitiful. Now I got a idea here and I want to know what y'all think. When it comes right down

247

to it, what we're dealing with, what we got that might work, is the fact that Mrs. Guthrie hit Mr. Guthrie with a pipe and now he's crippled up. The way I look at it is she should of killed him, but that's beside the point. Even as ignernt as she is, she must know she done something she could go to jail for if she was convicted, and . . ."

"Damn!" Daddy said. "I ain't one for blackmail."

"I don't like it," Doc said. "That woman's got enough burdens to carry without us doing that. I can't see as how there's ever gonna be any changes for her, but them littlest younguns might have a chance. She did change her mind about sending 'em to school. Maybe if we give her some more time she'll change her mind about Alice."

"I don't think we got any time to give her," Daddy said. "I'm scared for Alice. We ain't got no time to play with. I think everbody in this room knows that."

"I'm thinking you ain't giving Alice enough credit," Doc said. "We all know she's come a long way. We know she's suffering since she knows the difference in her life and everbody else's, but one thing we ain't considering—Alice loves her mama. I don't think she'd ever forgive us if we hurt that woman more'n she's been hurt already. I think Alice is to a point where we can set her down and talk to her. Reason with her. That youngun's smart. Ain't nothing stupid about that girl."

"Are you saying we tell Alice if she stays in that shed till she's twenty-one, then we can git her out?" Aunt Bessie asked. "My God, that's five years. That don't make no sense atall. I ain't in favor of telling her nothing. I'm in favor of taking her out come hell or high water. I'm in favor of doing what Will says."

Uncle Will nodded. He took his tobacco out of his shirt pocket. "I'm with Bessie," he said. "Them people been treating Alice worse'n a dog all her life and we seen already it ain't gonna change. Say Guthrie dies. Let's say that. Then

248

what? Then Alice gits to move into a house that ain't no better'n that shed. Gits to live a life of ignerence. Won't never have no schoolin. I say we git her out one way or another."

Everbody set quiet a little bit. Under come from under the table and whined to go out, so I got up and opened the door. I was wishing Sammy was there to talk to. I hadn't said nothing atall 'cause I didn't know the right thing.

"Tell ya what," Doc said, scratching his bald spot. "Let's let Ellie go git Alice. Let's talk to her and see if she has any ideas. If we can't work out nothing that makes no sense, then we'll do it Will's way. Jack, what you say?"

Daddy started to open his mouth but I said, "*I'd* sure like it myself if we started treating Alice like she's got enough sense to have a say."

They all looked at me. Doc smiled. Daddy stood up.

"Ellie, you stay. I'll go git her. You're right, honey. I reckon she sure deserves a say. Bessie, why don't you whip up a pie or something. I'll be back soon as I can."

Alice had on the overalls and shirt Aunt Bessie had give her, but her hair was combed nice and she was real clean. Daddy brung her in the kitchen door. We hugged her and I told her to set beside me at the table. She set with her head down. Everbody sort of looked at each other, wondering how to start. Daddy got the hearing aid and handed it to her. She put it on.

"Alice, we need yore help," Daddy said, reaching across the table and taking her hand. "We got a problem we can't figger what to do with and we need to talk to ya about it."

She didn't look up. Daddy give Doc a helpless look.

"We all know you want to git out of that shed, honey. We don't blame ya one bit. You need to be out of it. We want to git you a place to live. You understanding me?"

She nodded.

"What I brung ya down here for is for you to talk to us,

for you to tell us what it is *you* want to do. We want to know what *you* want. Will ya talk to us? Will ya tell us?"

She raised her head and looked into Daddy's eyes. "Wha *I* wan do?"

"That's right. What you want to do."

She turned and looked at me. Then she looked at Aunt Bessie.

"Tell us, hon," Aunt Bessie said. "You tell us anything you want to tell us."

"Wha I wan do hits goa schoolin." She bit her top lip and lowered her head again. "Ellie goa schoolin. Me, too."

Daddy grinned and patted her hand.

"Good girl!" he said. "That's what we want to hear. That's what we're here for, to talk about how to get you into school. Trouble is, yore mama, she don't want to send ya. You know why she don't want to send ya?"

"I too big schoolin, Mama say. I too big."

Doc slid his chair closer to the table. "How would you feel going to the same grade with little kids, Alice? If you started you'd prob'ly start in second grade, since all you know is your letters and numbers and a little arithmetic. Would you feel—funny, going with little kids?"

She didn't answer for a while. She bit her lip and played with her thumbnail.

"I wan go Ellie. I go Ellie?"

Aunt Bessie looked at Doc and shook her head.

"You could *go* with Ellie, but you wouldn't be in the same class with her," Doc said. "The first two grades are together. You'd be in the room with your little brothers. How would you like that?"

She didn't answer.

"Would you like that, hon?" Daddy said.

I leaned toward her. "Tell us. You can tell us."

"I—I too big schoolin."

"I wish she could live with us. She could catch up if ever—

body helped her," I said. "If we could just git Mrs. Guthrie to let her live with us."

Aunt Bessie got up and cut a piece of apple pie and poured a glass of buttermilk. She set them in front of Alice. Then she set a piece of pie in front of Daddy.

"I go schoolin, Sammy?" Alice asked Daddy.

"I'm afraid not, honey. It's the same problem, but you listen here. Problems is for solving and we're gonna figger this out. What we looking for is some time. What we're worried about is you. Is what—is gitting you out of this—ah—sad mood you been in."

I put my arm round her shoulder and give her a squeeze.

"We want you happy and smiling and being our beautiful Alice," Daddy said. "Now you eat that good pie there. Bessie done made it special. It ain't gonna be too long before we figger out this problem, is it, Doc? We gonna figger how to git you some schooling. You gonna be smart as Ellie or Sammy or anybody."

"Could Flossie Moore tutor her special?" Uncle Will asked, "Like that man's gonna do Sammy this summer? Flossie use to tutor Edgar Bruton's boy, didn't she? Reckon she'd tutor Alice here?"

"Damn!" Daddy said. "I didn't think of that. Reckon she'd do it, Bessie? How much would she charge, ya reckon?"

"Couldn't charge much," Uncle Will said. "Edgar Bruton never had two dimes to rub together."

"We could all chip in," Aunt Bessie said. "If we all chipped in it wouldn't be too much. School'll be out in two weeks. Maybe she'd do it all summer."

"Oh, I bet she would!" I said, gitting excited. "I bet she would do it! Can I ask her tomorrow? Can I, Daddy?"

We spent the next hour or so explaining to Alice what tutoring meant, and how she'd like Miss Flossie and all. She seemed happy, but then, like I told Aunt Bessie, with Alice it was still hard to tell if she was really happy or just wanted to please us.

After all the explaining, Doc asked Alice if she had ever told her mama how unhappy she was, living in the shed. Alice said no.

"I want you to tell her," Doc said. "I want you to set down with yore mama out there in the yard somewhere, or in the shed, so's yore daddy won't hear, and I want you to tell her you would like to live somewhere else. You feel like you could do that?"

Alice didn't answer.

"Listen, honey," Daddy said. "Maybe the reason yore mama won't agree with us about you living here is 'cause you ain't told her you want to. It might be she'd let ya if you begged her good. She ain't used to you asking her for nothing 'cause you ain't never asked her. You think ya could ask her?"

"I askin?"

"Yeah. You. You ask. Will you?"

Alice looked at me.

"*Please* ask her," I said. "Tell her you could come home to visit anytime. Tell her it ain't like you're going afar off. We could ride Poke up there for a few minutes ever evening if she wants us to. Will ya ask her?"

A funny look come on Alice's face. I knowed she hadn't never thought of somebody doing something 'cause she asked 'em. Her eyes lit up and she took my hand.

"I askin," she said, smiling.

"And listen," I said, "listen careful, if she says no, then that don't mean nothing. Ask her again. Ask her lots of times. That's the way you do, see. Sometimes I have to ask Daddy five or six times. Sometimes I have to drive him plumb crazy 'fore he says yes on something. What ya do is . . ."

Aunt Bessie laughed. "Looks like yore gal has got you

figgered, Jack," Aunt Bessie said. "Way I look at it, you're lucky. Five or six times ain't nothing. Morgan will ask till the cows come home and then ask some more. You just keep at it, Alice, you keep pestering yore mama and I'll be willing to bet a purty she'll give in."

"Wha pescherin?"

"Not wha. *What*. And it's *pesterin*," Aunt Bessie said.

"What pesterin?"

"What *is* pesterin?"

"What is pesterin?" Alice said it perfect.

"Tell her, Ellie," Daddy said.

Chapter 40

*M*iss Flossie said she'd be glad to help Alice all she could after school was out. She said she couldn't help her as much as she needed, though, but what she figered was if I set in on the lessons a few times, I could get the hang of the right way of making learning easier for Alice. Then between the two of us, and anybody else that was willing, and if Alice was as smart as I said she was, then she didn't see no reason why Alice couldn't git some education.

Aunt Bessie said she'd take me and Alice down to Miss Flossie's ever morning early in the buggy, then she'd pick us up about one. We would start two weeks after school was out. After Sammy come home and went back. That would be in three weeks. Everthing was happening so fast I couldn't hardly believe it.

Daddy had went and got his second batch of chickens and that was keeping us busy. Him and Mr. McClung had finished the cabin they was building for the man from Atlanta, and Mr. McClung said he had a contract on another one they'd start on around the end of July.

Three days after the meeting about Alice, I found out she still hadn't asked her mama.

"How come you ain't asked her? You scared?" We was cleaning the chicken house that afternoon and she hadn't been talking atall till I asked her had she asked and she'd said no.

"You scared to ask her?" I thought for a minute she might not have her hearing aid turned on, but she nodded.

I put down the rake and set down on a bench beside the door.

"Come on," I said.

She come and set with me.

"Now tell me how come you scared to ask?"

"I not know."

"I *don't* know."

"I don't know."

"'Fraid she'll say no? 'Fraid she'll git upset, be mad?"

She nodded. I thought about it a minute. Everthing in Alice's life is like starting from scratch. I just couldn't imagine it. Seemed like such a simple thing, asking yore mama something, but for her it wadn't.

"You help me askin, Ellie?"

"Will you help me ask? Say it like that."

"Will you help me ask?"

"Well," I said, "I reckon I could. I don't see what it would hurt. Ask yore mama to come to the shed tomorrow after school. I tell ya what. I'll not ask her. I really want you to do it. I'll be right with you to explain and talk about it, though. We think it's real important that you do the asking."

"What imp-tortant?"

"Important is—it's like urgent."

"What urgent?"

"Ah—well, it's like something that matters a whole lot. Something that means more than something else. See, it means a lot for you to ask for something for yourself. I ask for stuff. Sammy asks for stuff. It's time you done it."

Mrs. Guthrie was setting on Alice's cot when I opened the shed door.

"Hey thar, Ellie," she said. She had a spit jar in her hand. Under her bottom lip was a hump of snuff.

"Hey, Mrs. Guthrie. How ya been?"

"Tard. Tard out. Ormond's gittin worse'n any youngun. Wait on 'im hand an' foot."

"Daddy said he's got a big box of stuff he's bringing tomorrow. Aunt Bessie give some jars of berries. You can have ya a pie. You got plenty flour?"

"Got plenty. Close on sugar, though. Las' time he come he brung half a salted shoulder. Said the preacher sent it." She spit in the jar. "I'd shore like to fat me a hog next year. Good eatin, that shoulder."

"He got us two pigs in early spring. They's growing fast. First we had in a long time. He's gonna give y'all some when we kill 'em."

"Yore daddy's a right good man. Doc, he's right good, too. Ast too many questions, though. Never took to nosy folks. How's yore daddy's chickens coming on? I shore miss my chickens."

Alice fidgeted with her overalls. I could see she was nervous.

"Chickens coming along good. How you doing, Alice?" I smiled at her.

"I doin good," she blurted out, but she didn't look up.

"You wanna see me 'bout anythin' special, Ellie?" Mrs. Guthrie asked. "I can't stay out here all day. Ormond'll pitch a hissy."

"Yessum, we, that is, Alice, she wants to ask you something real important. She wanted me here when she asked."

Mrs. Guthrie eyed Alice with the side of her eyes.

"Huh! What you astin, girl? You know somepin em-portent, huh?" She put the edge of the spit jar under her lip and spit a loud glob of brown spit.

"Well? You gonna ast or not? I got better ta do."

"Ask her," I said, stepping up close to Alice. "Go on. Ask her."

Alice raised her chin. She stared at the wall.

"Ma-ma, I wan go liva Ellie. Can I go liva Ellie?"

"Oh, good grannies!" Mrs. Guthrie said, disgusted. "What's wrong with y'all. Ya know yore daddy done ast me that, Ellie. Ain't no sense in gittin inta hit no more. Now Alice, you jist hush up over hit, ya hear?"

"It's *real* important," I said quick. "Daddy wants to git Alice a tutor to . . ."

"What's that thang?"

"Well, it's a special teacher. We . . ."

"She ain't a-goin ta no school. She'd be the laughin stock. Now that's that!"

"No, ma'am. We wouldn't take her to school. We'd take her to the teacher's house."

"I never heared sech foolishness." She turned to face Alice. "This here gal ain't right. Ain't never gonna be right." She pointed her finger at Alice. "Now you quit gittin them fainsy idees, ya hear?"

Alice looked at me. I said "beg" with my lips.

"Ma-ma, please," Alice whined. "Please let me liva Ellie. We come ever day see you. We come. Please, Ma-ma." Alice was beggin real good.

"Huh! You git down there an you'd fergit y'ever had a mama, after all I went through!"

"We could ride Poke up ever evening after supper if ya want us to," I said. "Honest we could."

"I wanna learnin, Ma-ma. I wanna learnin. Be like Ellie. Please."

"Yore daddy ever found out you was gone, he'd kill us all. How you think we gonna keep him from a-knowing, huh? Them younguns'll blurt it out first chainct."

"But, Mrs. Guthrie, she comes down ever day anyhow.

They ain't never told, has they?" I said. "How did you git 'em to keep they mouth shut so far? You've done a real good job."

"I tole 'em if they tole I'd break a piece of stovewood over they bottoms. *That's* why they ain't tole."

Alice put her hand on her mama's shoulder.

"You hatea me, Ma-ma?" She was serious. I looked at Mrs. Guthrie's face change.

"Now don't go gettin plumb silly!"

"You lovea me, you let me git out this shed, huh?"

Mrs. Guthrie stood up fast.

"Huh! I know what y'all doin. Y'all gotta big plan ta git me changin my mind, ain't ya? Well, I done tole ya, Alice ain't goin nowheres and I ain't a-talkin no more on hit!" She stomped out the door. I waited till she was gone. Then I jumped at Alice and give her a hug.

"She's gonna do it!" I said. "Now you don't worry. You done good! I can tell she's gonna do it. All we gotta do is work on our plan! My goodness, for somebody ain't never had no practice, you nearly good as me at begging."

I told Aunt Bessie all about it later when she was setting on our porch.

"Funny the way things happen," she said. "I believe Alice is changing things."

"Whatcha mean?" I asked.

"I was just a-thinking 'bout yore daddy. How long it's been since he was drunk. It's been a long time. Let's see here. October," she helt up her fingers to count, "November, December, January, February, March, April, May, and here it is June. That's seven months. Ain't that a blessing! I told ya to keep believing. It'll work ever time."

She started the rocker moving back and forth slow. She leaned her head back and closed her eyes.

"Seems to me like I can 'member you telling me you

prayed for Alice and for yore daddy and for a lot of things that's happened."

"Yeah, but Alice ain't out of that shed and . . ."

"Just hold on a minute here," she stopped the rocker and looked at me. "You think Alice stopped yore daddy's drinking?"

"Well, I don't know. Maybe," I said.

"Who you reckon sent you up that mountain to find her, huh? The Lord works through people, Ellie. The Lord sent you up there."

"Yeah, well . . ."

"'Course he did. He gits a big plan going and we can't see nothing but little plans. One thing I've noticed about the Lord's doings is he thinks a heck of a lot bigger'n us. He used you to git Alice, but look how many things is changed on account of one little girl. Think on it."

I set thinking a while. I got out of the willow chair and set in the other rocker and rocked. Finally I told her I seen what she meant.

"You believing Alice is gonna git outa that shed?" she asked.

"Yessum."

"Then we might as well git Sammy's room ready, 'cause if you truly believing, then she'll be sleeping in Sammy's bed."

She started rocking again. "You ain't praying like ya use to, is ya, Ellie?"

"No'm. Not as much."

"God don't need no begging like us mamas and daddies. He knows what folks need 'fore they ask. All he tells us is to ask and then believe. We don't have to keep whining and begging. Took me a long time to understand that."

We rocked awhile, then I said, "You know something? A long time ago I 'membered about a verse that said something like "and a child shall lead them." Sometimes when I think of Alice and think of that verse, I git goose bumps. Know what I mean?"

"You a good girl," she said, smiling. "You my girl and now you gittin me another'n. *Two* girls! Ain't the Lord good!"

Chapter 41

*T*he next day at school Lisa Mae said she'd heard Sammy was coming home for a week. She wanted to know if Bertha was gonna date him.

"I'll just bet he'll be changed so much we won't even know him. Why, I'll bet he's got high-fa-lootin and he won't even speak to me. You think he'll speak? You think he'll date Bertha, or you reckon he's found somebody new so's her heart will break? Maybe he's got too high-fa-lootin for her. *That'd* sure be good news anyhow."

"He ain't wrote to her much," I said.

"Where's yore sack? Ain't you eating?"

"I forgot it. Left it on the table."

She helt out a biscuit with a piece of fatback in it.

"You want this or the one with jelly? I got a apple."

"Which one you want?"

"Let's break 'em and we'll both have each."

"All right."

"Bertha's half heartbroke already," she said. "She told Elaine that she cried ever night for three nights in a row after she quit hearing from him. She's claiming John and Richard and some days, she claims Mark to git even, even though Mark's too young. You still claiming Mark?"

"You know I ain't. I ain't had time to claim nobody."

"David looked at me twicet day before yesterday."

"He *did*?"

"Uh huh. And yesterday I walked up close to him and said hey, David, how're you doing, and he said real good, how're you, and I said oh, real good, too, and he said we'll see ya."

"Did he smile or anything?"

"Uh huh."

"Gosh."

"Mama bought me some Tangee. I tell ya? It's called rose pink. I had it on when he smiled."

"You got it on now? I can't tell."

"I guess I eat it off. I'll show you when we're done."

"Can I wear some?"

"Uh huh."

"Did David look at your lips real hard?"

"I think so."

"Gosh."

"Mama says when Daddy gits the money for that other cabin for sure, she'll buy me a bathing suit."

"You're teasing me! A bathing suit?"

"Uh huh. I seen it in the catalog. It's blue and white. Reee–al clingy. They's a drape that goes in front, over the stomach."

"David will pop his eyes out," I said. "How's the top made?"

She picked a pork rind out of her teeth.

"It's—" she looked around to see if anybody was close. Nobody was. "It's sorta gathered. You know, to make me look bigger." Then she whispered, "I could put cotton in and nobody won't never know."

"Well, I wouldn't git it wet then. Cotton gits all lumpy wet. And sides that, all the rest would dry before the cotton and you'd have wet bosoms!" I giggled.

"Oh, I won't git it wet. We'll plan some picnics down at the mill so's I can wear it."

"But nobody won't have a bathing suit but you. How's everybody gonna feel, you having a bathing suit? All the girls will hate yore guts."

"Uh huh, but think of the boys!"

I finished the biscuit half.

"I wouldn't wear it if I was you," I said. "I mean, that's like showing off. Don't nobody like a show-off, and they might think you are a harlot."

"A bathing suit don't make a harlot!"

"You finally know what a harlot is?"

"'Course I know."

"What is one?"

"It's a girl," she looked around again, "who does it," she whispered.

"I think Bertha is one." I leaned close to her ear to say it. She gasped.

I think when things start happening it's like rolling a snowball down a hill. It gits bigger and bigger. Seems like it goes in streaks. Like bad stuff brings on a bad streak and good stuff brings on a good streak. Least ways that's what I told Daddy when I got home from school.

"Me and Aunt Bessie was talking about it," I said. "We think Alice has done started a good streak, don't you?"

I was watching him split a oak log for stove wood. He had a piece about a foot and a half long up on the chopping block. I was setting on another piece I'd stood on end to make a stool.

Whack! He hit it and it fell in two fat pieces. Then he picked up one of the pieces and whacked it.

"Alice couldn't start nothing *but* a good streak," he said, wiping some sweat off his forehead with his arm. "Somebody sweet and good as that youngun couldn't start no bad streak."

"It'll be so much fun having her live with us. I know Mrs. Guthrie's gonna let her. It'll be like having a sister. I can't believe it, can you? Don't you think she's talking better ever day? I know she still forgets a lot, but if she lives here and is talking more, she'll catch on faster, don't you think? Aunt Bessie said that it was on account of Alice you give up the liquor. I think Alice started a whole streak of good stuff."

He laid the ax down and set on the block wiping more sweat off his face and neck.

"Did you quit drinking on account of Alice?"

He set a minute, then he started stacking the wood in a neat stack.

"I was ready to quit, Ellie," he said. "Alice or nobody else couldn't of made me quit 'less I was ready. I think I finally done what you said. I turned myself over to the Lord. Told him I give up. Liquor put us on a bad streak for a lotta years. All I'm prayin for, is I can make up for some of the hell I put y'all through."

I looked down at my bare feet and wiggled my toes. Under was sleeping next to my feet. One of our laying hens was pecking for a worm in the sawdust beside the chopping block. I glanced at the woodpile behind Daddy. I knowed a family of black snakes lived in the woodpile. Racers.

"I—well, everbody is proud of you," I said.

He picked up a piece of pine. He got out his pocketknife and started whittling on it.

"Use to make you little dolls outa pine. You 'member?"

"I 'member. I got a mama and a daddy and a little girl. They in the trunk in the front room."

"You still got 'em?" He was surprised.

"You know I have. They been there for years."

"Been a long time since I noticed much, I reckon," he said.

"It's all right. You gonna catch up."

"Can't ever catch up, honey. Won't never. I missed a lot of good years. Can't catch 'em up. Makes a man wonder—wonder how he could of been so stupid. So crazy. Makes a man wonder." He glanced behind him to the woodpile. "We got snakes in there this year? I heard something."

"Uh huh. Racers." He squinted his eyes and peered into the woodpile a few seconds. Then he asked, "You still got them rag dolls yore mama made you?"

"Uh huh. Well, I got two of 'em. Aunt Bessie's goat eat one. 'Member?"

He grinned. "Yeah, I do. I thought you was gonna kill that goat. Chased it with a hoe and the hoe was bigger'n you was. You was just a little 'un." He stood up and got another log off the woodpile.

"I wish we could of got Alice when she was little so's she could of had dolls, had stuff," I said.

"Damn shame," he said, standing the log on the block. "She lost a lot of years can't be caught up, neither." Whack! He split the log. "You gonna git her today?"

"I went up. She don't feel good. Had a fit this morning. I'm believing her mama will let her live with us. I'm believing hard as I can believe. You believing?"

Whack!

"I'm believing," he said.

"Won't Sammy be surprised? I can't wait to see his face when he sees Alice and how she's changed and all."

"He'll be changed a little, too."

"You reckon he's claiming some stuck-up girl at that school? Lisa Mae says Bertha's heart is broke 'cause he hadn't wrote to her. You think he's gonna marry one of them?"

Daddy laughed. "You girls!" he said. "All you think about is gitting these boys hitched up. You read Sammy's letters. He ain't mentioned no special gal. How come you don't like Bertha? She's a purty girl. Seems nice enough."

"She's a real harlot! Ah—ah—" I could of kicked myself!

Whack! He left the ax sticking out of the chopping block. He turned to me, wrinkling up his forehead.

"A harlot?" he said.

"I—I mean a snob. That's what she is, a snob." I wouldn't look at him.

"A snob is a little different than a harlot. You been going around calling that girl a harlot?"

I scrunched my toes into the sand.

"I was just teasing, Daddy. Honest."

"Answer my question. You been saying that word to anybody?"

"Only to Lisa Mae. She knows I'm just a-teasing."

"You know what that word means?" His voice had dropped to deep and scary.

"Uh huh. Aunt Bessie told me."

"I don't like you talking like that. You don't go teasing about stuff like that. You could do that girl harm. Bad harm."

"I—I won't say it no more."

"If you was little, I'd turn you over my knee. Been a long time since ya was spanked, ain't it? If you was little, I'd tear yore bottom up. I don't like you telling lies about something. Ellie, what you said is a lie." He was standing over me now, looking down at me. "Tomorrow I want ya to tell Lisa Mae you lied. You hear me?"

"Yessir."

I stared at his big brown work shoes. He stood there a long time. He didn't say nothing else.

Chapter 42

"I've made up my mind," Aunt Bessie said. "I ain't entering the buggy contest on Founder's Day this year. It's silly anyhow. What I'm gonna do is fix up yore and Sammy's rooms. Fix up Sammy's for Alice. Make lacy spreads and curtains. Will said he'd build Alice a dressing table. I'll put a lacy skirt on it. I ain't got a extra mirror. That won't cost much. Whatcha think of lavender for her room and green for yores? You like green? You look good in green with yore eyes and hair. And listen to this. I'm making Alice a lavender dress. Already crocheted the collar. Comes all the way to the belt. Won't she be a sight for sore eyes though? Told Will I was taking her and buying her a pair of white shoes. Bet she ain't never had a new pair of shoes. Won't she be a sight? She still begging her mama?"

"Alice has asked her mama *ever* day," I said. "She's begging and I told her to cry. I told her girls is 'spose to cry a lot. I told her to bawl loud and whine some, but I couldn't explain what whine meant."

Aunt Bessie laughed. She set down at the table. I set down, too. She reached in the old flour sack she carries her sewing in and pulled out the lavender dress. I sucked in my breath, it was so purty. "I'm gonna make you a green one. Kind of a blue green. Kind of a aqua, you know. Soon as I find some cloth. Ain't gonna make it like this'un. You and Alice is different as night and day. Can't dress you alike. You like this collar?"

"Oh, it's beautiful!" I said. "Alice will just faint!"

"Now, way I figger it, we got nine days 'fore Sammy gits here. This dress is nearly done. Gotta find some pearly buttons. I'll git yores finished in plenty of time. I'll take Alice into Bolton on Saturday for her shoes. You two girls is gonna knock Sammy boy's eyes out! What's the matter with you? You look like you done swallowed a hot pepper."

"Oh, Aunt Bessie. What if Mrs. Guthrie keeps saying no? What if she don't let her live with us?"

"I thought you was believing." She draped the dress over a chair. "Hush up that doubting now. One way or another Alice will be living here. Ain't a fleck of doubt in my mind. Now ride on up there and git her so's she can try this dress on."

When I got there, Alice's eyes was red from the crying and Mrs. Guthrie was in the shed.

"My goodness," I said, trying to look upset. "What's wrong with Alice?"

"This youngun's driving me slap crazy!" Mrs. Guthrie said. "She ain't never carried on so. She ain't got no re-spek fer nothing I says. What y'all learning her anyhow?"

"Just her letters and numbers. She's learning them real good. She can subtract doubles now. She's catching on."

"She ain't cried in years. Quit her crying. Now all she does is cry to live with y'all. I say no and no it is. Take her on down there fer a little while. I gotta git in 'fore Ormand busts his brain hollering. One of these days he'll have a dern stroke iffen he don't quit. Y'all gonna give her supper?"

I looked at Alice. She give me a teeny smile.

"Yes'm," I said. "We got poke sallet and cornbread."

"Y'all boil it 'fore ya fry it?"

"Uh huh."

"Fry it on down?"

"Uh huh."

"The best way. Some folks keep 'er too soggy. Like mine slicky. You brang me a bite or two. I ain't had none this spring."

"I'll bring you some. I'll bring you a mess to cook, too, if you want me to. We got a big bunch out 'hind our hog pen. You got plenty fatback?"

"Uh huh."

"I'll bring a big mess."

"Well, that's right nice of ye. I'd be beholden, and iffen ya don't mind, tell yore daddy I'm nearly outa snuff."

"Bruton, ain't it?"

"That's my kind."

"Well, looka here," Aunt Bessie said. "Here's the girls. Hey, Alice." She give us a hug. Daddy did, too. We all set down.

"Now tell us what happened," Aunt Bessie said. "Git a knife and help me peel these 'taters, Ellie. Did you cry good, Alice? What did yore mama say? Tell us ever word."

"I do it," she whispered and giggled.

"Talk louder, honey. These old ears ain't what they use to be."

"I cry."

"Hey! You *done* it! You cry loud? Real loud? What'd yore mama say?"

"She say shut up. She say I not liva Ellie."

"How many times she say it?"

"Lotsa time."

"Then what'd she say?"

"She say I driva her crazy. She say how you liva Ellie— you driva Ellie crazy, too."

"Well praise the Lord! Then what'd she say?"

"She say schoolin not cracked up to be. She say schoolin giva—giva—"

"Give what?"

"Hit giva bad thinkin."

"Uh huh."

"She say I git snickety."

"Per-snickety?"

"Mmmm. She say if I liva Ellie, I git per-sinickety of a snot."

"You mean snotty? You mean like stuck-up?"

"I not know."

"I *don't* know."

"I don't know. She say I fergit who Ma-ma."

Aunt Bessie slapped the table. "Bless Jesus! She's bending! She's almost there, honey. You keep at it and it won't be no time. Now what's our next move, Jack?"

"I think our next move is for Alice to keep her mama from thinking she's losing a chile. The pore woman's scared." He looked at Alice. "Honey, what you gotta do besides all that crying and begging is keep on a-telling yore mama that you'll be seeing her nearly as much as ya always do. And—it won't hurt to tell her ya love her. You ever told her that?"

"Nooo."

"She ever told you that?"

"Nooo."

"Then it's about time. Pour me some coffee, Ellie. We gonna practice."

"She wants a mess of poke sallet," I said. "I told her I'd bring her some. She needs some snuff."

"I'll take care of all that. Now Alice, I want you to practice saying 'I love you, Mama.' Think you can do it? You can practice on Bessie."

She bit her lip.

Daddy looked at Aunt Bessie. Aunt Bessie scooted her chair closer to Alice.

"We'll play like I'm yore mama," Aunt Bessie said. "Now I'll say it first. Look at me, honey." Alice looked.

"You ready?"

"Mmmm."

"Now, I'll say it first. Then you say it. I love you, Alice."

Alice covered her face with her hands. We all looked at each other. Then Aunt Bessie said it again.

"I love you, Alice."

For a long, long time you couldn't hear nothing but Under breathing. Aunt Bessie said it again.

"I love you, Alice."

Then she took Alice's wrists and pulled her hands off her face. "Say it, honey. You can say it."

"I—I lova you," she whispered, then she giggled.

Chapter 43

Well, wouldn't you know it couldn't last. All the good stuff had to be messed up with some bad. Mr. Guthrie had took a cold and his chest had got all clogged up. Mrs. Guthrie didn't hardly even git out to the shed, let alone long enough for Alice to pester her. Doc Murphy sent up some medicine. He said Guthrie was too mean to die. Prob'ly outlive all of us. Then Alice didn't go to Bolton with Aunt Bessie to git shoes on account of she panicked and run off at the last minute. Then Under got in a fight with a wild dog and got nearly killed and Doc had to keep him at his house. Then here it was three days before Sammy was to come home and school was out finally and it'd started raining and had rained till we was nearly flooded. I told Aunt Bessie if one more thing happened, I was going to bed and never git up.

But she rode up in the rain to help clean and cook for Sammy's visit. We had sheets hanging all over the house to dry and you had to duck down or around to walk in ever room. We hadn't seen Alice in three days on account of the weather. Bessie said she'd bring mine and Alice's new dress the next day.

"We might have to iron these sheets dry," Aunt Bessie said as she stretched another line and handed it to me. I was standing on a chair. I tied it to the nail I'd nailed into the windowsill. "At least it's nice and cool. One thing I hate is housecleaning in hot weather. What time is McClung driving up to git Sammy?"

"Said they oughta be back 'fore dark on Thursday," I said, and jumped off the chair.

"Let's pray this rain stops. Wish we could git Alice. Hate for her to be stuck in that shed in this weather. She scared of storms?"

"Nah."

"If it'd just slack some, you could take the buggy up. Doc say how Under is?"

"He's lots better. Daddy's gitting him today."

"You wanna take the buggy up? I didn't git wet coming. The sides is down. I could even drive ya up, come to think of it. How's the road on up thataway?"

"Same as down yore way, I reckon. Ya wanna do it?"

"Whatcha think?"

"I know she'd like to come, but what if it gits worse and we can't git her back? Her mama'd pitch a fit."

"Yeah. Well, that's right. We can't make that woman mad now we got this far."

Daddy come busting through the back door and run right into a sheet and it fell and covered him up.

"What the . . . ?"

Me and Aunt Bessie laughed and got him untangled.

"What's going on here?" He plopped into a chair, breathing hard.

"Can't dry 'em outside," Aunt Bessie said.

"You bring Under?" I asked.

"He's in the barn."

"Doc say how long it'll be 'fore he can run loose?"

"Said he didn't know. Guessed a week or two." He stood and took off his coat. "What y'all fixin for supper?"

"Ain't thought about it. Been too busy," Aunt Bessie said.

"I'm so hungry I could eat a bear."

"Yore appetite keeps on and you'll be fat as me."

Daddy reached inside his overall bib and pulled out a sack and set it on the table. The shape of it made me stare.

"What's that?" I asked.

"Liquor," he said, grinning.

Aunt Bessie dropped the dipper into the bucket. My heart sunk to my stomach.

"Doc sent it for me to take to Mrs. Guthrie. He rode up there yesterday and she begged him to git it. Says the old man is driving her nuts. Now the cold is better and he's hollering for liquor."

Aunt Bessie pulled out a chair and set down. A sheet blocked her view of Daddy, so she lifted it with her arm.

"Don't that beat all!" she said. "Looks to me like if liquor makes him meaner, she'd not want him to have it. I don't git it, do you?"

"She says he's mean with it and without it. Guess she wants to knock him out. Got any coffee made? To heck with Guthrie having his liquor. I got to rest awhile."

"Quit staring at that sack like it's got a snake in it, Ellie," Aunt Bessie said. "Doc trusted yore daddy with a jug of liquor. Now that's somethin'!"

"I thought so myself," Daddy said, smiling.

I got the coffee out of the cupboard. I felt real uneasy. It hit me I still didn't trust Daddy. The picture of Founder's Day was in my mind and of the next morning when Daddy was passed out in that wagon. I dipped water into the coffeepot. I thought of knocking the jug off the table. I thought of grabbing it and running out into the rain and pouring it out.

"Hadn't had the least temptation to open that sack,"

Daddy said. "You look silly holding that sheet up, Bess. Can't you hang it somewheres else?"

Thank goodness the rain quit that night. The next morning the sun rose over the mountains and made the world look fresh and new. I went up early to git Alice and Aunt Bessie said she'd be up about ten. We was gonna bake two cakes. While I was waiting for Alice to wash up, Mrs. Guthrie come out to the shed with Alice's breakfast, two biscuits with soggum and a cup of milk.

"Hey, Ellie," she said.

"Hey."

"What you up so early fer? Y'all gittin everthang fainsy fer Sammy?"

"We trying to. He'll be home tomorrow night, maybe 'fore dark."

She set the dishpan (she was using the dishpan for a tray) down on the wood box beside the washpan. Alice took a biscuit.

"Alice, you he'p 'em now. Don't you be gittin in tha way."

"Yes'm."

"Mrs. Guthrie?"

"Huh?"

"Did—ah—did Daddy bring you the liquor?"

"Shore did. Ormond got drunk as a skunk. Passed right out. Best rest I had in a month of Sundays."

"Ma-ma?"

"Huh."

"Sam-my, he not stay but week. He go back schoolin. Ellie say Aunt Bessie, she say she fixa me room nice. I want git outa shed. Please, Ma-ma."

Mrs. Guthrie plopped down on Alice's cot.

"Lord of mercy! Git one fool quieted down and another'n

starts up. What's a body ta do? I tole ya I didn't wanna hear no more foolishness. Now hush up 'fore I pore liquor down *yore* throat."

"Aunt Bessie say fixa room lace nice. Lace ona bed. Pleeeease, Ma-ma."

"Lace on tha bed? Godamighty, Ellie, that aunt of yor'n is a glutton fer punishment, doin up a bunch o' lace. Puttin lace on a bed. Ain't she got nothin better ta do?"

I set down beside Mrs. Guthrie on the cot.

"Aunt Bessie's got it all planned. She thinks Alice would like lavender. I just love lavender, don't you?"

She squinted her eyes and looked in my face.

"Lavender? It's right purty. Had a lavender dress when I was a youngun. Musta had four or five yards in it. Purty dress. My mama made it fer me. Dyed the cloth herself. Thank she used blueberries and ferget what else. My mama could do anythin."

"You must of loved her a lot."

"Uh huh."

"Alice loves you a lot, you know."

"Uh." She took her eyes off my face and looked down at her hands that was in her lap. She picked a tiny scab off a sore. I looked at Alice. She covered her face with her hands.

"Alice gets timid about it like I do, but she told me she loves you a lot. Didn't you, Alice?"

Alice shuffled her feet.

"Well," I said, standing. "We gonna have to git going. We gonna bake Sammy two cakes. You like coconut? I'll bring ya some."

Alice scrubbed the floor in Sammy's room while I scrubbed the front room. Aunt Bessie started the cakes. Daddy come in about one. He went on out to the garden. By six the house was shining and smelling like cake and pine soap. Me and Alice went out to sweep the yard. Daddy and Aunt

Bessie set in the rockers and watched. Alice was a nervous wreck. More'n me. She hadn't hardly said nothing all day, but worked like a beaver. After we finished the yard, we rode Poke down into the valley to pick bunches of wild-flowers. Honeysuckle and blue phlox and orange chigger weed. In the woods we picked arms full of pink wild azaleas as it was gitting dark.

By the time I finally set down on the porch, I was tired out. Aunt Bessie went in and made a pone of cornbread and brung it and glasses and spoons and a pitcher of buttermilk and a plate of spring onions out to the porch. We crumbled the bread into the milk for our supper. Then Aunt Bessie went on home to fix something for Uncle Will and Morgan. Daddy took Alice home. She carried her purty dress.

Chapter 44

Daddy rode with Mr. McClung to git Sammy. They said they'd be back by five or six. Doc couldn't come up on account of somebody was sick. Me and Uncle Will and Aunt Bessie waited on the front porch. The kitchen was piled up with food. I had gone to git Alice about two, but she was setting on that cot in her daddy's old overalls staring at the dress, and she wouldn't come. I never been so shocked. And not only that, she wouldn't say why. All she'd say was I not go, I not go. I set with her, begging her at least half a hour. Finally I give up. We was all real disappointed.

Never in yore life have you seen such hugging and talking and carrying on as we did till after one in the morning. Daddy was right. Sammy had changed. Seemed like he'd growed a foot. He was filled out and his hair was combed back and not hanging down. They was something else different, too. He talked more. He couldn't quit his excited talking. All about the school, the teachers, his studies. He had asked about Alice first thing and looked real funny when I told her she wouldn't come down.

Next morning we rode up to git her but she wadn't there, and Mrs. Guthrie didn't come out to tell us nothing. The little boys was playing in the barn. They said she walked thataway, pointing toward Yager. We went everwhere but we couldn't find her. We was both worried sick.

"Why don't she want to see me, Ellie? You *must* know why," Sammy said, when we had headed down to Yager.

"I don't know. Honest I don't. She's been as excited as me about you coming home. I just don't understand it atall."

"You gotta know something. Has she been sick? You think she's scared to see me?"

"She may be. That could be it. Since she's learned so much about things, she's different."

"Whatcha mean?"

"I don't know how to explain it. It's feelings. Feelings scare her, I think. She's learned so much. She's—well, she's just different."

"You think she's upset 'cause I didn't write her enough?"

"I don't know."

"I'm thinking you *do* know, Ellie." We both slid off Poke so's Sammy could lead him over some rocks. "You know her better'n anybody. I know she likes me. I don't see how come she run off."

"Maybe she's scared of liking you." I set down on a rock. Sammy set down on one, too. "Maybe she's scared of liking you like you're scared of liking her."

He jerked a leaf off a scrub bush and set looking at it, flicking it with his finger. He throwed the leaf down and stood up.

"Let's rest a minute," I said.

"Better not waste no time. We gotta find her." We got back on Poke. We looked all over the valley, then we went to Cherrylog. We rode to the clearing. She was nowhere. He kept after me to explain how she was different, but I really couldn't. We was quiet a while, then he said, "Maybe now that she understands things more, maybe she understands what I tried to do to her."

"She might, but she ain't never mentioned it, Sammy."

"I can't stand to think of it."

"I know. Let's talk about something else."

In a while he said, "Lotta things are different. Aunt Bessie says Daddy ain't had a drink in over seven months. I can't hardly believe it. And he's already paid Doc off."

"That's right."

"He's changed a lot."

"He ain't changed. We just got our daddy back, that's all. He's the same daddy."

"The place looks good."

"Yeah, it does."

"I reckon I've changed, too, huh?"

"Yeah, you have."

"Got me a good chance. Reading everthing I can git on reporting. On journalism. One of these days you gonna have a reporter for a brother."

"They teach it there? I didn't know that."

"No, not journalism, but Mr. Graves gets me books."

"Oh."

"You sure acting funny." He turned to look in my face. "You all right?"

"I'm just scared about Alice."

He dug his heels in Poke's ribs.

We give up about five. Sammy figgered she was hiding. After supper I rode up to the shed and she was there, curled up in them quilts sleeping. It was so hard to think of what to do. Should I wake her up or leave her alone? Aunt Bessie had said how important it was for us to let her make up her own mind about stuff. I wanted to git her up and make her come with me. I didn't. I stood looking at her a little bit, then I left.

"Dadgummit, Ellie," Daddy said from his rocker. "You know what's the matter with her. She must of give you a hint or something. This just ain't like Alice atall."

I had got back and set on the steps. Sammy was in the other rocker holding Under. A nice breeze was ruffling the leaves on the oaks. Half a moon was hanging in the starry sky and puffs of racing white clouds covered it from time to time, making long tree shadows in the swept yard.

"I think it's got to be me, Pa," Sammy said. "I think she don't want to see me. She's scared to see me."

"That can't be," Daddy said. "She's been too excited about ya coming."

"I think Sammy's right," I said. "I think she's got scared and timid."

"Is they anything *I* can do?" Daddy asked.

"I think we ought to think about it a while," I said. "I think—well—maybe she's gonna have to do what she has to do."

They didn't say nothing. Under whined a little and Sammy talked to him. We set staring into the valley. After a while I went and got us all some ice tea and cake. Then Sammy laid Under on the floor and went to the toilet. When he come back, he set with me on the steps.

"It's up to me, I reckon," he said. "I don't see as how it's up to anybody else."

"You can't go up there," I said.

"No, you better not, son," Daddy said. "I guess we better listen to Ellie. Let's just give her time. She'll be all right."

We talked about the garden. Then the chickens. Sammy told us about working in the dairy at school. Sammy couldn't set still. He stood and walked and then he'd set in the rocker. Finally he said, "Pa?"

"Yeah?"

"I like Alice a lot."

"We know."

"I didn't want to. I mean, like she is and all. I mean, she's—she ain't like . . ."

"She's like Alice," I said, gitting upset. "That's who she's like. She ain't like Bertha or all them and I'm thankful for it!"

"Ah, now, Ellie. I didn't mean . . ."

"I know what you mean. I know everthing you mean. You want one of them who's—who's like everbody else. Who ain't different. You want to git to be a big reporter and marry one of them. I know what ya mean, all right!"

"Now, Ellie," Daddy said in a warning voice.

"Well, it's the pure truth, ain't it? But you know yoreself that Alice is smart as anybody. You and Aunt Bessie and Doc all says it. You know she ain't all that different! She's learning quick. Catching on."

Sammy stood, then went past me down the steps. He walked to the edge of the road.

"Let him alone, Ellie," Daddy said. "It ain't easy on him."

I wanted to fuss at Sammy but I didn't. I shut up. Late that night Sammy walked and paced and drunk coffee. Daddy didn't git out of bed nor I didn't neither.

The next morning Alice was gone again. Mrs. Guthrie seen me come up and she come out. "She's acting plumb teched again," she said. "She was gitting better, lak a girl oughta be. Now she's actin teched again. Iffen the moon was full, I'd say it was that, but it ain't full. She won't talk ta me atall. She won't eat nothing. She ain't had no fits as I know of. You reckon the devil's after 'er?"

"Let's go set down a minute, Mrs. Guthrie," I said. We

went on in the shed and set on the cot. I said a quick prayer in my mind for God to help me. We set a few seconds, then I started off.

"Alice wants to be like a real girl real bad. She wants to be like you was when you was young. She wants to be like I am. She ain't teched by the devil no more'n nobody else, Mrs. Guthrie. She ain't never been like you thinking. Aunt Bessie says that *all* bad things is the devil's work. Ever single bad thing. *All* sickness is the devil's work, not just Alice's sickness. God loves us all the same. He loves Alice same as you. He wants Alice to git to be normal. You're her mama. You love her like God does. Don't you want her to be a normal girl? Don't you want her to be?"

Mrs. Guthrie turned her head and stared at the wall.

"She *was* gittin better," she said. "I could see she was gittin lots better."

"Yessum, she was. She is, and it won't take long till she'd be reg'lar as anybody. Reg'lar as you. You do want her reg'lar as you, don't ya?"

"Looks ta me like iffen He'd of wanted her reg'lar, He'd of made her reg'lar."

I sighed. I wished I had of studied the Bible like Aunt Bessie always said I should.

"You didn't understand," I said. "God *didn't* make her like she is. Honest he didn't. It's up to us to help her. God, he works through people. It's up to us. The fact is, Mrs. Guthrie, it's up to you."

"Me?"

"Yessum, you. Put yoreself in her place and put her in yore place. Wouldn't you want yore mama to give you a chance to be like everbody else?"

She stared at the dishpan. Her eyes got wet. I stood up. I patted her shoulder.

"Tell Alice I come," I said.

Chapter 45

The next day Daddy and Sammy went to Bolton to git Sammy some pants and shoes. I started to go up to Alice's, but I didn't. I argued back and forth with myself, then finally decided not to go. Aunt Bessie come up, then when Sammy and Daddy got home, Mr. and Mrs. Mc-Clung and Lisa Mae come by and set a few minutes. I couldn't git Alice off my mind. Aunt Bessie said I was doing the right thing. She said Alice was growing up, was gonna have to learn to face real problems, too—the way everybody else had to do.

That night after we was all in the bed I heard a knocking on the back door. Daddy heard it, too, and put on his overalls, yelling "Just a minute." The only time in my life we ever had somebody knock on our door after bedtime was one time when Mr. Hudson's wagon had got stuck in a gully down the road. I got up and looked.

Daddy toted the lamp high and opened the door and I couldn't believe what I seen. There stood Mrs. Guthrie with a big croaker sack in her arms.

"Mrs. Guthrie!" Daddy said. "Why, what's the matter? Is something the matter, ma'am?"

"Ain't nothing the matter," she said, setting the croaker sack on the porch floor.

"Here, come on in." He opened the screen. "Come on in and set down. Did you walk?"

"I ain't comin in, Mr. Perkins. I gotta git on back."

"It must be after midnight," Daddy said. "What you doing out such a time?"

"Couldn't sleep. I been thanking. My girl, she was acting good, doing good. Now she's acting funny. Won't eat. Won't say nothing. I—well, I brung her stuff here in this sack. I brung what stuff she's got. Y'all still want 'er?"

"We? You mean, do we . . ."

"Mrs. Guthrie!" I squealed and run to her. I throwed my arms around her so hard we both nearly fell. "Oh, Mrs. Guthrie, I just knowed you'd do it!"

She wiggled away from me. She wouldn't look in my face. She pointed to the sack on the floor.

"Her stuff's in thar." She moved toward the steps. Daddy run out on the porch.

"I don't know what to say," Daddy said. "We gonna git her a teacher—we . . ."

She went down the steps holding to the porch post. I flew past her in my gown to go git Poke.

"I'll take you back," I yelled.

Daddy helped her up on Poke's back. I looked and seen Sammy standing at the kitchen door, staring. She hadn't said another word. She wouldn't talk on the way to her house neither. All she said was, "Come get Alice tomorrow. Come early."

I can remember Christmases when Mama was alive. Mornings when I'd wake up so happy, so excited, so sure that the whole world was full to running over with more joy than folks could hold, that I'd bust from my bed to throw myself on a sleeping Sammy, to shake him and pound him and scream, "It's Christmas!" Then I'd run to Mama and Daddy's bed and do the same.

That night I didn't hardly sleep atall. I laid there planning and dreaming. I planned how I'd take Alice to the store. To church. To picnics, and how I'd show her off as my sister. Then I tried and tried to git to sleep but I couldn't. So I got up and got my tablet and pencil and started writing the first part of this story. I wrote till past three o'clock. Finally I slept.

And the next morning I tore into Sammy's room like in the old days. I jumped on him and squealed and pounded him and yelled.

"I got me a sister! I got me a sister! Git up! Git up, Sammy Perkins! Today's the day! Can you believe it? After all this time. After all this worrying. Today's the day me and you is been dreaming about for nearly two years. Today is the day we gonna get Alice outa that shed!"

She was gone again. We got there before seven o'clock but she was done gone. Mrs. Guthrie seen us and come out to tell us we'd have to come back. She told us Alice would come home a little after dark and for us to come back then. I had brought the croaker sack Mrs. Guthrie had left us with Alice's stuff in it. I had planned for Sammy to wait outside while she got washed up and put on the new dress. I had brought my black shoes. I had planned to comb her hair and to put a ribbon in it. I had planned to knock Sammy's eyes out, but she was gone.

Sammy moped around all day. Daddy had to go with Mr. McClung to lay foundation for the new cabin they was building. Aunt Bessie come up and we set on the porch and talked. It was the longest day God ever made. I thought night would never come.

The log was in the latch across the door. It hadn't been on the door since Mr. Guthrie got crippled. Sammy lifted it out easy and laid it on the ground. We tiptoed into the shed. The moon throwed light in through the open door. Alice was curled on top of the quilts. She was wearing the over-alls. I seen the hearing aid on the wood box. I touched her shoulder.

She turned and looked at me, then at Sammy. She raised up and set on the side of the cot. Her eyes was blank.

"Alice. Oh, Alice. I can't hardly believe it, can you?" I said hugging her. "You gonna live with us!"

Her eyes was still blank. Then I remembered she didn't have her hearing aid on. I grabbed it and handed it to her. She didn't put it on her ear. She put it on the cot beside her.

I started to scream to her, but thought of Mr. Guthrie. I looked at Sammy for help. He took Alice's arm and pulled her up off the cot. I grabbed her hearing aid. She let him lead her into the woods. Then I hugged her again. Sammy hugged her. She stood stiff.

"PLEASE PUT YOUR HEARING AID ON," he yelled. "I WANT TO TALK TO YOU, AND I WANT YOU TO TELL ME ALL ABOUT WHAT YOU BEEN DOING."

She stared at his face a long time, them eyes not hardly blinking. Finally she said, "Sam-my?"

"YES, ALICE."

"I learna cookin."

"YOU TOLD ME IN YOUR LETTER. DADDY SAYS YOU'RE A FINE COOK."

"I learna wash. I learna sweepin. I learna forkin, too. I learna he'p chickens."

"YEAH. I CAN'T HARDLY BELIEVE ALL THE STUFF YOU'RE LEARNING. ELLIE SAYS YOU'RE ADDING AND SUBTRACTING REAL GOOD. I'M PROUD OF YOU. REAL PROUD."

"I learna beggin Mama. I learna cryin." She stood straight facing him, her head high. She helt her arms stiff by her sides, her fists clenched.

Sammy patted her shoulder.

"I learna say I lova you. I learna make jelly, make jam. Aunt Bessie say I best sewin. I sew best. Ellie not sew best as me. Ellie say I be goin teacher's house alla time. Say I learna books to go schoolin. I do it. I do alla it."

Her eyes had not left his eyes. I'd never seen him stand so still, not moving a muscle. Not moving his eyes. His face looked like it ached.

"I do alla it, Sam-my."

He nodded. I seen tears glisten in his eyes.

"Sam-my?"

"HUH?"

"I do alla it to bein real girl."

He winced. The muscles in his jaws twitched. The moonlight coming through the trees fell in stripes and humps on his face.

"Sam-my?"

"HUH?"

"I scared when you come. I git scared alla it. I do. I say no. When you go back schoolin I come liva Ellie. I not come now." She unclenched her fists. For a minute I thought she might cry, but then she patted Sammy's shoulder and before he could speak or touch her, she turned and walked back to the shed.

Chapter 46

A different Sammy went back to school than the one who come home. He had seen a girl he'd thought was always gonna be helpless in lots of ways. He had seen her standing up for herself. Heard her bragging on herself even. Daddy says it's called self-confidence. He said he could tell she was gitting more ever day.

The day after Sammy left, Aunt Bessie come up and brung three buckets of paint and some leftover paints from her buggy.

"We gonna paint them walls, Ellie. They too dull. Yore daddy and Sammy said I can do whatever I want to purty 'em up. Wood gits too dark as the years pass. I got y'all's spreads and curtains ready. Will says he'll finish Alice's dressing table by the weekend. I'll make the skirt for it 'fore then. Git me a screwdriver to open these cans."

The cans had white paint. Two was full and the other'n half full.

"Gonna mix a little of this wine color from my buggy with one of them whites and make Alice's room a pink. Whatcha think? Jack can paint the ceilings white. Fer yores we gonna put in lots of green with a tad of blue. It'll match yore spread and all. We gonna stencil some flowers on both walls if I can git the colors right. Watcha think?"

289

"What's 'stencil'?" I was gitting excited.

"Ya make 'em with 'taters. My mama use to do it. Cut the end off a good-size tater and carve a flower. Then git another tater and carve ya a leaf. Then git another'n and make a stem. Then ya dip 'em in the color ya want and press 'em against the wall. Turns out real purty."

By night we had both rooms painted. I painted the high parts after Daddy done the ceilings. Then she painted the low parts. Sammy's—ah, Alice's room turned out a real purty, real pale pink. Mine was not as pale. It was a purty green. I liked them both. I couldn't believe what a difference paint made. They looked fresh as springtime. Daddy was real impressed.

Two days after we painted, we done that stenciling, or at least I done it with Aunt Bessie telling me how. About two foot down on Alice's walls, I put purple tulips with long green leaves. I put them in a row. Then everthing looked so purty compared to Sammy's homemade furniture that we painted the bed and chest white and Aunt Bessie said when they dried we'd put tulips on the wide boards on the top of the bedsteads and put one on each drawer of the chest.

In my room we got real carried away and cut 'taters to look like daisies and tulips and jonquils and tried iris, but couldn't git them right. I didn't put them in a row. I put them like bouquets. White daisies with yellow centers and purple tulips and yellow jonquils. Three big bouquets about two foot from the ceiling on two walls, and one between the windows on another'n. We left the door wall plain. When that was done, Aunt Bessie said something was wrong. It looked too blobbed out. She said we had to join them up some way.

I joined them by drawing, then painting a ribbon sort of draping across the walls and making bows on the bouquets. I never seen nothing so purty in my life. Aunt Bessie said she couldn't of done better herself.

And you talk about purty! You ain't never seen the like as when them rooms was all done up with the spreads and curtains and Alice's dressing table and skirt. Aunt Bessie brung a gold mirror that had hung in her front room. She said when she had the money she'd git another mirror and take hers back. I thought sure I was having a dream.

I was to git Alice on Sunday after church. I couldn't wait. Uncle Will took Morgan home so's Aunt Bessie could stay to see Alice see her room.

When I got to the shed Mrs. Guthrie and Alice was setting on the cot. She had on her new dress and she looked beautiful. Her feet was bare. She helt the croaker sack with her overalls and stuff in her lap. She was ready. I asked Mrs. Guthrie to come down and see the room but she wouldn't. Her eyes got cloudy and she jumped up saying she had to go see about Ormond. She touched Alice's shoulder and Alice sorta hugged her. Then she left.

When me and Alice got to the edge of the yard, I turned to see Mrs. Guthrie going on in the house. The two boys was setting on the back steps. I waved and they waved. Then I looked at the shed.

"Stay here a minute," I said to Alice. I run to the shed. I looked into that ugly room. Then I closed the door. I lifted the heavy log and turned to look at Alice. She stood there in that lacy lavender dress, in her bare feet, holding the croaker sack. Her shiny hair blowing in the gentle breeze. My heart leaped in my chest. I said thank you, God, and for the very last time in my life, and Sammy's life, and Alice's life, I dropped that limb into that latch.

When we got home Daddy and Aunt Bessie was waiting on the front porch. They was like two kids, they was so excited. They run out to meet us and hugged Alice, and Daddy took the croaker sack. They both was talking a mile a minute. When we went in the front door, Aunt Bessie said, "Now Alice, cover up yore eyes."

Alice put her hands over her eyes, and Aunt Bessie led her to the door of her new room. Me and Daddy was bumping them, we was so close.

"Don't look yet!" Aunt Bessie said, and run to turn the big vase of pink roses that was setting on the chest. She run her hand over the lavender spread, then stepped aside and grinned.

"Now look, honey," she said.

Alice took her hands off her face. I wish I knowed the big words to tell what her face looked like. I all of a sudden understood why Alice made up words. I felt like making up some myself.

She stood for a minute, staring. Then she started to giggle, but didn't git the giggle out. More like a he-he. Then she throwed her hands over her face for a minute. Then she slid them down so's her eyes was showing. Daddy had a grin from ear to ear. He put his arm around her.

"It's yores, hon. All yores," he said.

She kept her hands covering her nose and mouth. Daddy tried to move her into the room but she wouldn't budge. Aunt Bessie got misty-eyed. She turned quick and fiddled with the roses.

"And it matches that purty new dress," Daddy said. "Now don't that beat all? Yore dress just matches up with them curtains and all. Bess, you done outdid yoreself."

The sun come through the windows and the breeze blowed the fluffy curtains. I could smell the sweet fresh smell of roses.

My eyes followed Alice's. Her eyes moved slow as a snail from the bed to the dressing table to the curtains to the chest. Then they moved to the purple tulips high on the wall and stuck there and got bigger.

"I done the tulips," I bragged. "Aunt Bessie showed me how. I got a 'tater and I . . ."

Her hands flew to cover her eyes again. We stood staring at her like we was afraid to move. Then Aunt Bessie moved to Daddy and motioned for him to come with her. They left us. In a minute I said, "You wanna set down a while? You wanna set on the bed? Or on the stool? You gonna cry? If you want to cry, it's all right. I cry lots when I'm happy. Aunt Bessie is good at fixing stuff, ain't she? Me and you's got the purtiest rooms in this county, I bet." She dropped her hands. They wadn't no tears in her eyes.

"I—I not knowin how do it. I not knowin how stayin here. It hurta me. It hurta. I not knowin it." Her words was slow like she picked them one by one. "It purty. It too purty. I not know how. I pee ona bed. I makein it stinkin. I makein it scrumis. I go home, huh? I go back." She turned and walked to the porch where Aunt Bessie and Daddy was. I run and grabbed her. I told them what she said. She stood with her head down. For a minute, Aunt Bessie and Daddy looked stunned. They didn't know what to say. Then Aunt Bessie took Alice's hand and led her to a rocker. Alice set and Aunt Bessie pulled the other one to face her and set down.

"We been mighty dumb, honey," Aunt Bessie said. "I reckon I been the dumbest. All this is just too much at one time. I got carried away like I always do. It's a habit. I reckon it's 'cause I think I can fix up everthing purtier than anybody else." She looked at me and Daddy. "Go on in there and finish cooking. I'm gonna tell Alice the story of a tea set I got when I was little, and it was so purty and so delicate, I was scared to touch it. Y'all go on. We'll be in after a while. Ain't no big problem here. Heck, I'll just ride over to Ellijay and buy some rubber and make a sheet for

293

her bed. Ellie, I set the pie mixings in the bottom of the cupboard. Stir the beans 'fore they stick."

My Aunt Bessie is the smartest woman ever walked. She knowed just what to do. Before dinner was set on the table, she had Alice smiling and giggling and feeling the curtains and spread. She smelled the roses and counted the tulips and set on the stool at the dressing table and combed her hair with her new comb. She folded her overalls and shirt and bloomers and the gown Aunt Bessie had made her and put them in the chest. Then she stood looking. Them deer eyes, wet and wide. She looked and looked. She didn't want to leave the room to come and eat.

When we bowed our heads for Daddy to say the blessing, the tears finally started. They fell on her ruffled collar and when Daddy said amen, she wiped them on her fists and looked around the table at us.

"I not knowin what—what sayin."

"Don't you say a word, honey. We understand," Aunt Bessie said.

"What sayin Ellie? Say what sayin, what?" She looked in my eyes.

"You mean—well, you mean thank you? Is that what you mean?"

"What 'thank you'?"

"Thank you is what you say when somebody gives you something or does something for you or says nice stuff . . ."

"Not I lova you?"

I smiled and Aunt Bessie did, too. Daddy had to look the other way.

"I love you is good, too. Both of them's good."

She said them both.

Chapter 47

Life took on a feeling of a whirlwind after that. So much was going on I didn't hardly have time to think. Taking Alice to Miss Flossie's ever morning and me and Aunt Bessie setting in on the lessons so's we'd know how to help her. Me and Alice taking care of the chickens and the house and cooking and washing while Daddy worked with Mr. McClung on the new cabin. Going up ever night after supper to see Mrs. Guthrie for a few minutes.

We found out that Alice had a fit maybe twice a month. At first me and Daddy both would rush in her room. Mrs. Guthrie had told me Alice hadn't never showed no signs of swallowing her tongue, but Daddy always helt it down with a spoon anyhow. When the spell was over I'd change Alice and he'd change the sheets. And as strange as it sounds, we could nearly always count on Alice having a fit when they was a full moon.

Then come the first trip to the store. Alice had been wearing my old shoes. Aunt Bessie wanted to git her shoes and git cloth for another dress. We rode down in Aunt Bessie's buggy on a Saturday. I knowed Alice was scared, bad scared. Me and Aunt Bessie tried to say things to make her feel better.

When we got into Bolton and Alice seen the stores and the people, I thought she was gonna git out and run. I helt tight to her hand as we went into the general store and walked to where they keep shoes. She didn't look at nothing. Just looked straight ahead. Everbody was staring at her. In the first place, ain't hardly never no strangers comes to Bolton, and in the second place, Alice is so purty.

The thing we had decided to do was tell that Alice had been living in Waycross with her aunt on account of Alice hadn't been well, but now she was better and was going to live with us 'cause their house was so little and so's she could be close to her family.

Mrs. Guthrie had agreed to it. After all, we couldn't keep Alice a secret no longer if Miss Flossie was going to tutor her. Mrs. Guthrie said she reckoned it didn't matter nohow 'cause Mr. Guthrie wouldn't never know no difference.

Aunt Bessie introduced Alice to everbody and Alice done right good. She'd smile and say howdy-do. She sure did breathe a sigh of relief, though, when we was done and ready to go back home.

Morgan finally got to meet Alice that day. We stopped by Aunt Bessie's on the way back so's she could put on a pot of butter beans for supper, and Morgan was there. His stupid eyes bugged out of his head and he acted like he ain't never seen a girl before in his life. Aunt Bessie told him to git on back to the mill and she'd explain about Alice at supper. He didn't go. He didn't go till we left. He just kept staring. And after that, he was up at our house ever chance he got. Alice was nice to him just like she is to everbody. One day I caught him ogling her and I got this funny feeling, so I told him if he ever touched her I'd tell Daddy and Sammy both and they'd beat the slop out of him. He just snorted and went home.

We got letters from Sammy ever week. Alice could nearly

read them by herself. He'd got to where he wrote real simple so's she could read them. It tickled Daddy. Here was the boy who was gonna be a famous writer writing, "How are you? I am fine. The day is sunny. It rained on Monday." Stuff like that. He started off, "Dear Daddy and Ellie and Alice." She always giggled when she read them.

By August Alice had started going ever place I went. She went to church ever Sunday. Everbody treated her sweet, even Bertha, but I knowed that was 'cause her and John was claiming each other and she'd give up on Sammy.

The first Sunday we took Alice to church Lisa Mae couldn't believe her eyes. She was dying to ask me a million questions, but couldn't in front of Alice. She come home to eat dinner with us and seen mine and Alice's rooms and had a fit over them. At the dinner table, Alice shocked me and Daddy so bad we nearly fell out of the chair. She looked at Lisa Mae and said, "I don't lova the one, ah, Bertha. Do you?"

I started giggling so hard I had to hold my stomach. Lisa Mae did, too.

"We—we don't neither one of us like her," I said finally. "How come you didn't like her?"

"Now Ellie!" Daddy said.

"Ah, Daddy. Let her tell us."

He told Alice to go ahead and tell us.

"Bertha, she stare when y'all not lookin. She looka—she look at me and smile funny."

"Don't you never pay no 'tention to that snob," Lisa Mae said. "She ain't nothing but a two-faced snob."

"What a two-faced snob?"

"You tell her, Ellie."

"Well," I said, "two-faced means that somebody is your friend to your face and then talks about you behind your back."

Daddy laughed. "You two got a lot of room to talk."

"Ah, Daddy."

He got up and give me a pat on the head, then went out to the chicken house.

When he left, Lisa Mae said, "How long was you living in Waycross, Alice?"

Alice give me a scared look for a second, but then she said, "I live there three year."

"I'm just tickled to death you're living with Ellie! We can have a lotta fun. You in Ellie's grade? I'm a year ahead of Ellie, but we're together 'cause we're in the same room. Oh, you gonna just love the school. We got some *cute* boys, ain't we, Ellie?"

"Yeah, we . . ."

"I don't go to schoolroom. Miss Flossie, she teach me."

"She's, well, she got way behind 'cause she was sick," I said quick.

"Sick? Lordy mercy. What'd you have? You miss a lot of school? Oh, that's sorta tragic, I think, but you'll catch up! Miss Flossie will catch you up."

Alice got up and started clearing the table. I jumped up to help.

"I'll wash," Lisa Mae said. "Oh, I can't wait for Alice to meet David and Michael and them. I bet a purty she'll claim Michael right off. You can't claim Mark or David, Alice. Me and Ellie's claiming them."

"What claim mean?" She poured hot water from the kettle into the dishpan.

"You know. Claiming them for your sweetheart. Didn't y'all say claiming in Waycross? What did y'all say?"

I knowed Alice didn't know the word *sweetheart,* so I said, "Alice and Sammy is, ah, are—well, they're sweethearts." (Miss Flossie had been fussing about me saying is.)

Lisa Mae nearly dropped a plate.

"Sammy! You don't mean it! You like Sammy, Alice?"

Alice looked in Lisa Mae's face.

"I lova Sam-my," she said. She had never said it before. That was the first time. Lisa Mae raved on and on and we done the dishes and then we walked down to the valley and waded in the creek. We had a good time.

Lisa Mae started coming, in her mama's buggy, to see us a lot. She'd help us finish our work and then we'd do stuff. She took us to Bolton lots of times and Alice got use to going in stores and looking at stuff. One day Daddy give me and Alice a quarter each and I picked out two hair ribbons and a Tangee and a teeny bottle of Blue Waltz perfume. Alice kept fooling around, picking up stuff and putting it down.

"Can't you make up yore mind?" I asked. She took my hand and led me to the cloth section.

"I buy Ma-ma to make dress?"

"But you ain't got enough money. Looka here, this is twenty-nine cents a yard. A dress would take two and a half or three yards."

She pointed to a roll of blue cotton. It was nineteen cents a yard.

"You giva me quarter. I got quarter. That fifty. Two yard thirty-eight. Half yard not ten. I tell Daddy (she was calling Daddy, Daddy by then) giva you nother quarter. Will you do it?"

I looked at my Tangee and ribbons and perfume. I looked at her face.

"I'll do it," I said. She giggled.

"Ma-ma lova blue cloth. Oh, she just lova it."

"*Love,* Alice. For the zillionth time, the word is love. Say it. Say love."

"Love."

"Say it five times."

"Love, love, love, love, love," she counted on her fingers. "Now *you* do it."

"Do what?"

"Not say yore. Say what Miss Flossie tell you say. Say *your*."

"Your," I said and laughed.

"Say it five times."

"Your, your, your, your, your," I counted on my fingers. Then we went to the dress section to find Lisa Mae.

Chapter 48

Seemed like the summer was over before I knowed it, and I had to go back to school. The sessions with Miss Flossie was—were changed to three times a week and in the meantime Aunt Bessie would come up while I was in school and help Alice with the work and maybe help her study. (Aunt Bessie said if Alice kept up like she was going, she'd be ahead of what Aunt Bessie knowed.) Sammy wouldn't be home again till Christmas.

I couldn't wait to take Alice to the Founder's Day picnic. She made herself a dress for it and Aunt Bessie made me one. Mine was dark green with short puffed sleeves and a square neck. Alice's was deep blue like royal. It had a gathered skirt and puffed sleeves and a round neck that was sorta low. Me and Aunt Bessie looked at each other, not knowing what to say, when she picked out the pattern. I leaned behind Alice and said with my mouth, not out loud, that the neck was too low. Aunt Bessie nodded and started to say something, but Alice was so excited about the pattern, she didn't.

Aunt Bessie wadn't gonna be in the buggy contest. I could tell when the time come that she was sorry. Lisa Mae's mama had done her buggy up with light blue and dark blue and yellow. It was so purty, I just knowed she'd win.

Daddy stayed out in the yard the morning of the picnic so's me and Alice could bathe in the washtub. We made a awful mess that we had to clean up. We hollered back and forth from each other's room while we was dressing. I had decided not to roll my hair on account of it got so frizzy. I was just gonna wear it loose on my shoulders. It had a little natural curl so it turned out good. I was peering into my mirror when Alice called me.

"Whatcha want?"

"I can't git it right."

"What?"

"My hair. It's flying all ways."

I went in and looked. Alice's hair has a lot of 'lectricity so it was sticking up when she combed it. She had wanted to cut it, but Aunt Bessie talked her out of it.

I took the comb and she turned her back to me and I combed. It kept flying up.

"You think you plat it like Aunt Bessie did that time?" she asked.

"Well, I could."

"Will it look too—too—"

"We could put something in it. A ribbon."

She opened her chest drawer and got the movie magazine. She found a picture of a girl in a ad who had flowers in her hair.

"Think I have flowers?"

"Hey, that's a good idea! We could pick some . . . oh, heck, they'd wilt before we got there."

"You got lotta flowers in barn."

"Yeah! I forgot about them. The dried ones will work good!"

I run out while she put on her dress. I got bunches of dried yellow marigolds, white mums, purple mums, and a

302

few pink roses that didn't look too good. Alice was trying to figger out a place to put the hearing aid box since it couldn't go in the front of her dress. I put the box into the puff of her sleeve and then got a safety pin and pinned it underneath the sleeve and put the wire through the loop.

Aunt Bessie got there before we was done primping. She replatted the plat. She done it on top of her head instead of starting at the neck like I did. She tied it on top with a white ribbon and then platted the ribbon into the long plat that hung down Alice's back. Then she pinned white and purple flowers around the top of her head and at the end of the plat. Alice looked so beautiful I got jealous. She turned round in front of her mirror. The full skirt made her little waist look even littler. The top of her bosoms showed if she took a deep breath or leaned over. Me and Aunt Bessie stared.

"Don't be leaning over now," Aunt Bessie said.

"I look fine?"

"The way you look is making me a little nervous. Jack might not let you go."

Alice didn't understand.

"I not look fine?"

"I'm teasing you, honey. You look gorgeous. Now let's git Ellie fixed. Let's git some flowers in her hair, too."

I have to admit I looked purty good, too. Aunt Bessie pulled the sides of my hair up high and pinned the yellow flowers across my head. I thought I sorta looked like that picture in the magazine.

Daddy *was* shocked, but he didn't say nothing but how purty we looked. When we picked up Uncle Will and Morgan, I thought Morgan was gonna faint.

"Al-ice!" Lisa Mae squealed when we got there. "My gosh! Why you look—you look *real* purty."

"You purty, too." Alice looked at the ground.

"Why, you look so growed up with yore hair like that. You ought to fix it like that all the time. Ain't that right, Ellie?"

"I like it," I said.

"Y'all's dresses is so purty I wish I had a new one. Ellie, yore hair. It ain't frizzy!"

"I didn't roll it. You like it?"

"Gosh, I like it. Them flowers is a good idea. I look like a old dump." She leaned to my ear and pointed to David.

"Look over yonder. David's looking at us."

David was looking at *"us"* all right. Him and ever other boy there.

"I seen Mark over by the drugstore," Lisa Mae said. "And Michael is playing horseshoes. You ought to see Susan Hood. She's got on a see-through blouse! I'd of never thought. Where's yore daddy?"

"He's helping fix the stand."

"Mama's a nervous wreck. I hope she wins, but I heard Florine Attaway's buggy is a doozy. Alice! Gosh! You better not breathe deep. I see yore bosoms!"

Alice's face turned red. I think she quit breathing. I grabbed her hand.

"Come on. Let's go help Aunt Bessie unload the food."

Aunt Bessie tried to get Alice to take a number for a partner to eat with but she wouldn't. She stayed with Aunt Bessie. I had to eat with Milton Burgess, who's got bumps all over his face. Mark eat with Kemberly Brensfield and Lisa Mae with Darryl and David eat with Jackie Hayes. While we eat, I noticed that ever time I looked at Aunt Bessie or Daddy, they was looking over the crowd like they was looking for somebody. I waved at them, thinking they was looking for me, but they wadn't.

They done it all through the games. Me or Lisa Mae didn't win nothing. Alice wouldn't play. We all set together at the buggy judging. Lisa Mae was right. Florine Attaway won. Her buggy was silver and blue. It'd knock yore eyes out. Mrs. McClung told Aunt Bessie silver ought to be against the rules. It was too flashy.

By the time the dance started I was tired out. I'd played ever game and I'd eat too much cake. Me and Aunt Bessie and Alice went up to the Hoods to fresh up a little.

"Y'all seen Doc around?" Aunt Bessie asked as we was coming back.

"I ain't," I said.

"Me neither," Alice said.

We walked to the chairs that the women that ain't dancing sets in. Aunt Bessie plopped down in one.

"Y'all look around. I'm gonna rest my feet."

Everwhere we walked, folks looked and smiled at Alice. The boys couldn't keep their eyes off her. When the dance started, David run up first thing and asked her to dance.

"I not—I don't know how," she said.

"Oh, ain't nothing to it, is they, Ellie? Come on, I'll show ya." He grabbed her hand and pulled her up.

Mark come and asked me. I jumped up.

"Come on, Alice," I said. "We'll show you."

Me and Mark circled up four with Alice and David. Alice was so scared, her face looked like she'd seen a ghost or something. I kept smiling and nodding at her. Her face never did relax. She caught on to the dance step purty fast, but all the fancy calls mixed her up. David didn't mind. I kept yelling at her, telling her to watch what everbody else done.

David didn't get to dance with her long 'cause Lamar broke in. Then you ain't never gonna believe what happened. I looked over at Aunt Bessie and there stood Sammy! I fell all over Mark's feet. Then I run through the crowd and fell on Sammy.

"What you doing here? How'd you git here? Why didn't you tell us?" I screamed over the music.

Aunt Bessie was grinning. "Doc went and got him," she yelled. "They a little late."

"Did you know it?"

"I ought to," she said. "I asked him to do it."

"Oh, Aunt Bessie!"

Sammy was looking over my shoulder with his mouth gaped open.

"My God!" he said.

I turned. He was staring at Alice, who was dancing with Danny Haney. Her full skirt twirling. That long pigtail flying out. She was still scared looking, but her cheeks was pink and she was a mighty purty sight. Aunt Bessie laughed and winked at me.

"Thought you better git here quick," she said to Sammy. "Christmas may be too late." He looked from Aunt Bessie to me, then he run into the crowd of dancers. We watched him tap Danny on the shoulder. We watched Alice's shocked face when she seen who it was. Then some dancers blocked our view, and when they moved so's we could see, Sammy was standing there with his arms wrapped around Alice, her head laid against his chest.

Aunt Bessie stood up so's she could see better. We watched them standing there like wadn't nobody else in the world. I looked at the band. Daddy had let Mr. Frazier start calling and he was standing there grinning. Aunt Bessie put her arm around me and give me a squeeze.

"Ain't the Lord good!" she said.

YOU'VE SEEN THE MOVIE— NOW READ THE BOOK!

THE SILENCE OF THE LAMBS
Thomas Harris
_____ 92458-5 $5.95 U.S./$6.95 Can.

NOT WITHOUT MY DAUGHTER
Betty Mahmoody with William Hoffer
_____ 92588-3 $5.95 U.S./$6.95 Can.

THE NIGHTMARES ON ELM STREET PARTS 1, 2 and 3
Jeffrey Cooper
_____ 90517-3 $3.95 U.S./$4.95 Can.

THE NIGHTMARES ON ELM STREET PARTS 4 AND 5
Joseph Locke
_____ 91764-3 $3.95 U.S./$4.95 Can.

GREAT BALLS OF FIRE
Myra Lewis with Murray Silver
_____ 91641-8 $4.50 U.S./$5.50 Can.

SCANDAL
Christine Keeler
_____ 92070-9 $3.95 U.S.

BESTSELLING BOOKS FROM
ST. MARTIN'S PAPERBACKS—
TO READ AND READ AGAIN!

NOT WITHOUT MY DAUGHTER
Betty Mahmoody with William Hoffer
_____ 92588-3 $5.95 U.S./$6.95 Can.

PROBABLE CAUSE
Ridley Pearson
_____ 92385-6 $5.95 U.S./$6.95 Can.

RIVERSIDE DRIVE
Laura Van Wormer
_____ 91572-1 $5.95 U.S.   _____ 91574-8 $6.95 Can.

SHADOW DANCERS
Herbert Lieberman
_____ 92288-4 $5.95 U.S./$6.95 Can.

THE FITZGERALDS AND THE KENNEDYS
Doris Kearns Goodwin
_____ 90933-0 $5.95 U.S.   _____ 90934-9 $6.95 Can.

JAMES HERRIOT'S DOG STORIES
James Herriot
_____ 92558-1 $5.99 U.S.